SOMEWHERE IN THE DARKNESS WAS A PARADISE OF PLEASURE

in the form of a superbly sensual young woman whose sexual expertise stirred you to sensations beyond your wildest fantasies . . .

SOMEWHERE IN THE DARKNESS WAS A HELL OF AGONY

engineered by a master of torture who had begun to subject your flesh to his sadistic skills inch by hideously painful inch . . .

If you only knew which one was
the more dangerous. . . .

THE NIGHTTIME GUY

It will make you afraid to close your eyes!

"ENGROSSING!"—*Chicago Tribune*
"THE ACTION NEVER LETS UP!"
—*King Features Syndicate*
"IT KEEPS YOU GLUED TO THE PAGE!"
—*Natchez Democrat*

Big Bestsellers from SIGNET

THE
NIGHT TIME
GUY

TONY KENRICK

A SIGNET BOOK
NEW AMERICAN LIBRARY
TIMES MIRROR

For my father
who would, I think,
have been
happily surprised

I PROBABLY SHOULD HAVE WAITED awhile before writing this, let some time go by so I could back off it a little for a broader view of the whole thing, but I wanted to get it down while it was still fresh in my mind.

Not that I think there's much chance of its ever becoming stale in my mind—if you get zapped by a bolt of lightning or fall over a cliff, you're not going to forget it easily.

Neither of those things happened to me, but what did was just about as calamitous as far as I'm concerned.

To tell the whole story, I've been forced to guess at certain parts, although from what I've been able to gather since, it's pretty close to what actually took place. I've had to invent the settings for these sections, but most of them are geographically correct. I've had to invent some dialogue, too, and if it's not quite how the characters would have spoken, the sense of what they said, and the direction, has got to be fairly accurate.

The rest of the story, the remaining 90 percent, is as true as I'm sitting here, propped up in a poolside

1

lounger, scribbling away with a Paper Mate and a bunch of hotel stationery. All the same, I doubt you're going to believe it.

MAX ELLIS
Miami Beach, May 1977

1

The following three accounts are brief summations drawn from records on file with the New York City Police Department.

ON APRIL 18, 1977, A TUESDAY, a man named Ned Grady stepped into the elevator of his apartment house on East Sixty-sixth and nodded to Mrs. Ann Kronke, who lived two floors above. It had been a slow ride down, the elevator stopping for passengers three times before reaching the lobby. Everybody had got out except Grady and Mrs. Kronke, who continued down to the garage. The woman's car was in a parking spot near the elevator, Grady's at the other end of the garage near the door. Mrs. Kronke had trouble starting her car and was still trying when Grady reached his Continental, got in, inserted a key in the ignition, turned it, and set off a bomb powerful enough to send a piece of the engine crashing through a side window of Mrs. Kronke's car sixty feet away.

After the fire brigade had recoiled their hoses and

left, and the police were able to get a closer look at the car and its contents, they didn't have to ask around to find out something about Ned Grady. They themselves knew plenty. He was a lawyer with connections to the mob—very good connections. They put the murder down to Mafia business, which was none of their affair, and filed the case Unsolved.

A few nights later, on April 21, George Han, an usher at Madison Square Garden, had shown one of the regulars to his seat on the blue line, a man named Ellington, nicknamed The Duke. This man was also known to the police. He was one of the top packagers in the city, somebody who'd supply the talent for whatever endeavor you cared to name in return for a piece of the proceeds. The Rangers, playing the Bruins that night and trailing two to one, equalized late in the fourth period. The Duke rose from his seat along with fourteen thousand other fans, the cheer almost cracking the ice down on the rink. Then he sank back into his seat and seemed to lose interest in the game. When it ended a few minutes later, and the crowd trooped out, he stayed in his seat, which was unusual enough to make George Han, the usher, go down to check.

He thought the man had had a heart attack until he spotted the tiny round bullet hole in his neck.

On April 25 a man named Pierre Vasarely, an official of a French travel organization and newly arrived from Paris, had gone to an East Side health club he'd recently joined and taken a noon-hour workout. He'd played a game of paddle ball with a man named Baker; then they'd gone into the steam room together. Another man had come in, moved through the murky atmosphere, and sat down on the opposite bench, wrapped in towels.

Five minutes later Baker left the Frenchman, showered, dressed, and went back to his office.

Two hours after that an attendant, clearing up after the lunch-hour rush, found Vasarely slumped in the steam room and dragged him out quickly, but he was dead.

It wasn't the heat that had killed him; it was something long and narrow and very sharp that had been shoved down his ear.

The police thought the three deaths were related, and they were right.

But for the wrong reason.

A guy with mob connections, a man who found muscle for hire, and a foreign travel executive who could sail through customs—all three killed by pros . . . the police figured the deaths had to be connected with what was happening on the drug scene just then. A blockage had developed in the pipeline from Mexico, and they knew from past experience that when a billion-dollar business like that gets a loop in it, people start getting nervous and bodies start turning up.

Put in actual fact the three killings had nothing to do with what was happening south of the border. And at least one department of the U.S. government had a strong suspicion that they'd been precipitated

in exactly the opposite direction: north of the border
. . . perhaps no more than a week before Ned
Grady had gone down to the garage and turned the
key of his Continental.

2

It said April on the calendar, but on the streets of Ottawa it looked more like February. Plows made little headway against the snow that had been dumping down for the last two days, and it piled in drifts against the tall iron railings of the embassy fence.

In the late-afternoon light the embassy itself was just a thick, bulky shape squatting against a darkening sky, although there was a time when that shape had taken a different form. The original building, a high brick Victorian fantasy, had burned down one New Year's Eve, and been replaced by the present one, a severe, monumental structure that seemed a more accurate reflection of the tightlipped life lived in the country which owned the embassy.

Most of the staff liked Canada: the broad, flat expanses, the wind piling snow in miniature mountains, the whir of tires spinning on streets already dark at 5 p.m.—it was just like home.

Inside the embassy, in a room on the second floor, it was even more like home: heavy gray curtains over the windows, lights burning too brightly in the

7

ceiling, dull, efficient furniture, and not one window open a crack to cool the overheated air.

There were two men in the room, an embassy man behind the desk and a visitor seated in front of it. This man had just driven from New York, but he'd declined the offer of refreshment, preferring to get down to business.

His host, whose name was Plesek, opened a drawer in his desk, took out a large paper Jiffy bag that had been left unsealed, and passed it across. The other man accepted it, peeked inside, reached in, and brought out a bundle of money. There were a dozen more bundles just like it, and the man looked up when he saw them. "What's this for?"

He was a small, alert person whose skin seemed to fit too tightly over his face, making his features hard and sharp. He had a compact body, which he perched on the edge of his chair like an animal ready for instant flight, and he seemed uncomfortable with his surroundings.

Plesek was his exact opposite; he lounged in his chair, relaxed, stretched out. In his mid-forties, but appearing younger, he looked like a man who'd been an athlete once and kept his shape: flat stomach; long legs; bony shoulders. He had a strong face, the nose and jaw definite and pronounced, and above them his pale-yellow hair was worn short and parted high. The general impression was one of controlled energy, vitality. When he answered the man, he showed a slight accent, but a perfect command of North American speech.

"For starters."

"For doing what?"

"A very special job." There was a pause. "How much do you get for very special jobs?"

"Depends on what's involved," the New Yorker said. He had a voice like rocks grinding together.

"Three men."

"Then what?"

"Then you're out of it. Some other specialists take over."

"The job's here?"

"No. Your own turf."

The little man nudged the Jiffy bag. "How much is in here?"

"Fifteen thousand."

"For three heads I'd need that again."

"Another fifteen?"

"Yeah."

Plesek looked as if he were considering it. Then he said, "I'll give you another twenty."

The visitor frowned. "You bumping me *up?* Why?"

"So you know that when I say this job's special, I mean special."

The little man shook his head. "I got to tell you something. I don't like to work a job I don't understand. Nobody ever gave me a five-grand tip before."

Plesek tilted his chair back, put one foot up, very North American. He studied the low flat ceiling, then looked back at his visitor. "Let's see if I can explain it. Let's say we've heard that General Motors has come up with a great new invention, something they can put on an engine and get a hundred miles to the gallon. You can appreciate that we'd like to have something like that for our own auto industry. And so would a lot of other auto industries."

"They know about it, too?"

"Sure. But they don't know exactly what it is any more than we do. But they know it's something sensational, and they want it."

"So they're trying to grab it, too."

"Oh, yes. They're going to be trying very hard."

"Who are they?"

"GM's international competition. Jaguar, Citroën, Volkswagen."

The other man caught on but still had a problem with it. "But those people, I thought they're friends with GM."

"Everyday friends, yes. But when you get a new invention as big as this one, friends start acting like enemies."

The visitor nodded. "I get it. You want a little spadework done before you make your move. You want me to ace the competition, these three other outfits, before you take on GM."

"On the button."

"Okay then. Now I get it. You end up with this doohickey, and that's how come it's worth an extra five grand. Okay, fine. We got a deal."

Plesek sat forward, opened another drawer, took out a flat brown envelope, and shook out three photographs. Each shot showed a different man. The first one was getting out of a car looking as if he'd been surprised by the camera. The second was holding a golf club on his shoulder and smiling. The third was a police mug shot, front on.

The New Yorker took them, flicked his eyes over them, then passed them back.

"I'll identify them by company," Plesek said. He picked up a pen and wrote a name on the back of each. "Jaguar . . . Citroën . . . Volkswagen."

He handed them back to the little man, who said, "Any special order you want them down?"

"Whatever suits. But I'd like the job finished in ten days. Can do?"

"Sure, as long as they're all going to be in town."

"They'll be there. Their names and addresses are all in this envelope." He passed it across, and the other man dropped the photos into it and asked another question.

"Once they're down, the companies'll hire replacements, won't they?"

"You can bet on it. But it'll take time, and we'll have got a big jump on them."

"You want progress reports?"

"It's all in the envelope. Instructions on how and when to contact me."

Although he hadn't seen him do it, the New Yorker knew his host had pushed a button somewhere because the doors at the end of the room opened, and the same person who'd showed him in stood waiting for him. He tucked the envelope, and the Jiffy bag, under his arm and got up. Plesek rose, too.

"Careful driving back," Plesek said. "The roads are icy."

Four days later, when his secretary brought in the morning mail, the first thing Plesek reached for was *The New York Times*. He turned to the classified ads, the automotive section, and received the first of the progress reports.

Two days later he got the second. And three days after that, the third. Which read like this:

For sale: 1960 Citroën
Call Bill. 535-0196.

He folded the newspaper, sat back, and said in English, in an accent a TV comic might have used for an Austrian psychiatrist, "Now ve can begin."

3

THERE ARE TWO THINGS you're never supposed to take with you into the New York subway: a lot of money and a hangover. The first was no problem, I didn't have a lot of money to take with me. But the second . . . I can tell you, I had a hangover that day good enough to be nationally ranked, and a slamming, banging subway ride was the last thing it needed.

I was full of unneeded things, like the phone call I'd got around eleven. That was the reason I was riding the damn subway, a lousy phone call. Somebody named Logan, from Internal Revenue, and could I see my way clear to dropping in during the lunch hour with a view to straightening out a little matter regarding my tax return?

Great, huh? A fast little audit from those swell folks who brought you income tax. I really needed that. Always have a CPA handle your tax return, they say. The tax boys see his stamp and never question your return. Oh, sure. Maybe that's how it was once upon a time, but not since they switched to computers.

I knew what the problem was: They weren't going

to allow the deduction I'd made for home office space. And maybe one or two others as well. The hell of it was that once they find something to pick on, they're liable to go back through your past returns and rake those over the coals, too. If they did, then I had to be looking at a bill for three or four grand, and I didn't have three or four grand. I had about three hundred bucks in the bank, and a hangover in my head, as the subway train, roaring into Bowling Green station, reminded me.

I got into it and suffered in silence for a stop, thinking about how I came to have a hangover in the first place: Cy Greene's party last night. I still didn't feel right about that. Not just from drinking too much booze, but for letting my hair down with Cy.

I'd told him about the dream.

I'd never told anybody else before, and maybe I should have. Most people, with a problem like mine, would have hotfooted it to an analyst's couch long ago, but I've always shied away from that kind of thing, which makes me unique in New York. In this town everybody and his cat seem to go to a shrink. It's no big deal; it's just something they do once a week, like picking up the dry cleaning. Not that I have anything against psychiatry. I don't. I know it's a tremendous help for a lot of people. I've just never thought it would do *me* much good. But when the dream started getting really bad, I got to wondering if it wouldn't be such a bad idea at least to talk it over with someone. So I chose Cy Greene.

I told him everything. Not just the dream, but what was causing it: what I'd done to Ollie, my brother. Cy had listened quietly till I'd finished, then started talking about what he termed my imaginary debt.

I was sitting in that subway car thinking about it—my imaginary debt—and I was so engrossed I almost went past my stop and had to jump for the doors. I put it out of my mind going up the subway steps and wondered, instead, about a debt that couldn't be called imaginary: the one the IRS was going to hit me with. I was more than a little nervous, at the sight of the tax office, looking very stern and official, didn't do much to calm me. I've always disliked this part of town with its courthouses and state and city buildings; for me it's too much of a reminder of Them, the invisible people who send you letters in brown envelopes—franked brown envelopes, as if they didn't have any spit to lick a stamp with. I guess I'm talking about Authority, or the Authorities, and I've never been crazy about either of them. I can go through customs carrying nothing more illegal than pajamas and a toothbrush and still feel I'm going to be grabbed. It's not insecurity; it's just that all forms of officialdom make me uneasy, and I'd prefer it if the government went its way and let me go mine. That probably makes me sound like a conservative, which I'm not. I voted for Carter, although I'm not sure I will next time. Actually, I'm an old Stevenson man, which kind of leaves me out on a political limb these days; there sure as hell aren't any new Stevensons around.

As I went through the doors of the tax office, my hangover seemed to get worse; something fluttered in my stomach the way it does when I'm on my way to the dentist. Is there a parallel there, between the dentist and the tax man? Both probe. Both extract. Both are painful. Although your dentist can't put you in jail.

With that happy thought buzzing in my aching head I asked a receptionist for Logan's office and was directed down a long, echoing hall full of doors with hand-lettered signs scotch-taped to them. A zillion dollars to put up a building, and they can still manage only homemade signs.

I found Logan's office easily enough; it was in a corner of a room the size of a basketball court and full of deserted desks. I knocked on the opaque glass door and went in.

"Mr. Logan?"

"Mr. Ellis?"

I hate people who answer a question with another one.

We shook hands, and he motioned me toward the chair facing his desk, which was messy and strewn with papers. It didn't go with the man. He had a neat, almost natty look, and there was a palpable air of success about him as if he'd parlayed the Princeton tennis championship into a cushy job in investment banking. He was a surprise; I'd been expecting somebody like Charles Hall, the little guy who usually played a tax man in the movies, always following Ray Milland or Cary Grant around and writing down extravagant purchases in a notebook. But Logan was fairly well built and a very snappy dresser—hand-tailored suit, a Countess Mara tie, pale silk shirt, and with a haircut he'd paid at least twenty-five bucks for. I wondered if the tax boys were working on commission these days.

"Thanks for coming down, Mr. Ellis." Banker's voice, too—deep, crisp, confident.

"My pleasure," I said, hoping I sounded like a man with nothing to hide. Damn it, I didn't have anything to hide. I wasn't guilty of tax evasion, merely tax avoidance, which is legal and even recommended. The IRS itself urges you to minimize your taxes, which is all I've ever done. I decided to take the offensive. "I'd appreciate it if you could make this fast, Mr. Logan." I glanced at my watch. "I'm due in a meeting shortly."

That ploy has a lot more chance of working if your watch is a thin see-through Audemars Piguet. Mine's a Timex with big black numerals.

"I'll do my best," the man answered. But having promised that, he just sat there looking at me as if waiting for me to start talking. Was I supposed to give an embarrassed little laugh and come right out with something like "About that deduction, Mr. Logan," before he'd even mentioned it? If that was what he had in mind, he could think again. I wasn't going to play along. I decided to say nothing, and I stuck to my game plan for about four seconds.

"About that deduction, Mr. Logan. . . ."

He started talking then, but he didn't say anything I expected to hear.

"This meeting has nothing to do with taxation, Mr. Ellis. I'm not with the IRS. And my name's not Logan. I'm just borrowing his office for security reasons."

"Yes," I said, because I didn't want to say something dumb like "Oh" or "I see."

"My name's Gallo, and I'm with the Defense Department. I wanted to talk to you, so I borrowed Frank Logan's office. We're not supposed to, but he's a buddy of mine, and I didn't want you coming down to my office. Certain people make a habit of hanging around there."

"Oh."

I looked at the identification he showed me: a Pentagon pass with his photograph, signature, and thumbprint. So I knew he wasn't a nut who'd sneaked into the tax office one lunch hour. I cleared my throat. "Look, I think—"

"I'm going to explain everything, but there's a lot to tell, so we'll have to take it in stages. But basically, the reason you're here is that we'd like to ask your help on something."

"The Defense Department. . . ."

"Yes."

"I see."

"First, let me tell you why we've singled you out." He'd replaced the ID and taken out a long envelope, from which he now unfolded a closely typed sheet of paper. "Okay. I guess you're wondering how we even know you exist."

"I wonder myself sometimes." I wasn't trying to be cute, but the guy had floored me. The Defense Department?

"Five years back"—he was reading from the sheet of paper—"you were programming computers for the Klingman Company when they got a contract to do a piece of research for the Navy. You worked on the job, do you remember it?"

"Sure."

"You needed a security clearance. Which is how we know about you."

"And you'd like me to do a little free-lance for you again, is that it?"

"Yes."

"Why me? There are thousands of programmers. I'm nothing special. B average at best."

"The job has nothing to do with computers."

"Nothing to do with computers," I said. I didn't mean to sound like a parrot, but I wanted to make sure I was hearing him right. I went back over the ground to see if I had all the clues. "Your name isn't Logan, it's Gallo. This is the tax office, but you're not with the tax office, you're with the Defense Department. And you'd like me to help out on something, but not in the way I helped out last time."

"That's right," he said blandly. It all seemed perfectly logical to him.

I gave the embarrassed little laugh then, but for a different reason. "Um, why me?"

"We've chosen you because, as I've just pointed out, you've already been cleared, and we prefer to work with people we know. Less of a risk that way. But most important, you have the special ability we're looking for."

"What special ability? I don't have any special ability."

Instead of answering, he went on reading again. He was starting to annoy me, this guy, sitting there in his snazzy suit and Gucci underwear. I decided I didn't like him.

"Maxwell James Ellis," he read out, as if he were telling me something I didn't know. "Five feet ten, one-sixty pounds. Eyes, brown. Hair, brown. No distinguishing marks. Born Utica, New York, 1933." He looked up at me. "That sound like you?"

"Yeah," I said. It was exactly me, except for the height. I'm not five ten; I'm five nine and a half. I always tack an extra half inch onto my height because I'd like to be a little taller. At five nine and a half I'm not short, but I'm not what you'd call tall either. And these days, with all the chicks wearing platforms, a guy needs to be as tall as he can get. One or two young ladies have hinted that it'd be nice if I were a little higher, but on the whole, there haven't been too many other complaints. I've been told more than once that I look a little bit like James Caan, which is possible; I have the same kind of curly brown hair and the high forehead. But my jaw isn't quite as firm as his, and my nose isn't as fine. And with those shoulders he could certainly outmuscle me. But for all that, I suppose I'm not a bad looking guy on a good day. I just wish I was taller, that's all.

Gallo was droning on again. "No close family. Mother died 1972, father 1974. Brother died 1942." He looked up at me. "Must have been pretty young."

"He was eleven," I said, flatly.

He moved his head in a "tough break" gesture.

"Why did you ask about my brother?"

He was already looking back at the sheet of paper. "No special reason." He coughed and started reading again. "Married 1965, divorced three years later. Currently employed by Marshall and Lally, security analysts. Currently residing Five Seventy-five East Seventy-second. Lives alone, heterosexual A one."

"A one?" That pricked my ears up. "What does that mean, A one?"

Gallo allowed himself a little smile, his first since I'd known him. "Only that you have a pronounced sexual drive."

"How the hell would you know a thing like that?"

"Field agents."

"You're kidding. You mean you had somebody under my bed?"

"In your bed," Gallo said.

I was so surprised I didn't say anything. Can you beat that? One of those secretaries I'd picked up at some singles bar had been working for the Feds. Christ, is nothing sacred? I've always advocated screwing the government, but not that way.

Gallo read out a few more personal things: the fact that there are only two or three friends I'd call close, that I buy season tickets to Carnegie Hall, that I read a lot, and that I'm a sports fan as long as the Giants are playing. Then he got to the part which he must have been leading up to.

"Hobbies, none. Does volunteer work in rehabilitation for the blind." He put the piece of paper down and smoothed it. "I understand you do that three nights a week. At the Sight Center, isn't it?"

"That's right."

"What kind of work is it exactly?"

"I mainly work with the newly blind in an orientation class. Show them how to use a cane, how to get around. I teach braille, too."

Gallo nodded; he seemed satisfied about something.

"So?" I asked.

"So there's your special ability," he said. "Your knowledge of how to cope with blindness. We're looking for somebody who has that, somebody we know we can trust."

"I dig. The Defense Department wants me to work with blinded veterans. Okay, but why all the secrecy?"

"Blinded veterans? That's a reasonable assumption, Mr. Ellis, but that's not what we have in mind for you." He folded the piece of paper, taking his time over it. Christ, he was irritating. "I think I can explain it best if I sneak up on it a little. Will you bear with me for a moment?"

"Sure, for a moment." I underlined that by glancing at my Timex again. I wanted to get out of there. I was delighted to find I wasn't in trouble with the tax boys, but at the same time, I was annoyed at being dragged down there under false pretenses. I didn't like Gallo, and I've never been wild about the Defense Department, and whatever they had in mind for me I was pretty sure I wasn't going to want any. But I heard him out. I guess I was a touch curious.

"The history of warfare, Mr. Ellis," he said, pulling it out of left field. "A fast look at it demonstrates the almost total reliance on weapons technology for any kind of advancement. Once upon a time the best a soldier could do for a weapon was a rock he picked up and threw. Then along came technology and produced something that would throw it harder and faster for him, the slingshot. Then the soldier got even better things, steady improvements. Spears, bows and arrows, gunpowder and the wheel lock, the musket, the rifle, all the way to an antiaircraft missile he can fire from his shoulder. It used to take fifty men with a battering ram months to breach a castle wall, and now one man can wipe out an entire city ten thousand miles away with a touch of a button. But you know something?" Gallo asked. "All the time it was only the weapon that improved. The soldier himself stayed the same. So now we're thinking it might not be a bad idea to see if we can't improve the soldier, too."

"You mean make him smarter?"

Gallo shook his head. "No, I'm not talking about a mental improvement. I mean a physical one."

I didn't say anything, just waited for him to come out and tell me what kind of physical one, but he struck off into another part of the forest again. I felt like bending one of his fancy lapels.

"Mr. Ellis, it's generally accepted that the best fighting machine that ever existed is the Bengal tiger. It's got everything: speed, strength, weight, stealth, and terrific armaments—five knives in each paw and a jaw that can break stone. It can climb a tree, swim a river, and run all day. And yet none of these things would make a really big improvement in a soldier armed with modern weapons. Except one."

"What is it?"

"One I haven't mentioned."

I thought I might bend both of his lapels.

He leaned forward, and his voice lowered a bit. "A tiger can see in the dark. Imagine the improvement if a soldier could do the same."

"I thought they could," I said. "Don't they have those special binoculars?"

"Night scopes?" Gallo grunted a negative. "They're not the answer. A man can't use one and fire a weapon at the same time. And they cost a fortune, besides. But what if a soldier could see in the dark just with his own two eyes?"

"Right," I said, shifting in my chair. "That would really be a winner. But getting back to what you were saying about a physical improvement. What are you aiming at?"

"I just told you. Night vision."

"Oh." I coughed, scratched my cheek. "You're kidding, of course."

He shook his head.

"You've got to be."

"No."

"Come on, now. You really think it's possible for a man to see in the dark?"

"I know it's possible."

"How do you know?"

"Because," Gallo said slowly, "we've already done it."

There was no sound after that for quite a few moments; I just stared at Gallo, who stared right back at me. I was vaguely aware of traffic noise coming through the closed window and a telephone ringing somewhere that went unanswered. Then a door banged, and footsteps came our way. The door opened, and a man put his head in and must have been surprised to find two people he'd never seen before sitting each side of a desk, just looking at each other.

"Sorry," he said, "I was after Frank Logan."

"He'll be back shortly," Gallo told him.

The man left, and there wasn't any sound again; the office toilers were still at lunch, so there was no noise from them. And I certainly wasn't making any because what Gallo had told me stopped me cold.

He took advantage of my silence to deliver a little directive. "You understand that all this is highly classified, and you're not to breathe a word, not a syllable, to anyone."

I think I nodded.

"Okay, a few more facts. This thing's brand-new and hot as a pistol. It was tested on rhesus monkeys for a start, and when that was successful, we tested it on a terminal volunteer."

I asked him what the hell that was.

"Somebody who hasn't long to live and volunteers to help with experiments."

"God, you guys must have been desperate. A dying man?"

Gallo gave a little shrug. "He was more than happy to do it. He was an old man, late seventies. He had all his faculties, good eyesight, but a ticker that was running down. He had only a few days left, so he had nothing to lose."

"Except those last few days," I said. "Operating on somebody that old can be pretty risky."

"There wasn't any operation. This thing's way simpler than that. It's a chemical in a liquid suspension. Eyedrops. We gave them to the old man, then tested him in a blacked-out room."

"And he could see?"

"Perfectly."

"I just can't believe it."

"I know how you feel. I was in that room listening to the old man reading off an eye chart in the pitch-dark, and *I* didn't want to believe it."

"So now you're looking for a new guinea pig."

I don't think Gallo liked my choice of words. "We're looking for a new test subject, yes."

"Why not go back to the terminal ward, spread some joy around?"

"Because we want to run a whole series of controlled tests. Outdoor tests, all kinds. And we can't do that with a man in a hospital bed." He slowed for a second, then said, "We thought you might like to help us out."

"You'd like me to use my connections at the Sight Center to find somebody interested enough in vision research to volunteer, is that it?" I honestly thought I was taking the words out of his mouth. "Well, I can try, but—"

He cut me off. "Not exactly, Mr. Ellis. We want you. We want you to volunteer to take the tests."

"Me?"

"Yes. You'd be ideal."

"Hold it a second. Pull over." I was waving one hand in front of me as if I were polishing something. "One of the things I've always wanted to be is ideal, but I never thought I'd make it. How come I qualify now?"

"Because of your work at the Sight Center. Because of your knowledge of what it's like to be blind."

"Only a blind person can ever know that."

"Sure, I understand. But you know all about the problems of being blind and how to overcome them. You see," Gallo said, and he didn't even have the grace to pick some lint off his shoulder while he said it, "they haven't quite perfected the eyedrops yet."

I let out a long breath and did some slow nodding. "Here comes the fine print, huh? They haven't perfected the eyedrops."

"Not yet," Gallo admitted again.

"And they have a side effect, I take it." I had the guy pinned to the wall, but you'd never have known it; he came back at me as smooth and unruffled as ever.

"More of a frontal effect, I think you'd call it. Right now all the drops can do is reverse a person's sight. They can make you able to see in the dark, but they can't do it without affecting your daytime vision."

"You mean what you gain in night vision, you lose in day vision."

"Exactly. Your day vision would be impaired. This is something they're working to overcome, of course, and they're sure they'll be able to do it. But meantime, we want to go ahead and test what we've got."

I took that in, then said very slowly, so he couldn't possibly misunderstand me, "Say I did agree to take these drops. Just how impaired would my daytime sight be?"

"Quite a bit."

"What do you call quite a bit?"

Gallo gave me as close as he could get to an apologetic little smile. "Through the day you'd be totally blind."

For the second time that lunch hour I found myself staring at the guy and again hardly able to believe him. "You're asking me . . . let me get this straight. You're asking me to become a blind man?"

"It'd be easy for you. You teach blind people, you'd adjust quickly. And as it would only be in the daytime, you'd be blind only twelve hours a day. Less, in fact. And of course, it would only be temporary. You could restore your normal vision anytime you wanted to."

"I could?"

"Absolutely. You simply pop a pill, and it would reverse the process. You'd be able to see again normally."

"Then why would I have to be blind in the daytime? Why couldn't I have the drops, take the pill next day, then have the drops again that night?"

"Because they haven't got the drops to that stage yet. They're not sure why, but they won't work again after the pill. It's one of the things they're trying to solve."

"So these drops are only a onetime thing?"

"Right," Gallo said. "They work perfectly until the pill cancels them out."

I thought about that for a second, then asked him how long it took the pill to work.

"Ninety minutes, more or less."

"More or less, huh?"

Gallo shrugged a small qualification. "About that. With the monkeys it varied a little each time."

"Screw the monkeys. How long did it take to work on the old man?"

"I forget exactly, but certainly no more than two hours."

Then he said, hurrying on, "The main thing is, Mr. Ellis, we can restore your normal sight, so you wouldn't be giving up anything except a week of your time."

"Mr. Gallo," I said, getting to my feet, "thanks anyway, but I don't think it's really me."

"Why not?"

"Well, for one thing, I'd get fired if I gave up a week of my time."

"No, you wouldn't." Gallo had risen with me. "We'd fix it with your boss."

"And for another," I went on, getting to the real reason, "I don't think I'd like to be blind for a week of my time."

"It would only be for half that period. You'd be able to see at night remember."

"And for another thing," I said, sailing on, "I don't think I'd like to be blind for half the rest of my life either, which I'm damn sure could happen if something went wrong. I have only one pair of eyes, and I'm not about to risk them."

"But we've proved there isn't any risk. I've just explained that."

"All you've explained is that this thing worked on a bunch of monkeys and a dying old man. I'm no scientist, but I wouldn't call that conclusive proof."

"Mr. Ellis." Gallo paused, slowing the pace of the

conversation, which had been quickening. "You have my word that this experiment would be perfectly safe. And there's something I haven't mentioned yet. It wouldn't be without compensation. We'd be willing to pay you ten thousand dollars for your time."

"Ten thousand?"

"It's that important to us, Mr. Ellis. Vitally important."

When I didn't say anything, he said, "Most people could use money like that these days."

I went on watching him, and he added something else. "I mean, imagine if this had been a genuine trip to the IRS. For an audit, say. I don't know anything about your tax situation, but maybe it could've proven an expensive trip."

I said softly, "You rotten bastard."

"What?"

"Like hell you don't know anything about my tax situation. Let's cut the crap, Gallo. You're saying that if I don't volunteer for this little number, I'll get a call from you buddy Logan. I'll get an audit."

"That's not true." Gallo was shaking his head. "We'd never try to coerce somebody into anything like this."

"Bullshit you wouldn't. What about that old man? You probably twisted his arm, too."

"We offered him money, and he took it. For his family."

"Then he didn't volunteer like you said. You bribed him."

"It was a fair exchange. He needed money, and we needed a pair of eyes."

"I need a pair of eyes, too. And I'm not going to

THE NIGHTTIME GUY / 31

let you screw around with them." I shoved my finger at Gallo; I was plenty mad. "So go ahead. Sic your tax buddy onto me. I may end up broke, but at least I'll be able to see the red ink."

"Mr. Ellis, two of the top eye men in the country came up with this, and they don't have the slightest doubt about it."

"Maybe I wouldn't either if I wasn't being asked to test it. The answer's no, Gallo. Got it?"

Gallo waited a moment, then said quietly. "Look, officially I don't have to have your answer till tomorrow. At least think about it. Sleep on it. I'll call you at your office in the morning."

"You'll be wasting your time." I started for the door, and he took one last shot at me.

"Whoever does this would be doing it for his country."

I told him to try the American Legion and walked out of the office. I thought I was also walking out of his life, that that was the end of it—finished, kaput.

You live and learn.

4

TWO MINUTES AFTER PLESEK had opened his *New York Times* in Ottawa he'd gone in to see his section head.

"Still snowing," his boss said from his chair facing the window. "Well, at least it covers the place up." He swung his chair around, a gloomy, fat-faced man. He was one of the few in the embassy who didn't like to be reminded of home; he didn't care for winter. His idea of an overseas posting was a warm, sunny climate, and he'd gone so far as to become fluent in Spanish, hoping to be sent to the southern end of the operation, but five years later he was still handling things in the north.

Plesek tapped the newspaper in his hand. "It's time for me to go." They spoke in their own language.

His superior nodded. "How are you going to arrange it?"

"Same as last time. With Tula." When the other man frowned, Plesek said, "That bothers you?"

"I don't like doing the same thing twice in a row. It's always dangerous."

"Perhaps. But I think this one is worth one more

airing. 'Specially as tomorrow's Saturday. Besides, I won't be able to do it when summer comes."

"If it ever does," the fat man muttered. He pursed his lips, thinking. "All right. But you'll have to get Tula out of here a different way. We don't want to do everything the same."

"I was worried about that, too," Plesek said. "So I've thought of something."

His boss waited to hear.

"We arrange a trade delegation, a big one. Three cars, four men in each. Twelve men come into the embassy; thirteen leave. If they're bunched up together in overcoats, I doubt our friends will get an accurate count."

The fat man considered it. "No, they probably wouldn't. Very well, let's see how it looks. You make the switch with Tula in the mountains, and he comes back here as you. But when you don't come out after a couple of days, our friends will know you've flown. Officially you'll be ill and in the care of the embassy doctor, but they won't buy that, of course. They'll go looking for you."

"Yes, but in Los Angeles, because of the missile thing. They know we're onto that, but they don't know we're onto the eyedrops, so they won't be looking for me in New York."

The fat man made a slow swivel in his chair. By the time he'd come full circle he'd accepted Plesek's argument. He pointed a finger at the fair-headed man. "One question: If you're so sure this twelve-man delegation will get Tula out, why don't you use it yourself?"

"Because," Plesek answered, a little smile on his mouth, "I like to ski."

The snow had eased in the night, but Plesek still had to dig out his car next morning. It was parked in front of his apartment house, and the plows had covered it with snow.

He headed east, toward the Laurentians, keeping his speed down so as to take it easy on the RCMP car he knew would be behind him, as well as the one he knew would be in front.

The Canadians were well aware that the under-director for trade and development wasn't in Canada to promote his country's tractors. But they went along with it until such time it was convenient for them to learn, to their shock and disbelief, that he was actually engaged in spying, and to kick him out of the country. That wouldn't be till it suited them, perhaps in retaliation for one of their own men being exposed on the other side of the world. It was a game nations played. In the meantime, they never took their eyes off him for a second.

But it wasn't the RCMP, the Mounties, that both-ered Plesek; it was their opposite number across the border. If they caught him in New York, five hundred miles from where his diplomatic credentials allowed him to be, there'd be no public outrage— he'd just disappear. Plesek dimissed the thought; they'd have to catch him first, and they couldn't do that if they didn't know where to look.

He turned off at Montebello and took 57 heading north. There was no need to check on his escorts;

they knew where he was going. He always skied on Saturdays; everything would look normal.

He kept the car on the inside lane and steadily ate up the miles. Ahead of him the low line of mountains bulked against a background of snow clouds, and half an hour later he was in them, following the signs to Tremblant. He drove for another twenty minutes, then swung the car into the big south parking lot of the ski area.

He checked his watch: ten-fifty, plenty of time for some good runs.

He got out, slipped into a big red quilted parka, and pulled a white ski cap well down over his ears. He changed into ski boots, then fetched his poles from the trunk and his skis from the roof rack. He bought a one-day ticket, kicked into his skis, and took his place in the lift line, the cold grabbing at him after the warmth of the car. The Saturday crowd was a big one, and he was chilled by the time he reached the head of the line. A man next to him, who looked like his partner for the ride up, shook his head and said, "These lines, I tell you. I'm thinking about giving it away here and trying Grey Rocks next week. The runs aren't nearly as good, but at least you don't freeze your ass off hanging around." They positioned themselves and let the chair scoop them up and carry them away. During the ride they compared the relative merits of other ski areas, and Plesek, chatting easily, went along with it. He knew the man was a cop, and the man knew that Plesek knew; it was all part of the game.

Plesek figured there'd be three others besides this man, one of them probably a woman. But that wasn't going to be enough, not as long as Tula was on time, and he'd been right on the dot before.

From the chair lift they transferred to a tow bar which served the upper slopes. When they reached the top, it turned out, not at all to Plesek's surprise, that his partner intended to ski Ryan's Run, too.

"In that case, I'll probably see you around," Plesek said.

"Okay. Ski those moguls," the man cried, and pushed off, although Plesek knew he wouldn't be going far; he was the front tag, the others would be behind him.

He was right; he passed the man around the first bend in the trail, off to one side fixing a binding. Plesek put him out of his mind and concentrated on his skiing. The snow was good, deep-packed, easy to turn on. He got in three good runs, timing the last one so that he arrived at the top again just after noon. He used up a few minutes cleaning the lenses of his green aviator glasses, then adjusted the elastic of his gloves; this allowed him to take a peek at his watch.

Two minutes, ten seconds to go. He'd timed this section and knew exactly how long it would take him.

He counted to ten slowly, the snow squeaking in the cold as he moved his skis back and forth, set himself, then dropped down the trail. The second bend was a high, curving wall which he took wide so he could check back up the trail. He caught a fast glimpse of two figures he'd seen before, coming out of the first bend; they were staying closer than he'd figured.

He resisted the impulse to ski faster; everything depended on timing. Like a baton change in a relay, it was the smoothness of the changeover that made for speed, not the pace of the runners. The third turn bent to the right, then opened up into a bowl that stretched for a hundred feet before dipping out of sight again. Plesek skied a tight line through it, slanting toward the little warming hut which sat on the left of the bowl.

He spotted Tula's figure already moving on the slope above it, skiing fast to build up speed. It was like seeing his twin: same build, same red parka, same white ski cap pulled down to green aviator glasses, same skis and poles, same brown plastic boots.

Plesek turned sharply into the hill, shot around behind the warming hut, and bit his edges into the snow in a fast, shuddering stop.

Then his hands flew.

He dropped his poles, unzipped his parka, slipped it off, pulled it inside out, and slipped it back on again. In almost the same movement he whipped the ski cap off his head, reversed it, jammed it back on, snatched a pair of goggles from under his sweater, and pulled them down over his glasses. He retrieved his poles and pushed off immediately, but not with the expert control he'd shown before. The two figures coming down the trail flashed by without a second look at the beginner who'd bitten off more than he could chew. With his body practically bent in half at the waist, and his legs wide in a snowplow, what else could he be? He certainly looked like one in a sky-blue parka which was open, with the belt trailing, and a cute knitted Union Jack on his head, not to mention the dark plastic goggles which belonged on a sunny glacier in Europe.

Clumsily, Plesek sideslipped down the trail to the next bend and stopped. Down below, where the trail snaked back, he could see Tula's red parka swinging around a turn. The man had studied films of Plesek's style and learned to copy his slightly dated technique, the tight wedeln turns, and the stabbing use of the poles. Behind Tula, Plesek saw the same two figures that had flashed past him at the warming hut; they were still keeping that red parka in sight.

But Plesek, taking no chances, stuck to his new role and skied awkwardly down to a cutoff trail which led to another lift. He took it to the top and skied, in the same manner, down the Sissy Schuss, the beginners' trail, not because that was where he now belonged, but because it ran down the other side of the mountain, finishing near the north parking lot.

When he reached the bottom, he took off his skis, walked to the lot, and found Tula's car, a Monza with New York State license plates. He put his skis on the rack, took a duplicate key from his parka, and let himself in. He changed his boots for the shoes on the back seat, then started the car. While he waited for the engine to warm, he checked the glove compartment. Everything was there: money, driver's license, ID card. Walter Muller, photoengraver, 171 Humboldt Street, Buffalo. He'd been an engineer last time, Plesek thought as he nosed the car out of the lot. He was going down in the world.

*　　*　　*

THE NIGHTTIME GUY / 39

The hotel was in the mid-Forties, between Fifth and Sixth, the kind of place that catered mainly to long-term residents, but also ran a regular day-to-day hotel service. It was pricey enough to keep out the hookers, but not so expensive as to be high on the list of hotel thieves, so the atmosphere tended to be quiet and slow. What it lacked in service it made up by its solid security and its big old-fashioned rooms which had been renovated ten years back. There weren't any single rooms anymore, only suites, and all of them had their own service kitchens. It was clean, well run, spacious, and good value, and not one New Yorker in a hundred had ever heard of it. An hour after he'd checked in Plesek walked across the red broadloom to answer the door.

"Mr. Hines?"

The man outside nodded.

"Come on in."

Plesek stepped aside, watching the man as he went past. He was a sloppy-looking person, thick and flabby with pouches in his face and a receding hairline. With his big jaw and button nose and mild expression of disinterest, he would have looked like an Irish cop had he weighed another forty pounds. He wasn't a big man, but he moved as if he thought he was, slow and ponderous. His appearance troubled Plesek; this man was supposed to be the tops. He'd expected somebody slick and efficient, not somebody who looked like a bad horseplayer.

Plesek closed the door, came back into the room.

The man ran his fisheyes over him. "Who are you?"

"Somebody with money to spend," Plesek answered.

The other man grunted. "Who told you about me?"

"I'm very well connected. Sit down, Mr. Hines."

He took a long time over it, hitching up his creased pants and sagging into a chair. Then he sat forward as if he had a pain in his stomach. "So? What's the deal?"

Plesek, taking a chair opposite him, reached into his jacket, produced an envelope, shook out the snapshot inside, and held it up. "I'm very interested in this man. I have an idea he's going to be meeting somebody soon whom I'm even more interested in."

Hines pointed at the photograph. "Let's start with this guy. What do you know about him?"

"I know everything about him. All you need to know anyway."

"What's his name?"

"Gallo. James Gallo."

"And the guy he's meeting?"

"I know nothing about him. I don't know who he is."

"You got a shot of him?"

"No."

Hines moved his shoulders as if he had an itch he couldn't get to. His face looked uncomfortable, too. "You want to know all about a guy except you can't tell me what guy. How am I supposed to find him?"

Plesek tapped the photograph in his hand. "Gallo will lead you to him."

"How do I spot him when he does?"

Plesek tossed the photograph onto the coffee table

between them, then sat back. "Yes," he said slowly, "that's a point, isn't it? I'm going to have to tell you something about this thing."

"That would help." Hines looked almost weary when he said it.

Plesek put a hand to the top of his head and smoothed his fair hair as if he were getting his thoughts into place. He started with a confession. "I don't live in this country, Mr. Hines. I'm not American."

"I figured that from your accent. Where you from?"

"That doesn't matter. The point is I'm working for another country, and if you take this job, you'd be working for another country, too. Does that bother you?"

"You're paying me in American money, right?"

"Right."

"Then it doesn't bother me."

"Fine. Except there's one more thing I should tell you before we start. If, when this job is over, or anytime during it, I have reason to believe you've repeated anything of what I'm going to tell you"—Plesek smiled politely—"you'll be killed."

The other man reacted to that with a long blink. He said, with a tinge of disgust in his voice, "I don't make my money that way."

Plesek nodded; the subject was closed. "Now, James Gallo. He's a high-up in the Defense Department based here in New York. He's in charge of some kind of experiment they're running, a new development involving eyedrops. Just what these drops are supposed to do, I can't tell you."

"You won't tell me, or you don't know?" Hines asked.

"I mean I don't know. We haven't been able to find out."

"Uh-huh," Hines said. It was obvious he didn't believe Plesek, and Plesek didn't try to hide the fact that he didn't care one way or the other. He didn't like Hines, and Hines clearly didn't like him; too bad.

"Tell me," Hines said, "how did you find out what you do know?"

"There are two doctors working on these drops; we bugged the home of one of them. Just temporarily, though, because we didn't want to risk it being found. So we don't have all the details."

"Why don't you just put the bug back in?"

Plesek gave a fast shake of his head. "If you can find out a secret when the other guy doesn't know you're even looking, it's ten times more valuable."

"You just want the secret? You don't want the drops?"

"We'd love to get the drops, but we don't hold out too much hope of being able to do that. So we'll settle for finding out what they're supposed to do."

Hines reached for the snapshot on the table. "Then why don't you pick up this guy, what's his name, Gallo, and ask him?"

"We couldn't do that. There are certain rules in this game, and touching a government man is a no-no."

Hines only grunted, but there was a lot that could be read into it. It was clear that for him, rules were something that belonged on football fields.

Plesek continued, speaking faster now. "Even though it didn't tell us everything, that bug we planted told us a lot. We're pretty sure they're going to test those drops on somebody outside the government, somebody with a special talent, although what kind of talent is another thing we don't know. But Gallo will do the recruiting; that's part of his job."

Hines nodded. "So I stay on Gallo's tail, see who he talks to, and try to spot a likely candidate to test eyedrops. Somebody who's got something special going for him."

"That's about it, yes."

Hines ran a hand around his mouth, his sleepy eyes on Plesek's face. "That's a toughie."

"I know. That's why I came to you. You have a reputation for being good on the tough ones."

Plesek succeeded in keeping sarcasm out of his voice, but Hines seemed to hear it anyway. He gave his host a sour look and decided to hit him where it hurts.

"A job like this, I'm gonna have to use all kinds of men. I couldn't touch it for less than ten grand."

"I'll give you fifteen," Plesek said, and had to stop himself from adding, "And that's my last offer."

"Fifteen?" Hines, upstaged for a moment, tried to recover the initiative. "I don't see it anywhere."

Plesek took a key from his pocket. "You will once you open a locker at Grand Central. Lexington Avenue side. There's eight thousand dollars in it. You'll get the other seven when you come up with a name." He took the envelope from the table, dropped the key into it, followed it with the photograph, and held it out to Hines. "All the info on Gallo's in here, too. Anything else you need?"

"Yeah," Hines said, taking the envelope. "A little luck."

5

I GOT ABOUT AS MUCH WORK DONE, when I got back from seeing Gallo, as I usually get done Christmas Eve. Night vision . . . the idea was fantastic. But I wasn't doing any Gee Whizzing; I was too mad. I couldn't get over Gallo and his proposal and the cheap way he'd tried to hook me into it. Mr. Slick himself, calmly asking me would I mind risking my eyesight so the Army could kill more people next time they got involved in an Asian land war, or an African land war, or wherever they're going to hold it. And what really burned me was the guy saying I was ideal for the job. I think I knew what he meant by that, and it wasn't just because I could handle being blind on account of my training; I think it was because he knew what had happened to my brother. He knew everything else about me, why shouldn't he know? And he thought he had a pretty good lever there. That casual way he'd looked up and commented on Ollie dying young, as if it had just occurred to him . . . bullshit, that was a calculated little piece of psychology on his part, and he could take it and sit on it.

Who did he think he was fooling? Hell, once upon

a time maybe you could have believed a government man, but these days? Everybody knows that governments fight dirty, especially against their own citizens.

Anyway, I thought that Gallo's attempt to enlist me by using my brother was just about the lowest of the low, but I was underestimating him. I thought he was the kind of guy who went into the ring with weighted gloves, but I found out next day that he also bribed the referee as well.

When five o'clock rolled around and my boss still hadn't fired me, I left the office, grabbed a fast bite, then went uptown to the Sight Center. As I walked into the place, I wondered if it wasn't another little piece of psychology Gallo had tried, scheduling our meeting on a day he knew I'd be going to the Center. Probably. I don't know. I do know that walking in there seemed a little different to me from all the other times I'd done it. It occurred to me that if they really were able to make a man see in the dark, then it was a colossal leap forward, and one giant breakthrough can bring on another, like, say, restoring the sight of somebody with a damaged optic nerve. Maybe Gallo had counted on that occurring to me, too. Maybe he'd thought I'd start feeling like a rat for holding up a giant stride in vision research. Let him. There were plenty of people who'd jump at the chance of renting out their eyes for ten grand. There were people who'd do it for ten dollars. He wasn't going to be short of volunteers.

I couldn't get over the guy. If he'd known me a little better he would never have tried to strong-arm me into it. If he'd just simply asked me if I'd volunteer, I wouldn't have said yes right away, but I probably wouldn't have said no right away either. I've always disliked being coerced into anything, manipulated, maneuvered, call it what you will. I don't like bullies, and I never have, and that upright sentiment has got me into trouble more than once. Not so long ago, in a coffee shop, I heard a guy tearing racial strips off a Puerto Rican waitress because she'd forgotten his doughnut or something. I told this guy what I thought of him, and he invited me outside to confirm my opinion, and I stupidly went. I'm no fighter—the guy clobbered me. I'm too light and too old to play Galahad, and I know it, but sometimes, when the world gets particularly unfair, I tend to forget it.

I went through the reception lobby and upstairs to the recreation room. It's never failed to affect me, walking into this room where just about everybody's blind; it's like going to a party where all the guests are doctors or painters, and they're all talking about DNA or Larry Rivers, and that makes you the odd man out. On the street a blind person's an exception. Here, I'm the freak.

The Sight Center, in case you've never heard of it, is a funded society that helps the blind in a lot of different ways. It has a big rehabilitation program; it teaches skills; it's also a social center and, in general, serves as a sanctuary from all the problems a blind person has to face. It has a full-time salaried staff, as well as part-time volunteers, people who come in and read a book into a cassette recorder for the Talking Library, or take a group out on a field trip, or teach remedial skills, or, like me, work with the newly blind, teaching them how to adjust. The idea is that they can rejoin and, we hope, find a place for themselves in a sighted world.

There are quite a few members of the staff who are blind. They always get the best results because it's impossible for a sighted person ever really to understand how it is to be blind, which is why most of the big advances in this kind of teaching have been made by people who couldn't see. I had a braille class that evening, two beginners I'd never worked with. One was a kid of about eighteen, and from his pale, wispy look I guessed that he'd lost his sight to some disease in his body, diabetes, maybe. When that goes unchecked, the blood vessels of the eye start degenerating, sometimes badly.

I've picked up quite a bit of knowledge hanging around the doctors and the other pros, enough to know that there're a lot of popular misconceptions about blindness and its treatment. For example, a lot of people are under the impression that all a blind person needs to do to see again is drop by the eye bank and arrange for an operation, but it isn't that simple. An eye graft works only in certain types of blindness, like when the outside part of the eye has been scarred. It's possible then to graft on a new cornea. Or if the lens behind the cornea is affected, if, for instance, a cataract develops, the lens can be removed and a pair of prescription glasses will do its work. But generally speaking, the farther back in the eye the problem is, the less surgery is able to help.

I started the class. "Okay, let's see where you're at. Ron, why don't we start with you? What's the first word?"

We were in one of the small classrooms on the second floor. I stood at the kid's shoulder and watched his fingers move slowly over the embossed type of the braille primer. He held his head level but cocked to one side, as if he were trying to hear the symbols as well as feel them.

"Cat," he said at last.

"That's a *P*, not a *T*. The word is 'cap.' "

"Cap," he said, and went back over it. I got him onto the next word, and he moved his fingers over the raised dots as if he were feeling for a chord on a piano.

In actual fact, there's a link between braille and a keyboard in that its inventor, Louis Braille, was one of the top organists of his day. He's usually credited with the invention of touch reading, but it isn't true. A blind Arab, a professor of languages, invented a system five hundred years before Braille was born. And between his system and the one Braille introduced, there were a whole slew of others that have mercifully fallen by the wayside. A hundred and fifty years after the Arab died a Spaniard came up with a set of letters carved on a thin piece of wood; then an Italian took that a stage further by engraving the letters rather than embossing them. But both systems failed because the letters were too difficult to read. A German tried his hand next, using letters made of tin, but his successor promptly went back to the old method of cutting letters in a wax-coated tablet. It was a case of taking one step forward, then one step backward, and it continued. In the seventeenth century an Italian Jesuit got close when he devised a kind of cipher code based on a series of

dots within squares, but in Scotland they went all
the way back to the ancient Incas and introduced a
system based on knotted strings, a different kind of
knot standing for a different letter of the alphabet.
They ended up with the Bible translated into half a
mile of string and wound around a giant reel. But
then everything went ahead again when an Austrian
woman, with the marvelous name of Maria Theresa
von Paradis, learned to read letters formed from
pins stuck into a cushion. And when a German, who
was also blind, invented a system which used letters
pricked through cardboard, Maria took this system
to Paris, where a man named Valentin Haüy had
founded the world's first school for the blind. But
Haüy thought he had a better idea, a system made
up of ordinary large type printed in relief. However,
learning to read it took forever, and trying to use it
to write with was next to impossible. But things took
a big leap forward again, to stay this time, when a
French army captain, Charles Barbier, visited Haüy's
school around 1820. He'd invented a system using
dots based on phonetics which he called night writing, and he'd done it so his soldiers could communi-
cate with each other on the battlefield in the dark.
Now that I think of it, there's a pretty close parallel
between Barbier's invention and those eyedrops of
Gallo's. Both of them were invented to further the
art of warfare. Well, I'm not sure whether Gallo's
drops will turn out to be a blessing or not, but Barbier's invention certainly did because it gave Louis
Braille the idea for his system.

Why he needed a system is a bit sad. His father
was a Parisian shoemaker, and Braille, when he was

only a kid, blinded himself playing with one of his father's tools. He was put into Haüy's school, where he studied Barbier's night writing system, realized its value, and adapted it for his own system. He had it more or less complete by the time he was sixteen, but he spent another nine years on it till he was satisfied.

Basically, it's a series of dots embossed on thick manila paper, although a newer technique uses solid plastic dots bonded to the paper. But whichever, it still comes out as a kind of Morse code for the fingers. For example, the letter *A* is one dot, *B* is two vertical dots, *C* is two horizontal dots. No more than six dots are needed because you can get sixty-three combinations out of them, which is what you have in English braille: twenty-six symbols for the alphabet, one symbol each for "And," "For," "Of," "The," and "With," and the remaining thirty-two for contractions and punctuation. In other languages the arrangement is different, although you still have the same sixty-three symbols that can be used. And that makes braille the only universal writing, because whether a blind person's reading the Koran in Arabic or the *Kamasutra* in Tamil or Harold Robbins in Japanese, it's all written in the same script.

It's a great invention, all right, but not everybody can master it. The kid I was teaching in this class, for instance, Ron, was going to be okay once he got the hang of it, but I wasn't so sure about the other person in the room. I'd watched her trying to follow the lesson, and she was struggling.

"Mary, read the second word for me."

She was a middle-aged woman who looked like

any housewife you'd see lining up at a checkout counter. She was wearing dark glasses like a lot of newly blind people. Later, when they get a little more used to their condition, many of them find that a cane is all the badge they need, and they start leaving the shades off unless they're wearing them for cosmetic reasons. The ones this woman was wearing didn't quite hide some unhealed scars on her face. Auto accident, probably.

"Tap," she said very hesitantly. I knew she was guessing. I think she was embarrassed at even being asked. I could understand it, a woman her age, twenty years running a household in Queens or Brooklyn, suddenly thrown into a bewildering world of new rules. It couldn't be easy for her. Especially the braille; she'd probably do better switching to Moon, which is an embossed line system that's easier for older people whose touch isn't good enough for braille.

I spent the next hour with them and, when the lesson was over, changed classrooms and worked with a more advanced group before calling it a night. Coming out into the main lounge, I ran into Bev Jordan, a volunteer like me who taught an audio typing course. I wasn't feeling that great—my hangover was more than just a memory, and I was still shook up from my session with Gallo—but when I saw Bev, my troubles, as always, vanished in a stream of pure lust. Bev Jordan had to be one of the sexiest-looking chicks in New York, a walking *Playboy* centerfold, and just the sight of her coming toward me or going away, or just standing still, did more for my hormones than a six-week regimen of pills.

"Hi, Bev." I always tried to speak a little lower when I greeted her.

She smiled at me. "How are you, Max?"

"I'm all right now," I said, letting my eyes wash over her.

She got it and acknowledged the compliment with another little smile. Smiles are all I ever get from Bev Jordan. I've been trying for two years to get her up to my apartment, but I haven't even managed to get her as far as the front door of the Center.

"How are things?" I asked, being incredibly witty.

"Just fine."

"You all through for the night?"

"Uh-huh."

"Me too. What do you say we take in a movie maybe? Then grab a bean later on."

I got the same old shake of the head: I'm really used to it by now. "Thanks all the same, Max, but I don't think so."

"One of these days, Bev, you're going to say yes and I'm going to die of shock."

"Oh, I don't think there's much chance of that, Max."

"Which? You saying yes or me dying of shock?"

"Take your pick," she said, flashed another smile, and walked away. When I say walked, I don't mean walked, I mean moved off in a kind of many-sectioned glide.

She drives me crazy, and it must have been pretty evident because a voice beside me said, "You didn't miss much, Max."

I whipped my head around; it was Pete Withers, another volunteer.

"She's very disappointing," he said.

For a moment I believed him. "You've been there?"

He started to laugh.

"You bastard," I said. I had to laugh myself because it was no secret how I felt about Bev Jordan. I think all the male volunteers felt the same way, but I had the worst case of all.

"Come on," Withers said, "we're going to the movies."

"You're joking. If Bev won't go with me, you think I'd settle for you?"

"But I'll be buying my own ticket. Think of the money you'll save. Come on, it's supposed to be terrific."

Pete Withers is one of those good-natured, insistent guys who never recognize a turndown. All you can do with them is surrender.

"What is it anyway?"

He told me the title; I'd never heard of it.

"Faye Dunaway," he said.

"Don't miss it, Max. I seen it last week. It's a fantastic flick." This was from a guy named Benny who'd wandered up.

Benny is probably the happiest blind person I've ever met, and also one of the most capable. His handicap didn't seem to bother him any more than a broken fingernail.

"You went to the movies?" Withers asked.

"Sure, I go all the time," Benny answered. They love to kid each other, and they're always doing it.

"That's the last time I buy an apple from you, you goddamn fake."

Benny laughed. "Hey, you know that book that's set in the future, the one where they got these movies, only they call them the feelies? You just plug a gadget into your seat and you can feel what's happening up there on the screen. Well, lemme tell you, man, when that Dunaway's up there, I get the feelies. And I don't need no electronic help."

Withers came back at him. "Benny, you should enter for the next blind Olympics. You'd be a shoo-in for a gold medal in the pervert competition."

People were laughing around the room; these two were popular. Benny was an inspiration, the Center's unofficial champ, while Pete Withers had the knack of getting a blind person to feel a lot more confident about things.

"I'll tell you something," Benny answered. "I do a whole lot better with women now that I'm blind than I ever did when I had my sight."

"You'd do even better if they were blind, too," Withers replied.

Benny laughed louder than anybody. "Listen," he said. "I'm not kidding. The other night I was with this girl and I asked her if I could feel how she looked, you know, the way they're always doing it in the movies. She said sure, and five minutes later she said, 'When are you going to get around to my face?' "

Everybody broke up. Withers shook his head and said, "Maybe two gold medals."

On the way out I saw the kid I'd been teaching braille to earlier. He was sitting in a lounge chair practicing on an exercise card, and I went over and said good-night.

"Mr. Ellis," he said, "is this word 'ceiling'?"

"It sure is, Ron."

His face broke into a smile of delight. "How about that? My first big word."

I told him to keep it up and took a final look at him, sitting there in his dark closet world, his fingers moving painfully slowly over the braille card. Then I left with Pete Withers and went to see a movie.

I got back to my apartment around eleven and was happy to be home after the kind of day I'd had. My apartment isn't anything special, the standard two rooms, but after five years I've got it almost the way I want it. It takes some doing changing the personality of the standard New York two-roomer, with its inevitable cheap parquet floor, its curtainless windows, and its soulless white walls, but I've put down good broadloom and bought some nice pieces and covered up large sections of those walls with some Vuillard lithographs which I never get tired of looking at. Utica, New York, where I grew up in the forties, is a far cry from Paris, 1890, but there's something about his brown and gold room interiors that I find incredibly nostalgic, and I've always been a sucker for nostalgia.

Before I moved into this apartment, I lived in the Village because my ex-wife thought it would be romantic, but the Village she was thinking of, when the place had been a real neighborhood and full of writers and painters, had been gone for years, and we hated it. That wasn't the only romance missing from our marriage, and three years after we tied the knot, it went on the rocks. Well, maybe not the rocks; with me rowing one way, and her rowing the other, the marital boat just split in two and sank with all hands.

Still, there were some good times, and I miss them. Hell, I miss being married, although I'm not about to try it again unless I'm sure it's going to work. I've met a lot of women, and more than one has shared my humble abode for a time, but so far there's been nobody I wanted to spend the rest of my life with. I'm sorry about that because I'm not really crazy about living alone. I'm too old to do the odd couple bit and room with another guy, and I'm not old enough to say the hell with it and live with a cat. I'll get married again. It just may take awhile.

I fixed myself a glass of milk, caught the end of the news, took a fast shower, and got into bed. I must have been pretty whacked because I drifted right off and didn't know a thing till hours later, when I found myself sitting up straight with sweat popping out of every pore.

I'd had the dream again, stronger and more vivid than ever. It was so clear it could have been coming in by cable.

I got out of bed and went around switching lights on, sat down in a chair, and heartily regretted the fact I'd given up smoking. That rotten, lousy dream. It was picking me up, wringing me out, and hanging me up to dry. I knew I was going to get to a point where I'd start being afraid to go to sleep, just sit in front of the box all night, and gulp pills all next day so I could do my job. That's a fast way of ending up in pieces, but that's what I was looking at unless I could find a way to beat the thing. I thought about the conversation with Cy Greene at his party two nights back. Again I was surprised I'd told him, although Cy's the kind of guy you feel like talking to because he's such a good listener. It's his profession anyway, he's a psychologist, and he has the knack of getting people to let go.

I was a bit looped, I guess, and must have looked pretty down, and there was just him and me left, so when he asked me what the problem was, I explained that I'd been having lousy sleeps. And when he asked me why that was, I told him about the dream. He didn't comment till I'd finished; then he asked me, in that quiet, comforting voice of his, how old I'd been when it happened.

"Nine."

"How old was your brother?"

"Eleven."

"When did the dream start?"

"Not till I was eighteen. I'd have it now and then, and it would go away for a while. But in the last few years it's really started to come on strong."

"How strong?"

"Twice, three times a week."

"That's strong."

"I know it."

Cy, sitting opposite me, had taken a sip of his drink and said, "You know why you're having it, don't you?"

"Sure I do. But I don't know how to stop having it. And I wish I did because, I mean it, Cy, that goddamn dream's giving me fits."

"It's simple enough," he said. "You'll stop having it when you stop feeling responsible."

"But I was responsible. I am responsible."

"Max. You're sounding like somebody who got smashed out of his skull, piled into a car, and ran somebody down. You were nine years old, Max. What happened was an accident."

"Of course it was. But it was still my fault."

He finished his scotch and stood up, a big bear of a man but so gentle. I got up, too, and he walked me to the door.

"Give yourself a break, Max. There isn't any debt, and you're going to have to realize that. It's totally imaginary."

I asked him, "What if I can't help thinking there is a debt? A real one."

He smiled and shrugged. "Then you'll have to find a way of canceling it."

"What?"

"Find a way to cancel it, Max."

Cy Greene's suggestion bounced around inside my head, and it occurred to me, sitting there with my skin goose-bumping in the chill of early morning, that maybe it wasn't such a bad piece of advice. It also occurred to me that I knew a way I might be able to follow it. So when I got to the office later that morning, I did nothing but think about it till the phone rang around eleven. It was Gallo wanting to know if I'd changed my mind.

I took a very big breath and told him that I had. I told him I'd be his guinea pig. And do you know what the guy said? "Good. I thought you might."

Jesus, what a bastard.

6

PLESEK HEARD FROM HINES sooner than he expected; he'd been a bit surprised to hear from him at all. The man had asked him to come down to his office, which was good news. Not only did it mean that Hines might have something, but it was also a chance to get out.

He enjoyed the cab ride down Fifth Avenue; the spring weather had brought a snap and sparkle to the city that was a welcome change from the gray skies of Canada. The crowds on the sidewalk seemed to welcome the weather, too; most of the women wore sweaters and skirts. Back in Ottawa they'd still be bundled up like bears.

The taxi left him off on a street full of nondescript furriers and button shops that catered to the garment trade a little farther to the west. The building Hines had his office in was no different from any of its neighbors, a ten-story office block that looked as if the only thing holding it up were the fifty years of grime plastered to its exterior. The sight of it didn't make Plesek feel any better about the man he'd hired; he was New York's choice, and the New York office had been wrong before about people.

He went up in an ancient elevator to the seventh floor and walked down a dusty corridor. All the office doors were closed, and if it hadn't been for the faint sound of a typewriter, he would have thought the entire floor deserted. He stopped outside a door that had a number lettered in black numerals on its crinkly glass. Pinned to the wood above the knob was a small printed card that said Hines Commercial Photography. Plesek pressed the bell, and an answering buzzer sounded, releasing the electric door lock. The office he walked into didn't look as if it had been cleaned in a month, although he doubted that would have cured its air of drabness. An old box-shaped Underwood sat on a green metal desk, circa 1950, with a padded-back rollaway chair behind it. There was a filing cabinet in one corner, and in the other, an armchair that could have been bought at a hotel auction. Above it was a framed photograph of a small factory, and on the wall facing it a shot of a two-story suburban office block. The only touch of color was the picture of a tulip field on an airline calendar still open at the previous month.

The door to the inner office opened, and Hines, a half-eaten sandwich in his hand, motioned him in.

This office was almost a duplicate of the other but with a little more evidence of the nature of his business. A metal tripod was propped in a corner, and two cameras rested on a shelf over the radiator, an old fashioned Rollie, and an even more old-fashioned Speed Graphex. A plastic shoulder bag, lying open on the floor, contained a lens hood, some Kodak film, and a roll of white tape. Louvered blinds, layered with dust, were lowered over the window and slanted so that the view of the building opposite was almost closed off. In front of the window a Coke cup made wet rings on a square wooden desk, a folded newspaper next to it, and a brown paper bag from a delicatessen.

Hines locked the door and walked around behind his desk. He seemed more concerned with his lunch than his visitor.

"Thanks for coming down," he said.

Plesek was still looking at the Speed Graphex; it must have been thirty years old. He said dryly, "I'm sure it will be worth it."

Hines picked up the Coke cup, tipped it back, draining it, belched softly, then looked at Plesek. "You don't rate me, do you?"

"Somebody else did the rating, Mr. Hines. They said you were the best."

"They're right," Hines replied. "But you don't think so."

"I'll be happy to be convinced."

"What would you say if I told you I just took your photograph?"

Plesek gave him a tiny smile. "A wall camera, a foot button, it wouldn't be hard."

"Unh-unh. Hand-held."

Plesek looked at the man's hands and saw only the half-eaten sandwich. "In that case, I think I'd be impressed."

Hines gobbled the last of the sandwich, took a paper napkin from the bag, and wiped off his hands. He picked up the Coke cup, put two fingers on its base, and unscrewed it. He held it out for Plesek to examine. There was a tiny hole in the center of the base and, on the other side, a camera no more than an inch square fitting snugly into the fake bottom. Hines pointed to the seam of the cup. "The plunger runs up here to a little bulb in the lip of the rim. I work it by biting down on it."

"Did you make that?"

"I make everything I use."

"That's very clever," Plesek said, and began to feel a lot better about the man. The guy had an artistic temperament, he wanted to be appreciated, and that was good. Artists always cared more, so they took more trouble.

From the pocket of his baggy jacket Hines fished out a bunch of keys. "Come on, I'll show you what I got." He moved to a door on the other side of the office which Plesek had noticed and thought was a closet. But when he looked again, he saw that the door was made of steel and had no hinges showing. There were two locks, one near the top of the frame, one near the bottom. Hines put a separate key into each, pulled the door open, went in, and snapped on a light for Plesek.

The room was as long as the office but no more than ten feet wide. At one end, where a window might once have been, a movie screen was stretched against the wall. At the other end cupboards were built in on two sides, with a large cabinet backing onto the rear wall. It was six feet high with glass doors and black cloth-covered shelves, and standing on those shelves was a collection that could have gone on display at a photography fair.

The lenses alone took up half the space, brilliant blues and deep browns glittering like an optician's window. Wide-angle lenses, telephoto lenses, they ran all the way from a standard 35mm to a 1,000 mm monster the size of a man's arm. Most of the cameras were famous makes, shiny steel and black chrome, the finest that Japan and Germany could produce. The rest didn't look like cameras at all.

Hines slid back the door of a side cupboard and swung out a movie projector hinged to a metal arm. It swiveled laterally and locked into place with a precise click. From the cupboard on the opposite wall he brought out a carrousel projector mounted in the same way. When he locked it off, the two projectors sat next to each other suspended on their arms about four feet above the floor. Everything was beautifully designed and worked with an exact precision that was in amazing contrast with the man who'd set it up. Hines was turning out to be a surprise, and Plesek began to feel excited as he watched him thread film through the projector.

"You think you've found somebody?" he asked.

Hines said, "Yep. We got lucky. We got a break."

"What kind of break?"

"I had men covering Gallo's office building shooting everybody going in and out. We must've shot more film than *Gone with the Wind*. But then Gallo got cute. He left his office Monday, took a cab to Klein's, went in the front and came out the side, and got another cab. Might've lost him if I hadn't put three men on him."

"You would've needed five men if he'd really been trying. He was just being cautious."

Hines, finished with the film, was dropping slides into the carrousel. "Anyway, we knew something was up. We tailed him to the tax office and figured he was meeting somebody there."

"The tax office?"

Hines killed the lights, and the room went black for a second before the projector's beam cut a white path through the dark. The picture danced on the screen, then focused on people going up and down the steps of a building. It was shot from a low angle, and around the edge of the picture was a blurred image which Plesek guessed was a piece of whatever the camera had been concealed in.

"It was the lunch hour, so that was another break," Hines said over the whir of the projector. "A lot less people to cover."

The angle changed to the other side of the steps, the camera panning on people as they came down them, their faces distorting slightly as they went by the lens. None of them seemed remotely aware they were being filmed.

"Gallo was in there about an hour, then went back to his office. Which left us with about thirty or forty possibilities. Okay, next day, around about the same time, he does the cautious bit again, leaves his office in a car and goes uptown, switches to the subway, and heads back downtown."

The screen went blank for a moment; then a new picture popped on: trees and grass, people in a park. The image was grainy with little depth as if it had been shot from a long way off, and this time, it was only slightly below normal eye level. The picture jumped suddenly to two men on a bench talking.

"There's Gallo," Hines went on. "Rapping away

with the curly-headed guy. We tried to pick up the conversation, but it was no go."

"How come?"

"We put a mike in a paper bag and dropped it in that trash can next to the bench, but Gallo was wearing a multi-frequency scrambler. You know them? They're pretty new. A person can't hear them, but a mike sure can. Plays hell with reception, and it's impossible to filter out."

"I know them," Plesek said. "Gallo was taking precautions again."

"You don't figure he knew the tail was on?"

"No. He would never have met anybody in a park."

"Makes sense," Hines admitted.

"Who's the curly-headed man? Were you able to find out?"

"Name's Ellis. Maybe you didn't spot him, but he's on film going into the tax office."

"Is he now?" Plesek said. "What does he do?"

"Computer programmer."

"A programmer? Then I doubt he's the man we're after. I don't see the connection."

"Wait," Hines said. He cut the movie and switched on the slide projector, squeezed the remote bulb, and watched a still picture pop onto the screen. It showed the curly-headed man walking alone. "We followed this guy back to his office, waited for him to come out again, then tailed him home."

Hines squeezed the switch, again changing the slide. "There he is going into his apartment house.

We hung around there for a while to see if he had any other plans, and he did."

The picture changed again, a close-up this time, taken at night, of the curly-headed man standing at a bus stop.

"He went uptown. Fifty-sixth Street. This place."

The switch clicked. The new picture was shot from behind the man as he went through the door of a building.

"That's when I knew he was the guy you're after."

"Why?" Plesek asked quickly. "I don't understand."

"You want some kind of connection with eyedrops, right? Take a look what it says on those doors."

Hines changed the slide to a tight shot of the building's doors. The black lettering almost jumped off the screen.

Plesek read it out. "The Sight Center." Then he said slowly, with a lot of satisfaction, "Bingo."

"That's what I figured, too. I got a twenty-four-hour tail on him."

"What's his name again?"

"Max Ellis." Hines reversed the machine, clicked the switch twice, and went back to the frontal shot of the man waiting for the bus. He pulled focus so that the face filled the screen.

Plesek stared at it and smiled. "Okay, Max," he said.

7

SOME OF THE THINGS THAT turn heads in most cities of the world don't even get a second glance in New York, and one of them is an ambulance screaming through the streets. They're as much a part of the city as air conditioning, and they attract about as much notice. But this was one ambulance I couldn't have turned to watch anyway, because I was in it.

I couldn't see anything either—I was lying on a stretcher with my head bandaged from my scalp down to my upper lip, looking as if I'd just come off a Honda on the Major Deegan, which was exactly what was supposed to have happened to me. I'd even been dressed in clothes that looked as if they'd hit the road at sixty: a jacket with one sleeve torn away and a pair of pants with one leg ripped to the knee. I also had some authentic-looking bandages on my leg on that side. All this had been done to me in the back of a van that had picked me up at my apartment and driven me up to the Bronx. Two government men handled the job, both wearing white medical outfits. We'd switched to a waiting ambulance, then taken off in a burst of burned rubber, flashing lights, and wailing siren.

Gallo had surprised me. From his casual manner I thought I was going to be eased into this thing, but I'd been catapulted into it with dizzying speed. I'd met him again the same day he'd called me, which was that morning, come to think of it; in Battery Park this time. It hadn't been a long meeting, just long enough for him to explain how they were going to work it. For a start, he was going to square things with my boss as he'd said; next, I was going to get a new identity and a new address. That was a must, because I couldn't turn up newly blind at my old apartment, then, a week later when the tests were finished, confound friends and neighbors by suddenly not being blind anymore. I could hardly tell them I'd been to Lourdes.

And there was another reason I had to lose my identity, one which, when I thought about it, didn't make me feel like telling the driver to stop at the first liquor store for a bottle of champagne: I had to have a cover in case persons unknown checked on me.

When I'd asked Gallo who was going to want to check on me he'd frowned and said, "You have to understand something, Max"—he was calling me by my first name now, the hunter feeling a touch of love for the prey he's just bagged—"this thing's big. Top top secret. I'm running this show, but even I don't know what's in those eyedrops. Even my boss doesn't know, and he's been with the department for fifteen years. Nobody's taking any chances. I don't have to tell you what kind of advantage a country would have if its armed forces had night vision potential. A secret like this would be worth millions to anybody who had it to sell."

"But nobody knows we have it, do they?"

"Not as far as we know. But if somebody thought we did, they'd break down doors to grab it. That's why security's so tight. The trouble is, no security can ever be perfect, so if somebody does get wind of it and comes sniffing around, everything has to look kosher."

When Gallo told me that, I'd got the first little flutterings of anxiety. I'd been worried only about my eyes, but I was beginning to understand I might have to look out for my skin as well. So I was more than happy to have another identity I could hide behind. I was now Max Sinclair, born in Philadelphia and with a birth certificate on file there. I had a driver's license, Social Security number, Bank Americard, even a charge account at Macy's, plus college and high school records. Thorough man, Gallo. He'd even got me to call anybody who might have occasion to get in touch with me during the next seven days and give them a story about my being transferred to the Coast for a bit.

My sudden departure disrupted my life less than I thought it would, although it did mean I had to cancel a date with a young lady who I think was ripe for a meaningful relationship, and I hate to miss out on any of those. I also took a trip up to the Sight Center to arrange for a substitute to take my classes for a while. Then I seemed to be free to embark on this new adventure, and the way the ambulance was taking corners, the thrills had already started. I wasn't sorry when it skidded to a stop and I heard the rear doors bang open. I felt myself being lifted out on the stretcher, transferred to another one, and wheeled up a ramp into an echoing room. I didn't have much trouble visualizing the emergency ward of a big city hospital. Gallo hadn't said how I should play it, but I figured anyone who'd come off their bike hard enough to maybe fracture his skull wouldn't be sitting up and asking what time dinner was, so I lay very still and just breathed. I heard doors swoosh closed, and my stomach dropped away as we went up in an elevator; then I was trundled out of it and down what I assume was a corridor—I could hear the trolley wheels squealing on the linoleum and smell fresh polish. There was another door; then the trolley stopped, and two pairs of arms prized me up and laid me out on cool, stiff sheets. Somebody whisked my clothes off, slipped a pair of pajamas onto me, eased pillows under my bandaged head, and pulled a sheet up to my shoulders. I heard the trolley being wheeled away, the door opened and closed, and I seemed to be alone.

It must have been the fastest hospital admittance on record. There was none of the usual hanging around, bleeding all over the admittance desk while they checked your Blue Cross number against the delinquent list—bing, bang, and I was in. Gallo had told me they'd got the cooperation of the local fuzz; I think the story for the hospital was that I was wanted for questioning, which would explain the cop who was going to be sitting outside my door. He wouldn't be a real cop, he'd be another government man, and he'd be there to make sure no overzealous nurse would try to change my bandages.

There was still nobody coming near me, and I started to wonder if they hadn't got me mixed up with a genuine casualty, somebody scheduled to have a lobotomy, maybe—that would have been kicks. But I didn't get very far with this thought because the door opened and I heard Gallo's voice.

Somebody worked scissors at my bandage, snipping it at the sides, then unwound it off my face so I could see. The room was lit only by a bedside lamp, but I still had to squinch my eyes for a second to adjust.

I found I was exactly where I thought I was, in a private room: dressing table, washstand, folded screen in the corner. There were three men looking at me: one of the ambulance guys, who'd just cut away my bandages, Gallo, and somebody standing with him.

Gallo introduced us. "Max, this is George Weyland, my boss."

The man gave me a heavy nod. "Mr. Ellis," he said.

They were certainly a contrast, those two. Gallo had on another one of his suits that looked as if it had been tailored in London and dry-cleaned in Paris, while Weyland's looked like a red-tag special from Korvette's. He was much more the way I'd pictured a government man on a top secret project: a big guy with a neck, 1950s close-cropped hair, and a mouth that looked as if it had been drawn onto his face with a thin pale crayon. Gallo had said his boss had been with the department for fifteen years, and I was willing to bet he'd never called in sick once. He struck me as the solid, plodding type who went by the book and avoided bum decisions by making dull ones.

The guy was looking at me as if he were mentally flicking through a pile of Wanted posters; then, when the ambulance guy had left, he started talking. His voice matched the rest of him: stern and upright.

"Mr. Ellis, in a few minutes somebody will be here to put the drops in your eyes, and from that moment on you're going to be a very valuable man. Also a unique one. You're going to be the first man able to see in the dark."

"The second," I said. "The old man, he was the first."

"Yes. I was forgetting," Weyland answered. Which struck me as strange; this clearly wasn't a guy who forgot things. And something else bothered me, too. I got the impression that I'd surprised Weyland, which made me wonder if Gallo had told me more than he was supposed to. I imagined that Weyland would enjoy rapping Gallo's knuckles for that little lapse, although maybe I was being unfair to Weyland—I didn't know the guy, after all—but his type has about as much personality as a wire coat hanger.

He continued his little lecture. "I know Mr. Gallo has already explained the importance of this project, and that can't be too highly stressed. Secrecy is paramount. You'll have to guard against giving even a hint of what you're doing. Remember that because you'll be coming into contact with new people. Don't feel you can confide in anybody. We don't expect you'll have anything but a smooth ride, but you can't afford to relax for a moment."

"Right. Got it," I said, holding off on the salute.

Gallo was about to say something but stopped when the door opened. A younger copy of Weyland strode halfway into the room, gave it a fast once-over, got a nod from Weyland, then opened the door wide and stepped back.

Four men came in quickly; then the door was shut and locked, and I started to feel a bit uncomfortable. It was partly the sight of three of the men: each of them carried an airline bag over his right shoulder and had his right hand buried inside it. It was pretty clear there was something fast and deadly in them, machine guns, probably, those little ones that are fired like a handgun, what are they called, Ingrams? A single half-second burst can put ten little holes in you.

Their owners were pretty charming, too. They had the same slightly gone look of killer Dobermans—only one purpose in life. Those guys were upsetting, all right, but what really iced my insides was the man they were surrounding, a chubby little fellow carrying a metal box manacled to his wrist. It was smaller than a shoe box and bright green in color, and the way it gleamed in the light it looked as though it contained killer plague germs or some horror from another planet with a hundred eyes and a thousand teeth. Up till now this whole exercise had only been theoretical, but the dramatic arrival of that little steel box was about to shift it into the practical stage, and I was scared.

The Dobermans with the airline bags spread out and seemed to be keeping a wary eye on each other as much as anything else. Their leader, the junior

Weyland, pulled a small leather case from his pocket, snapped it open, took out a key, and unlocked the manacle from the chubby man's wrist. Then he unlocked the box itself, putting it down on the bedside table, and stood back watching it as if he expected it to sprout legs and make a dash for the door.

Gallo spoke. "Max this is Dr. John."

The chubby little man smiled and said hello. He looked exactly like a country doctor in a soap opera, balding, plump, benign. Under other circumstances, I think he would have driven to the hospital in a '38 Ford.

"How are you feeling?" he asked, opening the box, and I half expected him to take out a thermometer and start shaking it down.

"Fine," I said, not paying too much attention; my eyes were on the box. The inside was lined with a velvet-looking fabric, and I could see a squat little bottle cradled and cushioned by foam rubber. Beside it, fitting perfectly into its own special groove, a metal tube rested, very much like the kind good cigars come in.

The doctor lifted out the little bottle and held it up to the light. It was half full of a clear, viscous fluid that slid heavily to one side when he tilted it. He began to pick at the tape around the screw top.

There were eight people in that room, but the only sound was the tiny scraping of the doctor's fingernail on the tape. I had to say something just to break that eerie silence.

"Two teaspoons after every meal, that right?"

It got a chuckle from the doctor, zilch from everybody else. He finished picking, put the bottle down on the table, and very carefully unscrewed the cap. Then he picked up the metal tube, twisted it open, took out the eyedropper inside, dipped in into the bottle, and expertly sucked up a minuscule amount. He put the dropper down, recapped and retaped the bottle, and put it back in its frame inside the green box. Then he picked up the eyedropper again and turned to me.

"Would you sit up, please?"

What I felt like doing, with that evil-looking eyedropper coming toward me, was ducking beneath the covers and telling Gallo I'd had second thoughts, but it was a little late for that now.

The doctor tilted my head back and to one side and gently held my left eye open with thumb and forefinger.

"Quite still," he murmured. "This may sting a bit." Then he dropped something that felt like chili sauce into the corner of my eye.

Instinctively I brought my hand up to rub, but kindly old Dr. John parried it, and said in his kindly Council Bluffs voice, "It'll sting for only a second. Only one more to do now and we're all through."

Only one more to do? How many eyes did he think I had?

When he gave me the second drop, I had two balls of fire in my head, but the sting quickly faded, my vision cleared, and apart from some rapid blinking, my eyes felt normal again. The doctor put the empty dropper in its tube, put it back in the metal box, and shut the lid.

The snap of its closing was the signal for action

stations. The security captain, or whatever he was, stepped forward and locked the box, but this time snapped the manacle closed on his own wrist. He turned for the door, and the Dobermans gathered around him like linemen protecting a star quarterback. I don't think anybody was sorry to see them go; I've seen some pretty stony-faced payroll guards, but never anything like those guys.

I relaxed a little myself. With that little box gone it was as if a bomb had just been defused.

I watched kindly old Dr. John take some things out of his pockets: something flat, wrapped in aluminum foil, and a fresh bandage, from which he tore the wrapper. Inside the foil were two square pieces of heavy lint. He got me to close my eyes and laid a piece of lint on both eyelids. They'd been treated with something that smelled like hand cream. I thought they were a salve of some kind, but they turned out to be a sort of glue pad; my eyelids stuck together almost immediately, and when I tried to open my eyes a few minutes later, I couldn't.

"They're so you'll have a complete absence of light," the doctor explained. "The stuff needs it to work properly."

"How long will that take?" I asked.

"Less than twenty-four hours," he said, and started to rebandage my eyes.

Like a man who's been bitten by a snake and wants to know what color it was, I wanted to know about those drops, so I asked the doctor exactly how they worked. "Or is that information classified?"

"Not at all. The theory behind night vision's no secret, only the compound that makes it possible."

He went on bandaging and seemed happy to chat. "Do you know anything about the eye?"

"A little."

"Then you know what the retina is. . . ."

"Sure."

"What is it?" I don't think the good doctor believed me.

"The lining at the back of the eye. It receives impulses, and they're transmitted to the brain via the optic nerve." I would like to have seen the doctor's face when I came back at him like a med student, but all I could see was the inside of my eyelids, which was a very dark place indeed.

"Absolutely right. It's a mesh of nerve fibers and their light-sensitive endings, and it's these nerve endings that we're dealing with here."

You can imagine how I felt at the thought of anybody dealing with my nerve endings, but I said nothing and listened.

"There are two kinds of nerve endings, cones and rods. The cones function in good light, and the rods work when there's less light. You have to remember, light isn't just how we see; it's also why we see. Because what vision is, basically, is a chemical reaction to light. And the rods and cones in the retina are sensitive to the chemical products of these reactions. Are you still with me?"

"Just," I said.

"Go on." It was Gallo's voice. Apparently he was also getting his first lesson in how the stuff worked.

"Right. Well we know what the rods are sensitive to, a chemical called rhodopsin. In daylight it's inactivated. The rods switch off, and the less sensitive cones take over. If that didn't happen, we wouldn't be able to see because of the glare. At night the rods take over again. Now, what some genius has come up with here is something that produces a chemical reaction that boosts the rods so they can magnify even the tiniest amount of light. This allows the retina to relay information to the brain, which is vision. Only in this case, night vision."

I made a connection and jumped in. "But because the rods don't switch off in the daytime, I'll be blind because of the glare."

The doctor tapped me on the shoulder as if I were being awfully bright. But I wasn't being bright, just anxious.

"Exactly. This compound, whatever it is, inhibits the production of rhodopsin, and the rods go on functioning. So there'll be too much light for you. It's a lot like a camera. If you set the aperture too wide on a sunny day, all you'll get is a blank white print."

Weyland joined in. He'd been following it, too. "What they need then," he said, "is to find something that will do the same job on the rods at night, but not interfere with the other thing."

"The rhodopsin," the doctor said. "Right. Then you'll have both day and night vision."

"One more than I'm going to have," I said.

He finished the bandage then, and I asked him about the pill, the one that would return my normal sight, and he told me it was designed simply to reverse the process.

"It takes about ninety minutes, I understand." And I waited for him to verify that.

He said, "We think that should do it, yes."

That pricked up my ears. "You think? You mean it'll be different for me from the other man, because he was older?"

Gallo spoke. "Max, I think we'll have to can the questions now. Dr. John has to get back."

"That's right," the doctor said, but there was a moment's pause before he said it, and I got the impression that signs were being made in the air. And that bothered me, that really did. There was something about the old man, the first guinea pig, they weren't telling me. The doctor had inadvertently told me what it was, but I was thinking so fast I went racing past it.

He touched my arm. "Well, so long now. Be good."

I heard his feet crossing the floor, and the door open and close.

"Gallo? You still there?"

"Right here, Max."

"Mr. Weyland?"

"I'm here, too."

But both of them sounded as though they'd rather not have been, and as I pondered that, my subconscious backed up and slipped into the spot I should have seen before.

"Designed." I said it loudly. "That doctor told me how the pill is *designed* to work; that's the word he used. Doesn't he know about the tests on the old man?"

There was a silence; then Gallo said my name and followed it with one of the cruelest expressions in the English language. Cruel because it keeps you waiting for the ax to fall.

"I have something to tell you."

"Then tell me, for God's sake."

"The old man we tested the drops on died before we got a chance to test the pill."

In three seconds I went from a stupefied state to a red-faced, all-systems-go condition. I ripped back the covers and sprang out of bed, fully intending to nail the bastard right in his lying mouth before I realized you can't hit somebody you can't see.

I must have looked a fearsome threat standing there in pajamas with my head bandaged as if it were broken in two places. I called Gallo every kind of son of a bitch I could think of, and when I ran out of words, Weyland, in his official headmaster's voice, said, "I think it would be best if you got back into bed, Mr. Ellis."

There didn't seem much else I could do anyway, so I got back into bed.

Weyland said, "I regret the circumstances under which you were hired, but it was necessary."

"Necessary? Why didn't you tell me the *truth*?"

Gallo answered, "Because you might have turned us down, Max, and we needed you. You're the right man for the job, and the job has to be done now."

"Oh, you're beautiful, Gallo. Just beautiful. Jesus, I've been conned before, out of money, affection, all kinds of things, but nobody ever tried to rip off my eyesight."

"You're worrying about nothing, Max. The men who came up with the drops also came up with the pill. We know that the one works; it stands to reason the other one will."

"And if it doesn't," I said, "I'll be the one to prove it."

"Mr. Ellis. . . ." Weyland's turn again. "We're certain the pill will work. We've been assured of that. But if by chance it doesn't, you'll be amply compensated. You'll be a rich man for the rest of your life."

"Great. I'll put in my own fucking movie theater."

Gallo was still trying to soothe me and making a lousy job of it. "It'll be fine, Max. You wait and see."

"That's *exactly* what I'll be waiting for." At least I decked him verbally, not that it made me feel one whit better.

There wasn't anything very new said after that, just more reassurances of a happy ending on their part and more bitter recriminations on mine. When we all ran out of gas, they said they'd be back in the morning, added a few more words of cheer, and left me alone.

And I do mean alone. I had no friends who knew where I was—*I* didn't know where I was. I owned one pair of pajamas, there was an armed guard outside my door, my eyes were gummed up like a newborn kitten's, and all I had in front of me was the swell prospect of playing Oedipus for a week with a very good chance of my act being held over indefinitely. I guess you could say I was a touch miserable, but I didn't know what misery was. However, I got a little closer to it next morning.

I had a rotten night. I'd worry a bit, doze a bit, then wake up and worry some more. By the time the cop outside brought me some breakfast I had a fuzzy head and an upset stomach which was too nervous to take anything.

I was certainly no better an hour later when Gallo and Weyland and Dr. John arrived for the moment of truth. There were a few curt good mornings, then nothing but the snip of scissors cutting away my bandages, the outer layer quickly, the inner layer with a lot of care.

That left just the pads over my eyes.

I heard the clink of metal and the sound of water in a washbasin, then felt the cool moisture of a sponge on my eyelids. Nobody commented; maybe they were holding their breath as I was.

I could feel my eyelids loosen as Dr. John went on sponging; the lashes seemed to be curling apart. I felt his fingers on my lids, a few more wipes; then my eyes fluttered open in that nice, cheery, 10 A.M. room.

Spears, javelins, knives, daggers, arrows, all of them thumped into my skull, and I yelled out and clapped my hands over my eyes. It had been like standing up close to a searchlight and peeking in.

Somebody slipped some dark glasses onto my nose, and I tried it again.

The spears were gone, and there was no pain, but no matter where I looked, up, down or sideways, all I could see was a blank white wall. Instead of everything being black, as it is when you close your eyes, everything was white, but the effect was the same because I couldn't see a damn thing—I was totally, absolutely, 100 percent blind.

And brother, *that* was misery.

8

ACCORDING TO THE RECORDS on file at Lenox Hill Hospital, which, I found out later, was the hospital I'd been taken to, Maxwell James Sinclair had been admitted with abrasions, a suspected fractured skull, and sight damage. However, with the X rays proving negative on the fracture and there being no sign of concussion after a twelve-hour observation, he'd been allowed to leave at eleven the next morning in the care of a relative.

Gallo was the relative, and I'm glad he wasn't listed as a friend. The records had been backdated two weeks to give Max Sinclair a chance to recover enough from his accident to move into a new apartment, even though the accident had left him blind.

And boy, was I blind. Having your eyes bandaged closed so you can't see is a heck of a lot different from having them open and not being able to see, and I still hadn't got over the shock. My first taste of real blindness had been rotten enough in that silent hospital room, but it was far worse sitting beside Gallo in his car. I could hear the traffic and put names to everything—cars, buses, motorcycles, trucks—sense them moving around me, smell the

84

auto exhaust, feel the pattern of the traffic every time the car stopped and started. But, and this may sound crazy, not being able to see them, I had no proof they were really there, and that was more than a little scary.

Gallo had rented me a studio apartment in the East Twenties just off Second Avenue, and that's where we went. He told me it was a building that would suit the bank account of somebody who would now have to make baskets for a living, a place that had seen better days, although I got the impression going through the lobby that it hadn't seen all that many of them. It smelled vaguely of old newspapers, and I don't think the janitor swept under the furniture, although there couldn't have been much in the lobby anyway. The place didn't run to a doorman, so there was nobody to see us going in, according to Gallo. We went up in the elevator to the sixth floor and almost to the end of the corridor, where Gallo let us into an apartment. It smelled a lot better than the lobby because it had been recently cleaned, I could tell, but under the smell of Ajax and floor polish I caught the whiff of staleness that collects in old buildings if they're not looked after.

Gallo got me to change into some clothes which had been bought for me, because he wanted me to look as little like my old self as possible. So the clothes were things I'd never ordinarily wear: a suit and tie. Naturally I'm a slacks and jacket man; I don't think I've worn a white shirt and a suit in ten years. Being a nine-to-five wage slave has never really bothered me, but I've always resisted wearing the uniform.

He pressed a key into my hand, told me the refrigerator was stocked, the rent was paid, there were fresh sheets on the sofa bed, and a toothbrush and a new bar of Palmolive in the bathroom. I wasn't crazy about moving in, but I had to go along with it. Hell, I was going along with being blind, I could hardly carp over not having a dishwasher.

When I was ready, Gallo led me back down to the street, and we walked for a couple of blocks.

Most people get it all mixed up when they help a blind person, and Gallo was no exception. He took my elbow, thinking to guide me, but all he was doing was pushing me along awkwardly. A blind person holds the guide's elbow, not the other way around, and stays half a step behind so he has time to respond to direction changes or other instructions. When we got that straightened out, we made better progress.

The first place he took me to was a barbershop. When I came out of there and put a hand on my head, it felt like a five-day old beard—he'd got the barber to give me a real down-home Texas flat top. I knew he hadn't done it for a joke—he'd already played a pretty good one on me—so when we got back to his car, I asked him exactly why he had done it. He told me it was for the same reason I was wearing a suit and tie, to alter my appearance further. Clearly it would be a disaster if I were recognized, although Gallo doubted it would happen even if I did run into somebody who knew me; a blind man wearing dark shades and tapping a cane along the street is a pretty good disguise. But he'd had my locks shorn just to be on the safe side, and I do mean shorn—the way my hair felt I doubted that even James Caan's mother would have recognized me.

I'm making myself sound a lot more cheery than I felt. I was still at the bottom of the barrel, but I couldn't see what else I could do except do what Gallo and Weyland wanted. I couldn't just wash my hands of the whole thing, pop the pill, and hang around like Dr. Jekyll waiting to see if it would work. I didn't *have* the goddamn pill. Gallo had told me that the pill would be in my care, but he wasn't dumb enough to hand it over just then. He knew I would have gulped it like a Swiss liqueur chocolate and to hell with the project.

We drove uptown to a place called the Beacon, which operates in more or less the same way as the Sight Center. There was no fear of anybody's recognizing me here because the two places are in a kind of unofficial competition, and if you work at one, you don't work at the other. In fact, there's a bit of snobbism attached to working at either; the Beacon thinks it does a better job than the Sight Center, and the Sight Center thinks it has it all over the Beacon. In truth, both do a similarly good job.

Gallo filled out forms for me, turned me over to somebody, said he'd be back to pick me up that afternoon, and left me to it.

There were two reasons why I had to go to a rehabilitation center: one, that's what a newly blind person does anyway, and I still had to keep up my cover. And two, I *was* newly blind, and I could use the time to make sure I could get around okay.

I would say that the somebody Gallo turned me over to was a Westchester matron down for her day of good works. She kept up a merry stream of chatter as if I were somebody from *Vogue* who'd come to interview her in the Palm Court. She guided me through some doors, sat me down, and gaily announced that Mrs. Trumbull would be along in a minute to give both of us our first orientation lesson. I assumed that Lady Scarsdale didn't need an orientation lesson, so I gathered there was somebody else in the room. I checked the woman on that, and she gave me a little embarrassed trill and said how silly of her, and good heavens, where were her manners, introduced us and fled.

It was nothing to do with manners; she was clearly new to the job, and it takes awhile to catch hold of the fact that blind people can't see.

The other person was a man named Keitel, and I think from the sound of his voice he was around my age. We traded a few preliminaries, and it turned out we shared the same neighborhood; he lived only a couple of blocks away from me. It was a small point of contact, and when that subject was exhausted, I knew what the next one would be. I would have bet ten dollars on it and collected. He asked me how I'd lost my sight.

"I came off my Honda head first."

"You weren't wearing a helmet?"

"Sure. But I bought the cheapest I could find."

When he said nothing, I had to play the game and ask the same question. "How about you?"

He made the kind of sound that goes with a disgusted wave of the hand. "Aw, I got shitfaced and fell down some stairs. Shook something up in my eyes. They been trying to stick it back, tried hot things, cold things, everything but Elmer's Glue, but no luck so far."

"Tough," I said. It was; the guy had a detached retina, and that's surgically possible to correct unless there's a real problem.

The door opened, heels clicked across the floor, and a woman introduced herself as Mrs. Trumbull, our instructor for the day. A warm, warbly voice, mid-fifties maybe. I'd been hoping for somebody a little younger and built like Bev Jordan, my dream girl at the Sight Center. I could have had some real fun stumbling against somebody like that and clumsily recovering my balance. But I was there for a reason, and it wasn't so I could get my jollies.

I paid attention to Mrs. Trumbull, who was a mobility officer, her job being to teach the newly blind how to get around independently. She launched into a spiel I'd made myself a hundred times, all about the initial problems we'd be faced with and how we were going to learn to overcome them. And how we weren't to expect too much progress at first, et cetera, et cetera. Normally a blind person is started off with lessons in the basics: how to move with a sighted guide, how to use the sun to get a direction, posture training, auditory training, room orientation. But I'd been signed up for the crash course and was going straight into cane technique.

Mrs. Trumbull described the room we were in, which sounded like a duplicate of one I taught in at the Sight Center: a row of seats at the rear of the room and the rest of it taken up by an obstacle course a student has to learn to negotiate—simulated trash cans, lampposts, a curb, things a sighted person doesn't even notice but give the blind a hard time.

She gave us each a cane, although she didn't really give them, we borrowed them. A cane has to be made to measure to fit a person's height and length of stride, but the ones we got were approximately right. They were outdoor canes, which are longer and heavier than the collapsible indoor variety, and they're held differently. Mrs. Trumbull showed us the correct grip, which is a bit like the one you use for a tennis serve: The forefinger runs down the cane so it becomes an extension of your arm. She showed us the lateral wrist movement that works best and how to hold the cane in front of the midline of the body. These were the same things I'd been teaching for years, but I had to pretend it was all new to me.

When she was happy with the way we were holding the canes, she got us to try the course.

"Let's start with you, Mr. Sinclair." She guided me a few steps, describing the layout. "The wall's forty feet away, so you don't have to worry about walking into it. All you have to concentrate on are the obstacles. They're all made of styrofoam, so if you bump into any of them, they won't hurt you. Now, using the cane as I showed you, let's see you locate the first one and walk around it."

Then her hand dropped from my arm, and I was on my own. And I mean on my own. For the first time in my life I felt the utter vulnerability of the blind. There'd been somebody guiding me every second since I'd got out of the hospital, but now I was standing by myself with no one to lean on, and all I could see through my dark glasses was the same white snowstorm. I felt as if I were on the edge of a cliff, and I was afraid to take the first step.

"Go ahead, Mr. Sinclair," Mrs. Trumbull said. "There's nothing to hurt you."

I knew that, of course, knew I wasn't going to rack up no matter what I did, but I still didn't want to move. I figured that once I started I'd be fine; in fact, that was going to be a problem—I'd have to stop myself from looking too much like a pro. But I found out, when I finally did get started, that I didn't have to worry on that score.

What an enormous difference there is between teaching something and having to apply that knowledge yourself. I was terrible. I held the cane like a club and tried to fend off things as if they were going to leap at me. I ended up hitting everything, even stumbling over the "curb."

I used to wonder sometimes, when I gave this same class, why a particularly slow student would constantly hit an obstruction. I mean, there it was, plain as day. But now I was beginning to appreciate that to a blind person a sixty-story building is no plainer than a mailbox.

Mrs. Trumbull rescued me and led me back to the start. "Don't guess where things are, Mr. Sinclair; let the cane tell you. Try it again."

She was right about my guessing. I was mentally seeing the room I taught in at the Sight Center. The obstacles were similar, but they were placed differently.

I did slightly better on my second go, but not

much. Mrs. T. gave me a rest and had Keitel try it. He did pretty badly, too, but then very few people get the hang of it right away. On my third try I was way better. I'd calmed down and lost the feeling of panic, and I concentrated on doing everything right: held the cane properly, and in the correct position, and let it scan in front of me. I used that round to read the course, and on my next attempt I dodged everything.

Mrs. Trumbull was surprised, and excited, too. I think she thought she'd finally got one of the radar folk who come along once in a blue moon. I turned aside her praise, but to tell you the truth, I was pretty proud of myself.

Then Keitel went at it again and was obviously making zero progress, and Mrs. Trumbull, in an attempt to get a little healthy competition going, said, "Come on, Mr. Keitel. Mr. Sinclair's picking it up much faster than you."

That kind of brought me back to earth; very close to it, in fact. Poor old Keitel thought he was being shown up by a beginner like himself, and I stopped feeling tickled pink. The two of us spent another half hour at it, then were taken into the cafeteria for a sandwich. We did some more work after lunch, and around five, Gallo came for me. He didn't ask me how my day had been, as if what I'd been doing were perfectly normal, but merely told me I'd be going back again tomorrow, and that the day after they'd start the first of the tests. He wouldn't elaborate on what kinds of tests, putting me off with the assurance they'd be easy. Gallo had changed somewhat; when I'd first met him he'd been talkative, garrulous even, and quietly convincing about the project. But now that I was well and truly embarked on it, he apparently saw no need to give me any encouragement. After all, why should he? He still had that pill, so I was at his mercy. It sure didn't make me like him any better; the guy was a stiff.

He deposited me outside my apartment door, said he'd call for me in the morning, and left. I let myself in and, with the cane I'd brought from the Beacon, explored the terrors of the apartment. There wasn't much stuff to bump into: a few chairs and a sofa bed against one wall, a small dining table in the ell, and a tiny kitchen off. The bathroom was opposite the front door. Gallo had told me there was a radio on the kitchen counter, and I switched it on, found the FM band, and got some Handel, a person who's never failed to have a soothing effect on me. Another man who's always had a similar effect is John Barleycorn, but my search of the cupboards revealed nothing that felt like a bottle of hooch, which didn't surprise me; after all, I'd been vittled by the U.S. government, a notorious bunch of bluenoses. I would have killed for a drink, but I wasn't about to go out to buy one, so I tapped my way to the sofa, sat down, and thought about things instead.

A time check came up on the radio: five-fifty-five. I figured I had about an hour before it would be good and dark. I'd been effectively blind since six the night before, but it felt like forever, and I was busting to see again, desperate to, so I was getting awfully impatient.

Terrific, huh? I'd just spent the day with a guy who would probably never ever see again, and here I

was getting impatient. I was doing all right. Even if
the pill didn't work, if and when Gallo gave it to
me, I'd still have my sight half the time.

Six o'clock.

Dr. John had given me the drops around seven,
and he'd said they'd take about twenty-four hours to
work, so I had maybe an hour to wait.

I began to feel excited as the enormity of what I
was on the verge of doing crept over me. Night
vision . . . regardless of what had fostered it, a
military application, I now saw that ultimately, it had
to be a giant step forward for mankind. And I was
about to take that step, which made me a fully
fledged pioneer. When night vision became a recognized fact of life, maybe I'd be mentioned as one of
the first to experience it. Maybe my name would get
into the history books. What an overwhelming
thought that was. But why not? After all, I was going
to do what had been done, as far as anybody knew,
only once before since the dawn of time. More men
had walked on the moon than had done what I was
about to do. I was struck by the different circumstances of the two events: The entire world had
known about the moon landing, millions of people
had watched it happen, while my accomplishment
wouldn't have one single witness.

I sat there listening to the music and waiting out
the clock. On a sudden impulse I closed my eyes. I
didn't want gradually to start seeing as the dark
crept into the room, I wanted it to be really black,
then open my eyes and get the full effect. I forced
myself to wait, thinking back on what Dr. John had
told me about the nerve endings in my eyes, the

cones and rods. I was beginning to get a clearer understanding of the theory. Because they'd been artificially boosted, the more sensitive rods had overridden the cones and been in use when normally they wouldn't have. That's why everything was white in the daytime; my eyes were taking in too much light. But once the daylight faded and the dark came on, the rods would do what they were designed to do, only a hundred times more efficiently; they'd magnify the merest glimmer and allow me to see.

I stayed as I was with my eyes squeezed shut, listening to the Handel finish. Then they started playing some Bach, which I thought, in this case, was a spooky coincidence on account of the fact they both went blind. Had they been helping their government with an experiment, too? When I recalled that both composers had been operated on, unsuccessfully, by the same quack eye surgeon, I wondered if Gallo's great-great-grandfather had been in charge of the project.

All this helped me get through another half hour; then I couldn't wait any longer. I stood and groped my way to the end of the room and turned around. It was a shame that the first thing a pioneer of night sight would see was going to be a sofa that needed re-covering, but hell, what did Armstrong see on the moon? Rocks.

It was also a shame that a historic occasion like this wasn't going to get TV coverage, some breathy-voiced announcer building up the tension. "He's on his feet, ladies and gentlemen. . . . He's starting to move. . . . He's walking down to the other end of the room. Now he's turning. And now he's—yes, he's moving his hand toward his dark glasses. His hand is going up to his shades. Now he's gripping them—we're very close, ladies and gentlemen—he's gripping them with his right hand, and I believe he's getting ready to. . . . Yes, he's taking them off. He's taken them all the way off. Now we just have the eyes, ladies and gentlemen, just have the eyes to go. . . . They're still shut tight, still closed tight. But wait . . . I think I see a flicker of movement. . . . Yes, I think. . . . *He's opening them! They're open. Max Ellis has opened his eyes!*"

I'll tell you something: If it had been on television I would have laid the greatest egg since Lost in Space.

And do you know why?

Sure you do.

All I could see was the same wall I'd been looking at all day, only now it was totally black.

The fucking drops didn't work.

9

I READ A THEORY ONCE that said the reason most of us don't go insane somewhere along the line is that a little circuit in the mind shuts down whenever the brain is in danger of blowing a fuse.

I assume something like that happened to mine.

I didn't rant, rave, sob, fall down in a heap. I took it pretty calmly and did what I always do when I'm hit by, shall we say, adverse news: went out and headed for the nearest bar.

I put my shades back on, found my cane, and tapped my way along the corridor to the elevator. I made it down to the lobby okay and out onto the street, but then I was lost. I heard a bus rattle by on what I knew was Second Avenue, and from its direction I at least could tell which was north, south, east, and west. But that was all; I knew nothing about the area, and the first two people I asked just walked on by without a word. So much for my debut as a blind man on the streets of New York.

A woman stopped for me, finally, and told me there was a bar at the end of the block, so I set off to find it. I took it very carefully and slowly, fanning my cane in front of me as if I were sweeping a minefield. I made it without falling down any open man-holes and knew I'd found the bar because the beer smell was unmistakable. I was feeling my way toward the entrance when a man spoke behind me.

"You goin' in? Lemme help you."

He took my arm in a grip that was almost painful, steering me ahead of him. "Here you go. Coupla empty stools right here. What're you drinking?"

I told him I didn't care as long as it was a double, and he said that the place was having a special on Four Roses, and that a double Four Roses would be an Eight Roses, then laughed and half punched my shoulder, almost putting it out of joint. I could have done without him, but at least he got the drinks fast, which was all I cared about, and I knocked mine right back.

"Hits the spot, huh?" he said.

"Yeah. Listen, if the barman's still there, I'd like this again."

"Hey, Jimmy. Same again for my buddy."

A gravelly voice growled at him, "The name's Charlie."

My new friend waited a moment, then said to me low, "Jimmy, Charlie, what's it matter long as they bring you the stuff, right?"

I heard the clink of a bottle on a glass in front of me, carefully felt for it, and tossed that one off, too. A nice, warm feeling started up through my body, gently cradling my brain.

"You hear the one 'bout the guy had one of them operations so he couldn't have no more kids?"

I didn't hear the story. I was thinking about the beautiful fix I was in. That Gallo—what a sweetheart. He'd lied all the way. Weyland, too. There'd been no old man at all, no first guinea pig. I was the first guinea pig. And the eyedrops were a failure, so it was back to the old drawing board and thanks a lot, Max, here's your check.

I thought bitterly about my grandiose thoughts of a little while back, about my going down in history as a pioneer. I wouldn't be making it now; the failures never did. Everybody's heard of the Wright brothers, but what were the names of all those guys before them who jumped off cliffs with homemade wings?

The analogy was an apt one; that's what I'd done, thrown myself off a cliff and landed crippled at the bottom, which had never seen a ray of sunlight.

". . . And then he says to the cop, he says, 'Do I have any visible scars? Sure, I got a visible scar. I got one ten inches long.' "

The guy broke up at his own joke and, when he'd finished laughing, asked cheerily, "Been blind from birth?"

"It sure seems like it," I said.

"Yeah? How long's it been?"

"Couple of weeks."

"Gee, that's tough. What do the docs say? Any hope?"

That was a good question. Was the change in my eyes permanent or temporary? If it was temporary, how long was that? A week? A month? A year?

I knew how long permanent was.

I ordered another double. When it arrived, I raised it and said to my friend, "Here's looking at you," and drank it down.

The guy laughed. "Hey, you're okay, you know that? Somebody else, blind like, they might just sit around and mope."

"Yeah, I'm real brave."

"My name's McCone. You just call me Jake."

"Max Sinclair."

"I ain't seen you around before, Max. You just move in?"

"Right."

"Then this'll be your friendly neighborhood bar. Good. I'm in here all the time."

I told him I was delighted, then got unsteadily to my feet. I tossed a bill down—I think it was a ten—refused his offer of a helping hand, and tapped my way out into the street. Three quick doubles had done wonders for my confidence, and I had a lot more to worry about besides lampposts, so I got back to the apartment pretty fast.

I didn't even attempt pajamas, just stripped down to my underwear, found a blanket, fumbled open the sofa bed, and stretched out on it. The combination of the booze, the emotional shelling I'd taken, plus the swell future I was facing, combined to knock me out fast, and I fell asleep with a vision in my head of a little glass bottle with a $2 million price tag on it, only the figure had been crossed through and replaced with $1.99.

I guess that must have been around nine o'clock or so, and I didn't know a thing more till I found myself, hours later, sitting bolt upright with the sweat running down me, breathing as if I'd just run two blocks for a bus.

That rotten, lousy dream had survived the move

intact. I'd brought it all with me: the lake, glittering in the sun, but somehow solid as if it were made of green ice. It took me an age to run across to the other bank and find what I always found there: the pile of clothes. Only they weren't just thrown-down, tossed-aside clothes; they were one-dimensional, like pictures of clothes, very precisely stacked one on top of the other. This was the only part of the dream that had ever varied, the part where I spot the clothes. And the variation was a particularly horrible one.

For a second I didn't know where I was; then I remembered the new apartment.

I'd actually made it halfway to the bathroom before I realized something that shook me to my back teeth: I wasn't feeling my way across the room; I was seeing my way across it.

The walls, the furniture, the closet door, I could see them all perfectly.

And there was something else I could see: the streetlights of Second Avenue. And every detail of the avenue itself—cars, apartment blocks, a few early-morning trucks. I could even make out the sign on the window of the deli on the corner and, above it, the leaves of a pot plant in somebody's living room. The colors were a little off, a little like the too-bright results you get with a cheap camera, but everything was in the same sharp focus as it would have been in the daytime.

In a daze of discovery I wandered out into the kitchen—cupboards, counter, stove, pots, and pans; in spite of an inky 3 A.M. darkness, I was seeing all these things.

I tried an experiment. I opened the door of the refrigerator, and the interior, lit by the shelf light, was just a blurry white haze. It was incredible. Everything was the exact reverse of what it should have been. I closed the door, and my eyes picked out things again, the radio on the countertop. I could read the numerals on the tuning dial easily—it was almost pitch-dark in that tiny kitchen, but I was standing there reading a row of figures some people would have had trouble reading at high noon.

I understood now: the drops were everything Gallo and Weyland and Dr. John claimed, only they'd taken a few hours longer to work.

What a wild thing human nature is. I'd almost been ready to slash my wrists at the possibility of the pill's not working, leaving me only with night sight for the rest of my life. But when I'd thought I wouldn't be having even that . . . right then if somebody had offered me a choice between keeping what I had and a 99 percent chance of regaining my normal vision, I would have settled for the night sight only and been ecstatically happy to do it.

I was pretty ecstatic anyway, and I wanted to rush out onto the streets, wake everybody up, and show them what I could do, tell the world that it was possible for a person to see in the dark. But I knew I couldn't share my news with anybody. If I so much as let out a peep, Gallo would have me put against a wall.

Gallo. At least I could tell him. I found my jacket and the number he'd given me to call if I needed him. At three in the morning, or whatever time it was, I knew there might not be an answer, but the phone was picked up on the first ring. A crisp voice repeated the last four numerals I'd dialed, and when I asked for Gallo there was a series of clicks, and I figured the call must be going through a switchboard. Then Gallo said a very sleepy hello.

"Gallo, you son of a bitch. It's me, Max."

"Umph," he said.

"It works, Gallo. It's fantastic."

"I know," he said around a yawn. "Anything else?"

"Yeah, something really important. I thought I'd lost the cap off the toothpaste, but I found it. Jesus, this is the biggest thing since night baseball, and you ask if there's anything else. You're some party pooper, you know that?"

"See you in the morning," he said, and hung up.

His sleepy reaction cheered me even more. It meant that the story about the old man had to be true. If I'd been the first to test the drops, I would have had Gallo and a team of doctors on my doorstep in nothing flat. So that was something anyway. A big thing. Mentally I was clicking my heels. All I needed now was for the pill to work, and I'd be home and dry. Laughing all the way to the bank.

Yes, sir, that's all I needed. Then I'd have it made.

10

HAD PLESEK BEEN IN THE LOBBY of his hotel the next morning he might have got a surprise. He didn't know more than a dozen people in America to talk to, but he'd memorized at least fifty faces, and had he looked out at the sidewalk at just the right moment he would have seen one he knew. The man walking by the hotel didn't go far, just a block and a half west to Broadway to an address he'd been given. It was a penny arcade he must have passed a thousand times, but this time was different. This time he stopped and went in.

It sounded like a prison break: Bells jangled, a siren screamed, a machine gun roared, and rifles fired in a loud, erratic volley. But the people there didn't seem to hear a thing. One man in particular, hunched over a pinball machine, looked as if he would have been surprised had somebody asked him how he stood the noise. Every ounce of his attention was focused on the game he was playing. He was small and energetic, with a thin, wiry body that looked undernourished. His eyes were quick and bright, and there was something birdlike in the way they flitted to and from the flashing scoreboard. He wore a baseball cap, an orange sweat shirt with the name of a new hit musical printed across it, sneakers, and a pair of narrow, chalk-striped pants that could have been the bottom half of a suit.

He pumped a ball into play, pulled and released the shooter, and, fascinated, watched the ball being shoved and belted and bullied down to the bottom of the machine.

"Mr. Page?"

The little man didn't seem to hear.

"Mr. Page. . . ."

He glanced up, took a quick look at the man at his shoulder, then went back to his game. "Naw," he said. "That ain't my name."

"I was told it was."

"You was told wrong."

The shiny silver ball caromed off a spring, rat-tat-tatted between two buzzers, then zoomed toward the exit slot. The little man frantically jabbed the side buttons, but the ball shot between the barriers and vanished. On the scoreboard the lights behind the drawing of a high-kicking majorette had an electric fit, and a numerical counter spun crazily.

"Twelve hundred seventy-five. That won't win you a cigar."

"Goddamn balls," the little man said. "They're just like the ponies. Some days they don't wanna run for you." He glanced at his visitor again. "Joe Percey sick?'"

"Who's Joe Percey?"

The little man pumped another ball into play and launched it. "Mister," he said, "I only ever get two types comin' up to me. Cops and customers. Take you now, you don't look like a cop. But you don't look like a customer either."

"I'm not a cop."

The pinball player bumped his thin body against the machine, jarring a stuck ball into flight. "Who told you my name was Page?"

"Somebody named Jackie."

"What's this Jackie look like?"

"Short and fat. He has a speech impediment."

"Jackie Stammers. That's his name, sort of," the little man said. He seemed to relax a little. "Yeah, I know him. Only he didn't tell you my name was Page. He said Pages. That's what they call me. It's short for Yellow Pages on account of all the info I got."

The other man had to raise his voice as a pounding jukebox opened up. "Is there somewhere we can talk?"

"This is my office right here. Ain't nobody gonna overhear you, and most of my customers like that."

"Okay. I need some of that information you're famous for. I need a name."

"Sure you do. You wouldn't be rappin' with me otherwise. Jackie tell you the rate?"

The visitor brought out a wallet, slid a bill from it. "Is a hundred all right?"

The little man took his eyes off the pinball machine long enough to pocket the money. "Fifty would've done. You ain't been around much."

"I suppose not."

"So? What can I do you for?"

"I need a doctor."

"No kidding. Now that really surprises me, that

really does. You don't look the type would want one of them. Course it ain't my business why a customer wants any name I give 'em. I just give and don't ask questions."

"A smart policy," the customer said.

"A doc, huh? Well, you come to the right guy. I got maybe ten, fifteen on the list. All of 'em got great hands and bad memories."

"Fine. There's just one thing. I don't want an ordinary MD. I'm looking for a specialist."

"Specialists is all I deal in." The pinball player forgot about his game, dug under his sweat shirt, and pulled out a diary. "You wanna left-handed lion tamer or a electrician speaks Japanese, I got one for you. I got one or two of everybody, and all of 'em go to work for money." He leafed through the book, making a great show of wetting his fingers to turn the pages. "You want a sawbones, right? What kind?"

"A surgeon."

The little man nodded as if he'd been expecting the answer. "No problem. You got a friend maybe shot hisself in a hunting accident—I'm just making a maybe now—I got docs can whip that bullet out of him just like that."

"What I'm after," the other man said evenly, "is an eye surgeon."

The diary pages riffled. "Eye man, huh. Yeah, well, I think I maybe got one of them. Lemme take a look here." The man found the place he was looking for, scanned the entry, and tapped his finger on it. "Sure, here we go. Knew I had one. You wanna write this down?"

11

When Gallo picked me up at 10 a.m., the solid white wall was back in front of my eyes, but I felt a lot better about it now that I knew for sure it was only temporary. Driving me up to the Beacon, Gallo was just as unexcited about this minor miracle as he had been several hours earlier; to his way of thinking, I guess, things were merely going according to plan.

I spent another day knocking Mrs. Trumbull dead; she took me and Keitel, my classmate of the day before, out onto the street for our first practical run. I didn't tell her I'd had one the night before. I thought she was rushing things taking Keitel out so soon, but I didn't say anything, of course, just concentrated on my own performance.

I was a lot more relaxed knowing I was going to be seeing again that evening, and I did everything right. I stayed in the middle of the sidewalk, as you're supposed to do so you miss the bus stands and the No Parking signs, and the fireplugs on the curbs, and the trash cans and the stairwells, and even elevators, the freight elevators in the sidewalk that are often left open and unguarded. Of course, staying in the Center has its own problem, too, one that all New Yorkers face, and that's dog crap. It may sound funny, but it's real hazard for blind people. You're supposed to curb your dog, but a lot of fidos just adore the center of the sidewalk, and their doting owners think that's cute.

Another hazard is one so obvious it tends to be overlooked, and that's people. An amazing number of them just don't recognize blind persons; a white cane just doesn't seem to register. And the level of understanding is worse with a Seeing Eye dog. They don't notice the special harness; all they see is a man out walking his dog, and they make no allowances. The trouble is a lot of these people are drivers, and that's when problems really start.

In the afternoon Mrs. Trumbull let me solo, gave me my wings, and said I was the best pupil she'd ever had. And so I should have been. Gallo picked me up again, drove me back to the apartment, and told me that tomorrow I'd start the first of the tests. He asked me if I'd like to have dinner out, but I knew that he was just doing his duty. I don't think he wanted to have dinner with me any more than I did with him, so I took a raincheck. As it turned out, I had a dinner date anyway. I was hanging around the appartment, waiting to come out of the long white tunnel I'd been traveling through all day, when the doorbell buzzed. I asked who it was, and a muffled voice said something about a neighbor, so I opened up.

"Hello there. My name's Carson. I live next door." He had a meek little voice, and as he didn't sound as if he'd come to complain about anything, I introduced myself back.

"Muriel and I," he said, "that's my wife, we wondered if you'd have time for a drink. A welcome to the building, such as it is."

I didn't particularly want to go, but the guy was trying to be nice to a blind man, so I went along.

Although we were only going next door, I took my cane with me; even with somebody guiding me I felt more confident if I had it in my hand. Carson led me along the corridor and into his apartment, and straight away the impression I got was a good one. The place smelled clean and looked after, and there was also a fine aroma of something cooking. Carson introduced me to his wife, who sounded like a counterpart of her husband, a little shy, but warm, and I got a mental picture of a smiling gray-haired woman in her fifties, the type that always has flour on her hands and a pie cooling in the kitchen.

They told me a little about the building for a start, about how they were trying to get a tenants' association going and force some improvements. Then Carson told me what he did—he was a semiretired accountant—asked me what I did, and I told him about the rehabilitation program I was undergoing, which got us onto the whole subject of my accident and subsequent blindness.

"Maybe Mr. Sinclair would prefer not to talk about it, Ralph."

"Of course," he said. "Let's talk about something else."

However, it wasn't long before the talk drifted back to my infirmity, and I could understand—it would have been like sitting in the same room as someone wearing a leg cast and not asking him how he got it.

Ralph Carson fixed some drinks—he made the weakest Bloody Marys I'd ever tasted—then we had another, and they invited me to stay for dinner. I really wasn't thrilled at the idea of going back and opening a can of soup for myself, and those great smells were still coming from the kitchen, so I accepted and had my first real sit-down dinner as a blind man.

I did okay. I kept my movements small and contained and, as far as I know, didn't cut a hole in the tablecloth or pick up somebody else's water glass. The kind of food helped, too: a clam cocktail I could eat with a spoon—the easiest utensil for a blind person—and scallopini which Muriel Carson brought already cut up and with very little sauce so I wouldn't gloop it everywhere. There was fresh cheesecake for dessert, which I managed to keep from forking onto my nose, so all in all, I was very glad I'd stayed. But I was itching to get back next door and take off my shades and start seeing again, so I tried to say good-night pretty early, but they wouldn't let me go.

I had another cup of coffee and told them some more funny stories about my two years in the Navy. I didn't have to make up these stories; I didn't understand the Navy, and the Navy didn't understand me. I must have been the worst sailor in the history of the service. Once, in Japan, I went AWOL for about five minutes when I fell off a destroyer while it was anchored in Yokosuka Bay. A buddy finally threw me a rope, but there was no time to change because I had to go on parade. I remember this lieutenant we had who was a bug on shipboard cleanliness going down the line, asking men if they'd showered that morning. When he got to me standing rigidly at attention, soaked through and dripping water, his mouth dropped open, but he didn't say anything. He didn't have the guts to ask the question he'd asked everybody else. He just moved on, and I got away with deserting the ship.

The Carsons enjoyed the anecdotes; I got the impression they didn't have too many friends, and they didn't mention any children, so they were probably a little lonely.

I finally escaped, thanked them both for the good cooking and the hospitality, and said I'd see them later. They saw me to my door, said good-night again, and as their door closed, I opened mine.

Now I don't want you to think that in two very short days I'd acquired the extra perception of the blind. All I can say is I knew beyond a doubt that somebody was in my apartment.

The noise came a fraction later, a soft, rustling sound from the kitchen. Then absolute silence. It was the kind of noise a mouse makes nibbling through paper, but I didn't figure this was a mouse. With a cold prickling creeping down my neck I somehow knew it was a burglar, and not your ordinary garden variety type either.

Very slowly and very quietly I pulled the door closed again and even more slowly and quietly released the key so the lock moved back into place without clicking. That left me out in the corridor with a fine trembling running through my body and a very large question mark over my head. Calling the cops might be a mistake. I had to call Gallo. But where was I going to do it from? I couldn't see how I could talk to him from the Carson's without breaking security, and he and Weyland had brainwashed me into putting secrecy first. The nearest phone I knew I could get to and use without being overheard was the one in the noisy bar I'd been to the night before.

I went along the corridor feeling I had a target pinned to my back, called the elevator, made it to the lobby, and started down the block. It was good and dark, but I couldn't see all that well because of the shades, and I couldn't take them off because I still had to appear to be blind. So I couldn't run to the bar the way I wanted. But I moved as fast as I safely could and reached it without hitting anything.

For the second night running the door was opened for me, and by the same guy.

"Max, baby. You and me are keepin' the same hours."

"Hi, Jake. Listen, do me a favor. Show me where the phone is."

"Sure thing, kid. Stick with me, you'll be wearin' radishes on your ears."

He took my arm in one of his pincer grips and propelled be down the bar. It was crowded, a lot of talk going on, and with the Knicks game booming from the TV nobody was going to overhear me on the phone. I had Gallo's number in my pocket, but of course, under the lights I couldn't see to read it.

I thrust the piece of paper at Jake what-was-his-name, McCone, asked him to dial it for me, and dug for some coins.

"If a guy answers, you want I should hang up?"

I gave that a laugh it didn't deserve and listened to him dialing.

"It's okay," he said, shoving the phone into my hand, "it's a broad."

I didn't want McCone to hear what I had to say, so I said it another way.

"Hello?"

The same crisp woman's voice repeated the last four digits.

"Do you have any Gallo wine?" I said into the phone.

"Would you repeat that, please?"

"Gallo."

Beside me McCone said, "Hey, Max, you don't wanna drink at home. Let's do it here."

"I got a friend coming. A wine freak."

Then Gallo came onto the wire. "Fine," I said. "Sinclair. Three Twenty-five East Twenty-fifth. I'd appreciate it if you could come soon as possible."

"Fifteen minutes," Gallo said, and I hung up.

"Max, baby," McCone said, taking my arm again, "you're a real swinger. C'mon, I'll buy you one for the road."

I had fifteen minutes to kill, so I let him lead me to a stool and order for us. This made the second night running I'd sat there; I was getting to be a regular, and I didn't even know what the place looked like, although I doubted it'd be much different from any of the other Third Avenue bars I knew: There'd be a row of booths behind me, probably a broken bowling machine at one end, the standard beer signs above the standard spotty mirror in back of the standard line of bottles, a long dark-brown wooden icebox installed in the thirties, and, perched up high near the front window, an oversized TV set which the customers would be watching simply because it was on. I've yet to go into a bar, outside of World Series time, and see anybody getting excited watching the box. The booze is always the main attraction.

"Hey"—McCone dug my ribs with a heavy elbow—"what's it like bangin' a broad you can't see her?"

"Sometimes it's an advantage."

He laughed loud, said, "Max, you're okay, kid," and gave me the elbow again. He sure was the physical type, and I didn't have much trouble visualizing him either: built like a stevedore and with the map of Ireland on his face, dented here and there no doubt by a variety of knuckles.

I knocked off my drink when it came, said I had to go, but McCone wouldn't let me leave till I'd had another one with him. The booze calmed my anxiety, and I was beginning to wonder if I hadn't been a bit hasty calling Gallo. After all, it had only been an impression I'd got that somebody was in the apartment; the noise I'd heard in the kitchen could have been a mouse after all. Or something could have fallen down. I had a sudden vision of Gallo with a gun in his hand creeping up to the kitchen, then charging in, then coming out a moment later, holding a dishcloth and saying, "Good thing you called me, Max. I had to pistol-whip it to the ground."

I broke in on whatever the hell McCone was rattling on about. "Listen, Jake, got to go. Thanks for the drink, huh?"

I left him, found my way back to the apartment house, and rode up to my floor. I wanted to get there ahead of Gallo and somehow explain my call.

I stopped outside my door and listened—I knew it was my door because I'd counted them off from the elevator—but I couldn't hear any sounds from inside.

I felt for the keyhole with one hand and soundlessly slid the key into the lock, turned it slowly, and eased the door open.

I listened some more.

Nothing. If there'd been somebody in there, he'd gone now.

I closed the door, let out a large economy-sized breath of relief, and was reaching for my glasses when somebody rushed me.

I felt him coming at the same time I heard him and reacted instinctively. I grabbed my cane and brought it slashing around with both hands.

I'd got a mental picture of some faceless guy coming at me, and I aimed at where I thought his head would be, but either I swung too early or it was Toulouse-Lautrec in front of me because all I did was fan the air.

Then a horse kicked me in the stomach.

A little lower then that, in fact.

I jackknifed over, and he was out of the door and gone, but I'd lost interest in him. I stumbled the two steps to the bathroom and made the bath in time to say good-bye to Muriel Carson's clam cocktail, her scallopini, and her freshmade cheesecake. Then I lay down and got in some real good groaning.

When Gallo arrived five minutes later, I'd recovered enough to get rid of the mess in the bath, splash water on my face, rinse out my mouth, and hobble out of the bathroom bent over like a safety pin.

He could see me because of the light coming in from the corridor. "What's wrong with you?" he asked.

I was pretty mad at myself for not waiting for him, so I took it out on Gallo. "Menstrual cramps."

He picked up my shades from the floor, put them onto my face, closed the door, and turned on the lights. "You run into something?" He didn't sound too frantic.

"A knee."

"Whose?"

I groaned, and it wasn't only because of my physical discomfort.

"I don't know. Look on the telephone pad; maybe he left his number."

It seemed impossible to get a rise out of Gallo. He blandly asked me to tell him what had happened.

"I thought there was somebody in here, so I called you from the bar down the block. Then I thought I'd been mistaken, but when I came back here, I found out I'd been right."

I felt my way to the sofa, slumped down on it, and listened to Gallo poking around the apartment.

"He got your radio," he called from the kitchen. "Unless you hocked it."

I heard him move into the bathroom, come out again.

"He went through your bathroom cabinet, too."

"He was after the eyedrops," I said.

"Impossible. Nobody knows about them except the people who are supposed to."

"You told me yourself that no security's perfect. Maybe somebody's found out."

Gallo wouldn't accept it. "Even if you were right, they'd have to know a thing like that wouldn't be left lying around an apartment."

"Maybe. But they'd still check it out, wouldn't they?" I shifted into a less painful position and kept on at him. "And another thing, he was in here for at least twenty minutes, maybe longer. Why spend all that time poking through the kitchen and the bathroom?"

"Because he was after your stash. Most of these break-in artists are on something. If you're clean, they'll still take anything they can find, codeine, Seconal. They get more for stuff like that than they get for radios."

"I don't buy it," I said.

Gallo sniffed. "Max, I'm afraid I've turned you into a suspicious old man. Your first thought was the drops, and that's good, shows you've got your priorities right. But you're forgetting that this is New York, burglar capital of the world. A building like this, no doorman, standard locks on the doors, anybody with a piece of plastic could just walk in."

"You could have thought of that," I said with more than a touch of bitterness, "when you put me in here."

"You're right," Gallo admitted, although he didn't sound at all repentant. "I'll have the super install a mortise lock in the morning. Incidentally, I have something for you."

I heard the rustle of paper; then Gallo pressed something into my hand.

"Is this what I think it is?"

"I'm trusting you not to take it before we're through with the tests."

"You're not taking much of a chance. The goddamn thing probably won't work."

"Just don't try to find out too soon," Gallo said. "And put it somewhere safe. It won't tell anybody anything, but you don't want to lose it."

"Gallo," I said, still clutching myself, "if I thought there was a chance of a repeat performance of tonight's little episode, I'd gulp it down now."

"You don't have to worry on that score, he won't be back tonight. Those guys only come back when there's something left to steal." I heard him move toward the door. "Now get some sleep. Tomorrow we start getting our money's worth out of you."

I changed position again and winced. "You're doing okay."

"You want the light out?"

"Please."

The door opened and closed. Good-night, Mr. Gallo. Always a pleasure, I thought. I left off holding my throbbing parts, reached up, and did what I'd been about to do earlier on, before I'd been so rudely and effectively interrupted: I took off my shades.

The first thing I saw was a piece of faded wallpaper which had come unstuck and needed gluing, but it didn't matter; after the second day in a row of blindness that crummy little apartment looked as good to me as a room at Versailles.

Getting my sight back every twelve hours was something I was never going to get used to. It was spooky and gorgeous at the same time, but I didn't care, just as long as I could do it.

I examined the pill in my hand. It was the size of an ordinary aspirin and didn't look any more talented. I decided to hide it away, eased myself up from the sofa, moved slowly into the bathroom, and found a spot for it in the cabinet. There wasn't much in there, but what there was had been raked over. It would have been a logical place to look for eyedrops, but also the place a junkie would search for a stash, so I figured there might be something to Gallo's theory after all.

I thought I'd better do something about my wonderful front door, so I got a chair and wedged it under the knob. If Gallo was wrong and I was going to have more callers, I didn't want them getting too close.

As a matter of fact I did have another caller, although not that night, it was the next morning. And as it turned out, she got very close indeed.

12

"MR. SINCLAIR? MY NAME'S KAREN PETERSEN. I work at the Beacon. May I come in for a minute?"

The voice was low and smooth and with a smile behind it.

"Sure." I stepped back, and she moved past me. The perfume was nice, too: sweet-sour expensive. Whoever Karen Petersen was I was glad she'd come to call.

"Why don't we sit down?" I suggested. I've always found that the first step in getting a chick together is to get her relaxed and off her feet, and when I heard myself immediately suggesting we sit down, I realized that, blind or not, I was lining up this girl. That stopped me for a moment; high on the list of things I thought I wouldn't be having for a while was sex. I guess I never thought I'd have room for it in my new life. I suppose I should have realized that sex is like Jell-O, there's always room for it.

"Let's take the sofa," I said to her.

"May I help you?" she asked.

"Thanks, but I'm pretty good around the apartment."

"I understand you're pretty good everywhere. That's why I'm here."

Instead of following up on that one, I concentrated on finding the sofa. I was moving a lot better than I had been the previous night, the shot in the groin had sidelined me only temporarily, and everything seemed to be back in working order down there, as my reaction to Miss Petersen was proving.

We sat down, and I asked her to expand on her last statement.

"Mrs. Trumbull tells me you're a very fast learner. She says she's never seen anybody adapt so quickly."

"She's a good teacher."

"That's true, but she's taught hundreds, and she say you're the best student she ever had."

I wondered what this was leading up to, not that I cared much. It seemed like twenty-seven years since I'd been alone with a great-looking chick, and with a voice like hers there was just no way Miss Petersen was going to turn out to be fat and dumpy with spiders in her hair.

"We're constantly trying to improve our teaching methods," she went on, "and when we get a star pupil like you, we'd naturally like to find out what it is that makes you adapt so fast, so we can pass it on to other students."

"I see," I said, wondering if they smelled a rat. Maybe I shouldn't have been quite so spectacular.

"If it's all right with you, Mr. Sinclair, I was wondering if I couldn't spend a little time observing you to see where you found the shortcuts."

"How do you mean, observing me?"

"Maybe that's a bad choice of words," she said, laughing. "What I mean is, I wouldn't be any bother. I'd just stick close for a few hours a day and see how you do it. Ask you some questions, that kind of thing."

The prospect of having this yummy young lady, with her warm laugh and delicious smell, sticking close to me was a delightful one, but I could just imagine what Gallo would have said if I'd turned up for the tests with a dolly on my arm.

"That might be a bit difficult through the day, Miss Petersen. I'm about to start a braille course, and I doubt you'd learn much watching me try that."

"How about after your lesson? Maybe I could pick you up."

"My brother-in-law usually drives me home."

"Well, look. I really don't want to give up on this. I think you could help us quite a bit. Would it be all right if I dropped around this evening? As I said, just by observing you, watching how you handle yourself in different situations, and by asking you questions, I'll be able to find out a lot."

"This evening," I said, as if pondering the root stem of the word.

"If you're free, we could have dinner. That's always a good time to talk. And if we went out to a restaurant, it would give me an opportunity to see this famous mobility of yours." She touched me lightly on the back of the hand. "Come on, Mr. Sinclair, what do you say? It'll be my treat."

I tried to think of the last time a nubile young woman had pleaded to take me to dinner. Apart from Raquel Welch there hadn't been anyone for ages.

"Well, er, I guess so. Okay."

"Great," she said. "You're really doing me a favor."

"Fine," I replied, trying the waters. "Maybe you'll be able to do me one in return."

"I'll be glad to. All you have to do is ask." She said it innocently enough, but it was an ambiguous choice of words which could be taken as either a polite answer or a promise of future delights.

We both got to our feet then, and she started to ask me if six o'clock would be all right when I heard her stumble, heard her cry, "Oh!" and got my hands up in time to steady her right breast. It was nicely firm and didn't need any steadying.

"I'm so sorry," she said. "I caught a heel in your rug."

The contact had only been for a half second, but it left no doubt in my mind that Miss Petersen had the kind of body I'd imagined. I mumbled something about the rug's being a bit old, said I was looking forward to seeing her at six, and off she went.

Looking forward to it was putting it mildly; I was tingling with anticipation. I remembered Benny, one of the guys at the Sight Center, saying that since he'd been blind, he made out like a bandit. Why not? Maybe a certain type of woman was drawn to a man who was blind; not for kinky reasons, but for sympathetic maternal ones. Maybe they felt a need to protect. It was fine with me; if Miss Petersen felt that way, I'd be happy to have her protect me all night long.

I was still thinking about her an hour later when El Gallo arrived and drove me up to the Beacon. On the way he explained the new setup. I was going to start a class for a while, to make it look good; then I'd be spirited away for the tests. When I got in the door, a voice I knew said good morning to me.

"Mrs. Trumbull, how are you?"

"Fine, Mr. Sinclair."

"I just met a friend of yours."

"Oh?"

"Miss Petersen."

Maybe in the back of my mind I half expected her to say, "Who? I don't know any Miss Petersen."

"Karen," she said, "Yes, I told her all about you. I think you could really help her, Mr. Sinclair."

I told her I'd try and let her lead me into a classroom, very pleased that Karen Petersen had turned out to be legit. I think my brush with the burglar had made me a little sensitive to people suddenly dropping into my life, and though I hadn't admitted it to myself, I'd been a bit suspicious of her.

I had Keitel for a classmate again, and Mrs. Trumbull started us off with a different mobility technique: how to move safely without a cane. A blind person has to give first thought to protecting his face and head, so in a room he doesn't know he moves with one arm bent across his body at an angle; that way the hand extends in front of his face. His other arm is held out in front of him, as low as possible, with the back of the hand foremost. Thirty minutes later Mrs. Trumbull had us walking into tables and chairs and doors without hurting ourselves, an accomplishment Keitel sounded particulary pleased with. I think Mrs. Trumbull had tapped a vein of confidence in him, and he seemed to be adjusting a lot faster than he had.

We broke for coffee an hour after that; then somebody came and led me through a side door and into an elevator. We went up a couple of floors, then down a corridor and through more doors. Gallo and his merry men had rented some office space in the same building, which they'd turned into a little test center—very smart. I was guided into a room, the door closed, the lights clicked off, and a voice told me I could take off my shades.

There were two men in there with me. They couldn't see me now because it was almost pitch-black, but I could see them. One looked like a librarian, the other like a phys. ed. major, but I think they were doctors.

They chatted with me for a while and gave me some idea of what I'd be doing, then asked me questions about my general health, noting the answers down on clipboards which they saw with the aid of penlights. I thought it was a little late to find out whether or not they had a healthy guinea pig.

Then we got started on the practical stuff.

The first test was the same kind an optician gives you, reading off an eye chart, the difference being that, in my case, I was reading it in the dark. I could read it down to the second last line from the bottom, the same as I would have been able to do normally. Then we did some color separation tests and some tests involving depth perception.

All this took quite a while, and we quit when lunch arrived. I elected to stay in the dark, and they left me sitting at their desk, reading a copy of that morning's paper one of them had put there. I think my lunch break impressed the doctors more than anything else I'd done so far—me, sitting there munching on a ham and swiss, and reading a column by Bill Buckley in a blacked-out room, although a lot of people would say that that's the best way to read his stuff anyway.

We got to it again an hour later, moving into another room. This one was blacked out, too; a much longer, larger room. The only object in it turned out to be a tennis ball launcher, of all things, one of those machines you set up on the other side of the net to practice against. The doctors explained that this test would check my perception of moving objects and my reflexes and reaction time.

They stood me at the end of the room, lighting their way with the penlights, had me take off my jacket, then handed me, not a tennis racket as I'd expected, but a baseball mitt. It was attached to a lead that ran back down the room to a machine they'd rigged up. The idea was that the tennis ball launcher would lob balls to me, and I had to try to get a glove on them. Each time I did it would register on the machine.

My old high school teacher had always said I'd end up as a fool; I'm only glad he wasn't around to see me standing there in the dark, facing a tennis ball launcher and wearing an electric baseball glove.

They asked me if I was ready, switched on the launcher, there was a boing! and a tennis ball came through the air toward me in a slow, looping arc.

I hardly had to move my glove. The ball popped

into it and popped out again, too light to stick. I heard a ping from the doctors' machine behind the launcher and saw a dial light flash on, registering the hit.

I knew it didn't matter whether or not I caught the balls, but I still felt like a bush leaguer dropping that easy one, so when the next ball floated to me, I made sure I held onto it. Then the launcher was adjusted, and the balls started coming with a little more speed, but I could see them plain as day, and they were no problem.

I was feeling like Max the Infield Marvel when they changed the launcher again. The balls came harder still and a varying heights, and I had to go up on my toes for some and bend for others, and a couple got away from me. One of the doctors made another adjustment, and when the next ball came, it was as if the launcher had been yanked and Catfish Hunter sent in—the damn thing brushed me back.

"One more of those," I said, "and I'll lay down a bunt and come after you."

"Sorry," they said, and slowed the launcher, but not by much.

I managed to get a glove on the next four balls, but the fifth zinged by my ear. "Lost it in the sun," I said.

Then they let up on me and turned the launcher off.

They told me it was a wrap for the day, and we'd be moving onto other things tomorrow, but I could tell they were delighted with the tests. They didn't say as much, but I think they'd given the drops a triple A plus.

They returned my shades and my cane, then led me back downstairs.

Mrs. Trumbull didn't comment on my absence, so I assumed she'd been given some kind of plausible story. I joined Keitel for the last half hour of a class; then Gallo called for me, drove me back, and left me off in the lobby.

When I got up to my apartment, Ralph Carson was there.

"Hi, Max. I've been waiting for you. The super changed your lock and gave me the key to give to you."

"Thought I might as well get a good one," I said. "No sense in taking chances." I didn't want to tell him what had prompted the lock change, so I didn't.

"Come on in for a drink," Carson said. "I bought a new record today. Mozart. I know you like the longhair stuff, too. I heard your radio playing night before last."

What I wanted to do was go into my apartment and spruce up for Miss Petersen's arrival, but I thought I could spare thirty minutes, so I went along. I had another of Carson's terrible Bloody Marys, listened to one side of the Mozart, and ate a slice of fudge cake Muriel Carson had made specially for me because I'd happened to mention, the night before, how fond of it I was. I was going to miss these people; my neighbor in my regular apartment was an old crab who thumped on the wall if I brushed my teeth too loud.

I finally made it out of there, went back next door, and tried out my new lock. It slid back with a comforting solid sound. Nobody was going to get through that in a hurry.

I double-locked it behind me, went into the bathroom, undressed, and took a shower, leaving the light off so I could see. I shaved carefully but didn't enjoy it much because I hated my reflection; that stupid brush cut was spikier then ever and made my ears stand out like an Airedale's.

I was back to being a blind man when Karen Petersen arrived. She'd changed her perfume for a slightly sweeter one, but her voice was just as smooth.

"Hello there. Am I too early?"

"Not at all. Come on in while I get my jacket."

I stepped back, hoping the rug would be good to me again, but I was out of luck this time. We chatted about what I'd been doing that day, the class with Mrs. Trumbull, and about the Beacon in general and her work there. It turned out she was a physiotherapist and taught an introductory course for anybody thinking of studying it at college. A lot of blind people take up physiotherapy, and always have. You'll find blind masseurs as far back in history as you care to look.

We left half an hour later and went uptown to a hotel bar, where we continued the conversation. She asked me all kinds of questions about how I'd been before my accident, which I'd told her about, and whether I'd always had a good sense of direction, what sports I'd done well at, and which problems I was now finding hardest to overcome. They were exactly the same kinds of questions I'd asked people at the Sight Center. She really knew her stuff, and I even got a little wrapped up in my own case.

She took me to a French restaurant in the East Eighties, where I ordered frog's legs, not just because I love them but because I could eat them with my fingers, so I didn't have to worry about stabbing a fork into my thumb. Even if I had, I doubt anybody would have noticed; it was a loud, bustling place, the kind that's too enthusiastic to be snobby, and it was impossible not to have a good time.

We got off the clinical stuff, found out about each other's background, got into a game of movie trivia with the next table, beat them and won a couple of cognacs, beat them again and won a couple more.

We arrived back in a very happy state, and Miss Petersen insisted on riding up in the elevator with me.

"Karen," I said, as we went down the corridor, "I haven't been escorted to the door since the last time I was in P.J. Clarke's."

"All part of the service," she said.

We reached my apartment. "Well," I said, "this is where I say thanks for a wonderful evening. And I really mean that, I had a ball."

"Then why don't we do it again tomorrow night? If you're going to be free, I still have dozens of questions I want to ask. We don't have to go out, I could cook for us here."

"Sold," I said. I hate keeping people in suspense.

"You know, if the positions were reversed, if it was you walking me to my door, I bet you'd play it cool. I don't think you'd try to overpower a girl on the first date. I think you'd do something casual, like kiss my hand maybe, then walk away and leave me intrigued."

"Absolutely right," I said. "I used to get great results that way."

"Okay then. So I'll see you tomorrow night." And she took my free hand, lifted it, pressed her lips into my palm, and left me standing there.

I let myself into my dark apartment, took off my shades, and looked at my palm. Jesus, what a sexy chick. If she figured I wasn't a first-date presser, she had to know I'd be a second-date presser. Nobody waited any longer these days. So she'd not only invited herself for tomorrow night, but also written the scenario.

I went into the bathroom and checked my reflection; my hair hadn't grown any since before dinner. Maybe my ears turned her on.

For the first time since I'd started the project I went to bed feeling good. Things were starting to pan out. I was getting around okay through the day, the tests were fun, and it was a tremendous kick when night came on and I could see again. Also, everybody I'd met so far had treated me kindly—the Carsons, Mrs. Trumbull, old Jake the barfly, not to mention Karen, who I was pretty sure was on the verge of treating me *very* kindly. The only cloud on the horizon was the question of the pill working, but I refused to think about that; I'd been going down and down on the yo-yo string, but now I'd bottomed out. From here on in, I had nowhere to go but up.

13

THE CADAVER, COVERED TO THE NECK BY A SHEET, lay on a table in the smaller of the medical school's two demonstration rooms. The room had the same white tile floor as its larger counterpart next door but lacked its circular observation gallery. It was ideal for a small class that needed to be close to the lecturer.

A dozen students ringed the table, watching a lab assistant work on the cadaver's face. He cut away a section around the left eye, clamping the flesh back, and the exposed eyeball, huge in the head, seemed to condemn the man for this horrible disfigurement.

The students, talking softly, fell silent at the clipped approach of long, striding footsteps, and the man who came through the doors entered a room as quiet as a tomb.

Extremely tall and gaunt, with a pale, waxy skin, he looked as if a tomb was where he belonged—until you saw the flash in his eyes. They glared at the group, resting for a tiny moment on a face, then darting on to the next. His hair was gray going into white and worn long. Everything about him was long: his body, his arms, his legs, his beaky nose. He strode toward the table, the students quickly making room for him, watched his assistant critically for a moment, then began his lecture.

"Good morning," he said, and even the salutation was full of sharp little claws. "Gentlemen, if I may have your attention. . . ." It was a needless request; the students knew that to look away for even a moment was to risk a tirade of scathing insults. There wasn't one of them who hadn't been flayed by that tongue in the past, and nobody wanted a repeat performance.

It was also an inaccurate request in that two of the students were women. But this was a point the man always ignored; to his way of thinking the only thing women were good for in medicine was carrying bedpans.

"If my assistant has finished his knitting, perhaps we can begin."

There was some nervous laughter as the assistant stepped back. "All ready, Dr. Bonnard."

The lecturer selected a scalpel from a tray, picked it up, and pointed it just below the exposed eyelid. "But first, who can tell me the name of this fascia?"

Nobody answered.

"A classful of dunces then. Very well, I shall tell you. And please listen because I'll be asking again. Aponeurosis of levator palpebra superioris. Got that?"

Silence.

"Very well then. The eye. First discovered in 1790 and named after its discoverer, Sir Henry Orb."

The class started to laugh but stopped immediately, silenced by a savage look.

The voice was icy. "If I want you to laugh, I'll hold up a sign."

They stared back at him, hardly breathing.

"The eye is a sphere with a slight bulge in front, and a stalk behind a little to the inner side of the midline. So, working from the front. . . ." Bonnard held the scalpel easily in his fingers—long, bony, beautifully manicured. He gently brought the blade down and, with near zero pressure, ran the razor edge along the exposed eyeball, slicing it, almost imperceptibly, from top to bottom.

Angry, he tossed the scalpel aside, glared at his assistant. "I butter my toast with sharper knives."

The assistant quickly changed the instrument for another, passed it to the lecturer, who quietly asked a question of the room.

"What have I just cut into?"

Nobody answered.

"*You!*" Bonnard shouted at the student next to him, an intense-looking young man with heavy-lensed glasses.

"The—the cornea."

"And was there nothing else before that?"

"The conjunctiva."

"Then *say* so. I want correct answers or none at all."

The student blinked back at him, swallowing hard.

Bonnard bent to his work again and, with incredible dexterity, sliced through the cornea. A watery fluid appeared.

"Next man. Name it."

"Aqueous humor."

"From the . . . ?"

"Pardon?"

"Where does it come from, a *tap*? Where am I now?"

The answer tumbled over itself. "Anterior chamber. It comes from the anterior chamber."

The doctor moved the scalpel again, scraping at something with immense care. "What's this? Next man."

The next man was a woman, a good-looking one in a skirt and sweater that hugged her full figure.

"Iris." The voice was shaky.

"That's your name? Iris Smith? Iris Jones?"

"The iris muscle."

"What does it support?"

"A pigmented diaphragm."

"Yes. I'm sure you know all about diaphragms."

Red-faced, the girl bit down on her lip.

"What famous song was written about the iris of the eye?"

The woman was flustered. "I don't know."

" 'When Iris Eyes Are Smiling.' "

There was some faint laughter, which was cut off immediately. "*Quiet!* This isn't a pep rally."

A long, hushed interval followed, the students not knowing what to do. Nobody had ever figured out Bonnard; he was a superb surgeon who knew his theory backward, but as a teacher he was fifty years behind the times, driving students instead of leading them. And his moods . . . he was happy one second, furious the next. Some people said he was crazy.

They watched him demonstrate his talent as he deftly severed the iris from its supports.

"What's its function?" he asked.

The girl stammered and coughed, then got it all out in one breath. "The iris contracts or relaxes to adapt the size of the pupil to the amount of light received. It also enlarges the pupil when the eye is focused for near vision."

Bonnard held out a hand, into which his assistant pressed tweezers. He lowered them to the disk he'd just freed, pincered it, lifted it up, and placed it on a porcelain dish.

He glanced to his left and saw the other woman student standing next to the one he'd just been grilling.

"Next man. Tell the class why you have such pretty blue eyes."

The girl had been ready for him and was determined not to be intimidated. She answered in a firm voice. "Because of the presence of pigment at the back of the iris."

"You're not explaining it to your boyfriend," Bonnard snapped. "I want its *name*."

"The posterior epithelial layer."

The doctor pointed to the porcelain dish. "But this iris is brown. Why?"

"Because pigment was also present in the middle layer."

"Which is?"

"The stroma."

"Amazing," Bonnard said sarcastically. He pointed the scalpel. "Next man. What are we looking at now?"

"The lens."

"Function?"

"Varies focus. Its curvature is adjusted by the sur-rounding muscle and varies focus."

"What muscle?"

"The, er . . ." The man floundered.

"Idiot! Don't you know anything? What muscle? Next man."

"The ciliary muscle."

Bonnard quieted. "Well, let's just sever the ciliary muscle." The blade moved. "And the suspensory lig-aments." The blade moved again. "What's this space called? Or do I have to tell you?"

None of the students replied.

"The canal of Petit. And this ligament here? Next man, for a hundred dollars, what's this ligament called?"

"I don't know, sir."

Bonnard snorted with contempt. "The zonule of Zinn. A ninth grader would know that."

The scalpel completed its smooth, even slice, and the tweezers came down, pinched the clear, egg-shaped lens, lifted it away, exposing the interior of the eye.

"Next man. What are we looking at?"

"Vitreous humor."

"Correct." Bonnard's thin mouth stretched a frac-tion. "Something I'm often accused of having."

The scalpel blade cut deep, slicing into the eye-ball down and around in a wide circle. The doctor accepted the instrument that was passed to him, a long, thin, spoon-shaped thing. He carefully dug it into the eyeball and scooped out a blob of clear white jelly.

"Next man. Where am I now?"

"The optic nerve."

"And this?"

"The retina."

"Name the layers," Bonnard ordered.

The student thought for a moment, started confidently but stumbled halfway through. "A layer of pigment cells, a layer of rods and cones . . . um, a layer of dendrons—"

"*Two* layers of dendrons, you idiot. Two layers of axons and a layer of ganglion cells. Physiology. Ever heard of it?"

The student dropped his gaze to the gleaming tile floor. Bonnard turned from him in disgust and went back to his work.

The scalpel picked and pared. "Next man. Where am I now?"

"The vascular coat."

"Which contains?"

"The choroid membrane."

"Which is composed of? Next man."

"A layer of blood vessels."

"That's all?"

"And a layer of pigment."

"Which does what? Do I have to drag the answers out of you?"

"Prevents light being reflected back into the retina."

Bonnard straightened, pointed at the tissue layer he had identified for them at the start of the lecture. He nodded at the student who'd flubbed the answer. "Name it."

The man's hand went to his glasses, adjusted them nervously.

"The er, apon, aponeurosis of . . . of. . . ."

"Get out! Get *out!* I can't teach *cretins!*"

With a sudden movement Bonnard scooped up the eyeball jelly from the dish and threw it into the student's face.

In its headlong rush toward summer the spring weather had stumbled momentarily, and the day was cool with a chilly wind that hid around corners and sprang out at people.

Coming into the campus parking lot, Bonnard bent his tall figure against a sudden gust and had to clutch at his black homburg to save it from being blown away. As he hurried toward his car, he didn't notice the man waiting up ahead until he'd drawn level with him.

"Dr. Bonnard?"

"Yes?"

"I'd like a word with you."

Bonnard flicked his eyes over the man; he'd never seen him before. "About what? I'm in a hurry."

"A medical matter."

"My office is the place for that. I suggest you call for an appointment."

The doctor began to stride off, but the man's reply halted him. "I don't think you'd want to discuss it there."

"Why not?"

"Could we talk in my car?" The man opened the door of the automobile he was standing next to.

Bonnard hesitated a moment, made an annoyed sound in his mouth, strode back, and got into the car. The other man got in beside him and closed the door. The windows were up against the sharp wind, and their voices sounded loud in the enclosed space.

"Please make this fast. I'm due in surgery."

"I need your services, Doctor."

"Who referred you to me?"

"A man they call Pages."

"I know nobody of that name," Bonnard answered curtly. But he paused a fraction of a second before he said it.

"I need an operation performed that can't be handled in the regular manner."

"If you're talking about an abortion—"

"Nobody pays five thousand dollars for an abortion."

"Five thousand?" Bonnard said, the edge off his voice. He watched the man reach back to the rear seat and pick up a small briefcase, set it down between them, and click it open. Inside were crisp, neat packets of one-hundred-dollar bills.

"Count it if you like."

Bonnard looked at the money, looked at the man who was offering it. "You have a friend who needs surgery?"

"Yes. He has to have something extracted."

"A bullet?"

"His eyes."

Bonnard stared. "I don't understand."

"Let's just say his eyes are rotten. Like a bad tooth. It would be best if they came out."

"You're offering me five thousand dollars just to blind a man?"

"He's already blind."

"Blind?"

"I want his eyes."

"I still don't understand."

"No need to. A pair of eyes in exchange for five thousand dollars." To underline the offer, the man nudged the briefcase an inch closer to the doctor. Bonnard looked at it; he could smell the new ink of the bills. Fresh from the bank, like buns fresh from a bakery.

"Where is this operation to take place?"

"That's up to you. It shouldn't take a man of your skill more than a few minutes, should it?"

Bonnard reached out a long hand, picked up a packet of bills, riffled it quickly, tossed it back, closed the briefcase, and took it by the handle.

"I'll need help. An anesthetist, shall we say?"

"I'll arrange it."

"When do you want this done?"

"Would tomorrow night be all right?" the other man asked.

14

THE MORNINGS ALWAYS BROUGHT two things I didn't like: the great white wall in front of my eyes and Gallo.

I'd already got the first around 8 A.M., and when somebody knocked on the door an hour after that, I thought it was going to be the second of my dislikes, but it turned out to be Muriel Carson. She was on her way to the garbage chute and wanted to know if I had any to go. When I told her I hadn't done enough eating yet to rate any good garbage, she bundled me into their apartment and cooked me flapjacks and ham, which was a slightly better breakfast than the cup of Nescafé I was going to settle for. I just made it back to the apartment in time to let Gallo in, and he had news for me. I wasn't going back to the Beacon for more tests; I was going to give a demonstration instead.

"What kind of demonstration?"

"An easy one."

"Whereabouts?"

"The Police Academy."

"I'm going to shag tennis balls at the Police Academy?"

"It's going to be simpler than that."

"Like what?"

"Simpler," Gallo said.

Gallo the clam. I wondered if his passion for secrecy carried over into his everyday life. I had a picture of him going up to the betting window at the track. "Two bucks on the nose," he'd say to the clerk. "On what number?" the clerk would ask. And Gallo would say, "I'm sorry, I'm not allowed to tell you that."

As we drove downtown, I asked him what had happened to change the plan. He told me there was a Washington senator in town whom they wanted to show me off to. He mentioned his name, and if you'd been living in a tent in Sumatra for the last ten years, maybe you wouldn't have heard of him. He was a real biggie on the Armed Services Committee, and according to Gallo, that was why I had to impress him.

"How so?"

"Because if he's impressed, we'll get a nice fat budget so we can hold some real tests."

"Aren't I real tests?" I think I must have sounded hurt.

"You're doing a great job, Max, but it's just a start. What we want to do eventually is get a couple of hundred men—soldiers, sailors, fliers—take them out to the South Pacific say, give them the eyedrops, and test them under simulated battle conditions. Put them in tanks, destroyers, fighters, and see how they perform at night. And that kind of thing carries a pretty hefty price tag."

"Okay, but how are you going to keep the drops a secret giving them to two hundred servicemen?"

"It won't be a secret by then," Gallo said. "It's impossible to keep anything secret for very long. And it won't matter anyway. You don't develop super-weapons to use them; you develop them to get what you want."

"You'll have to explain that one."

"They're tools, that's all. Something you use to get somebody else to see things your way. It's like taking your father to the sandlot when the kids have stolen your ball. When they see you've brought your old man along, they hand it back."

I thought about Gallo's theory, and I didn't like it. To me the idea of weapons development as just so much muscle flexing seemed more than a little dangerous. What happened when a country got tired of getting all greased up and striking manly poses? And what happened when one country came up with something which put it way ahead of its competitors? As night sight would. Was I helping push along World War III? That was a charming thought. "What did you do in the war, Daddy?" "I helped start it."

I didn't have much chance to worry about it because the Police Academy was only a few blocks away near Gramercy Park. I'd never been there before and didn't know what it looked like, but I envisioned something like a cross between a small college and P.S. 19. It certainly smelled like a school—blackboards, chalk, and books—and it sounded like one, too. Everything echoed the way it does in big rooms and long corridors.

Gallo led me to what he said was the indoor pistol range and told me it had been secured and the area cleared so nobody would wonder what a blind man was doing going into a pistol range.

We went through two sets of double doors; then Weyland's voice greeted me. His only other appearance so far had been at the hospital the night I'd been given the drops, so I gathered that Gallo's boss was going to be on hand for only the big occasions.

He asked me a question. "You ever done any shooting, Mr. Ellis?"

It was so blatant I knew for sure they didn't know the facts about Ollie. Nobody could be that much of a crud.

"Not outside Coney Island," I said.

"This isn't going to be much different," Weyland answered, and elaborated. "You're going to be firing a bench-rest rifle at a stationary target. There's no way you can miss." Then he said, to somebody else, "Can we have the lights off, please?" I took my shades off and took a look at the place. It was like a long, low cave. A counter ran the width of the room, and on the other side of it an open space that looked like several bowling alleys stretched for a hundred feet. At the end of the alleys large cutout figures of advancing thugs were propped up, their snarls peppered with bullet holes. I thought it was pretty sporting of the cops not to have placed them facing the other way.

Weyland asked me could I see the rifle, but I was already looking at it, a little .22 fixed to a stand which had been rigged up on the counter. As Weyland had said, it wasn't much different from a penny arcade gun, the electric ones that turn a bear around if you hit it in the right spot. I looked around at Weyland and Gallo. It was a nice change to be seeing them without their seeing me, but it was still hard to believe they were one and two in the same department section—Gallo as sleek as an investment banker and big, lumpy Weyland looking like an extra in an old FBI movie.

I asked them what I was supposed to fire at. "One of the figures?"

"There's a target on the counter near the rifle," Weyland replied. "Take a look at it."

It was a two-foot square of heavy cardboard with one big circle filling most of it. This was quartered into sections, one red, one blue, one white, one yellow. There were no other markings.

"Somebody left out the bull's-eye," I said.

"You won't be needing one," Weyland answered. "Not in the dark."

I started to ask him to explain but didn't get very far because somebody put his head in the door and said, "He's here."

Gallo told me to don my shades, and everything went white again when the lights came on. I heard the door open and close, and footsteps, then Weyland greeting our VIP. He didn't introduce me. As the world's only genuine see-in-the-dark sideshow freak I thought I might have rated a handshake, but I guess I was still only hired help. I knew the guy pretty well anyway from his twenty years of making news. He was a senior senator from one of the New England states, one of the last of the Down East cracker-barrel sages, famous for his salty sayings and his dry wit. He had a razor tongue and plenty of clout to back it up with, and I think his motto was, Talk saltily and carry a big stick. But evidently all this was just for his public image because in private, where he was now, he was quick and businesslike with no frills.

"Okay," he asked, "what have you got for me?"

Weyland went into his sales pitch. "Senator, we're going to show you something you're going to find hard to believe, and just so there'll be no doubt in your mind it's for real, we're going to make it fool-proof." I heard him move past me. "This is the target Mr. Ellis here will shoot at. It'd be pretty hard to switch it on you, but just so you'll be sure we haven't, would you write something on one of the corners, sir? The name of a friend or a relative, perhaps."

"Right."

I heard the sound of a pen scratching. If this had been a media event, I'm sure the senator would have written the name of his dog or his old grade-school sweetheart, but as it wasn't, he probably wrote the name of his bookie.

"Fine," Weyland said. "Mr. Gallo, would you do the honors?"

I heard Gallo attach the target to the overhead wire, then the electric whine as it was whisked down to the end of the range.

Weyland went on explaining. "There are ten rounds in the rifle, Senator. Why don't you decide where you'd like them placed? Write them down on this, sir, so you'll have a record."

I heard the pen scratching again; Weyland must have passed him a note pad.

"Okay, then we're all set. You happy, Senator?"

His voice came back, decisive. "Let's see it."

"Could we douse the lights, please?"

The room went black, and I took off my glasses again. The senator looked the same as when I'd seen him on TV, alert, narrow-faced, mustachiod, and with a full and flowing head of hair. He'd been quoting Mark Twain for so long he'd begun to look like him. He was peering into the darkness suspiciously; he must have known about the project, since Weyland hadn't explained any of it while I'd been there, but that didn't mean he had to believe it. He was right to be suspicious; he must have thought we were all out of our heads.

My sight blurred for a moment when a flashlight beam hit me.

"As you can see, Senator," Weyland said, still showing he had nothing up his sleeve, "no infrared devices of any kind."

The light winked out. "Mr. Ellis, you may fire when ready."

My God, Weyland injecting a touch of humor. Amazing.

I bent over the rifle. It was a pump action, no problem, and with it fixed to the bench there'd be zero kick. Through the peep sight the target looked huge, and I didn't see how I could miss it from fifty feet.

Behind me Weyland handed the flashlight to the senator and invited him to read off the placements he'd written down.

"Two in the red," the senator called.

I swung the rifle onto the red section, pumped a slug into the spout, and squeezed the trigger. It made a sound like a sharp handclap, and a hole appeared in the target exactly where I'd been aiming. I pumped up another bullet and put this one an inch to the right of the first one.

"Four in the blue," the senator announced.

I spread four holes around the blue section. I could have written my initials with that rifle.

"Three in the white."

Bang, bang, bang.

"One in the yellow."

I put it in dead center.

Beside me, Gallo had his finger on a button, which he now pressed. The target came singing toward me, and Gallo told me to put my shades back on, so I didn't get to see a close-up of my marksmanship.

Weyland called for the lights. I heard the target being unclipped, then Weyland asking the senator if he'd care to check the pattern.

There was a few moments' silence before the senator spoke. He didn't use any of his colorful Vermont/New Hampshire expressions; he just said, "Jesus Christ Almighty!" in a very awed voice.

We left on that note, Gallo and I. Weyland stayed behind to conclude his sales pitch, although I don't know what he could have added. It must have been abundantly clear to the senator what a platoon of soldiers with night sight could do to an enemy.

Gallo congratulated me on the way back, happy with the way the test had gone. I guess he felt certain he'd get the money now for his big-scale combat trial in the South Pacific.

I was happy too, but for another reason: I had the rest of the day off and Karen Petersen coming for dinner. And if I'd been reading the signs right, she was going to be the dessert.

"Hi," she said when I opened the door, "I've been shopping. Where's the kitchen?"

"Past the billiard room and through the library."

When she walked by me, whatever she was wearing swished with a silky sound, which, combined with the musky perfume she wore, was a great introduction to the evening.

"What's on the menu?" I asked, following her in.

"Shrimp cocktail, steak, red wine, lemon meringue pie."

"I'm staying," I said.

"Very wise. It's starting to rain," she answered. "I got a little wet."

"Well, as Bob Benchley said, we'd better get you into a dry martini." I told her she'd find them in the refrigerator—I'd bullied Gallo into buying me some hooch—and she came back a minute later and put a frosty glass into my hand.

We drank; then she said, "Mm, good. You make them?"

"Yep, it's my grandmother's recipe. One ice cube for everybody drinking, add the gin, let it steep for five minutes, then pour and serve with lemon."

We never really reined up after the fast start, and a few more martinis didn't do a thing to slow the pace. By the time she had dinner ready we were a merry little twosome.

The steaks were great; the wine was great; Miss Petersen was great. She'd even brought along a transistor radio, having noticed the day before that I didn't seem to have a record player or anything. She went around the dial and found some WPAT stuff, not too funky, but nice.

"All right," she said, "that's enough fun for one night. Let's get back to your mobility talent."

I was just a touch dismayed. "Sure."

I heard her chair scrape back. "Let's see if your blindness affects your dancing any."

I got up feeling suddenly better; then she melted into me, and for the first time I got some idea of what she looked like. She was only a little thing, and very, very soft. It was like holding a five-foot-three marshmallow.

We moved around doing a kind of forties nightclub shuffle, the greatest dance step ever invented for bringing boys and girls together. I said, with my face in her hair, "I'm not crazy about this, but anything for research."

We shuffled and swayed some more; then she murmured, "Well, your dancing seems to be okay."

I had only to move my head a little, and then I was kissing her, getting a taste of the marshmallow at last.

It was delicious.

When we finally broke, she said, softly, "That seems to be okay, too."

I started a circuit of her nose and ears and eyes. "I

think we owe it to science," I said, "to push this experiment as far as we can."

She said, her voice low, "What did you have in mind?"

For a crazy moment I was tempted to say "Indian wrestling"—I often tended to self-destruct with women—but I held off and, instead, bounced the ball back into her court.

"I don't know. Got any ideas?"

She had a lulu.

I felt her hand creep up my chest and start to unbutton my shirt.

"Wait," I said. "I'll get the light."

I knew exactly where that was, moved to it, and clicked it off. Behind me I heard zips unzipping, snaps unsnapping, and elastic being slipped down. God, what a gorgeous sound. It had been some time since I'd taken anything to bed besides a lot of doubts.

I got out of my clothes quickly, took off my shades, turned around, and got my first look at Karen Petersen.

It wasn't completely dark in the apartment; a red glow in the night sky, diffused slightly by the rain, lit the room softly. She could see me, so I couldn't let my eyes roam as I would have liked to. But I was smart enough to level them where I could take in the more fascinating parts of her body, and they were well worth taking in. But when I saw all those parts start to move toward me, I realized it wasn't my eyes that might give me away; it was another organ altogether. I think I was the first man in history who was in danger of being betrayed by his penis.

She glided into me, and we moved back together and crumpled down onto the sofa. Since I'd met her, Miss Petersen had taken the dominant role—taking me to dinner, guiding me around, buying groceries, and cooking for me—and she saw no need to change now, so I lay back and let her dominate me some more. And believe me, she was a great little dominator.

I still hadn't got a look at her face, and I was in no position to then. All I could see was shiny blond hair on the top of her head as it moved slowly up and down, and I certainly didn't want to interrupt her by asking her to look up. She couldn't have replied anyway.

But she had other things in mind, and she stopped what she was doing, gently pushed me back, and mounted me as prettily as you please.

I had a grandstand view of her then, and I could look all I wanted without fear of her catching me at it, because she had her eyes closed and her head tilted back. I let my gaze travel over her at about twelve inches an hour, rising slowly from her dark triangle, into which I kept vanishing, to the soft, high curve of her belly, the deep scoop of her navel, her sensationally firm and full breasts, which were moving up and down a beat behind the rest of her body.

The face was a travel poster for Sweden: wide mouth, high forehead and cheekbones, strong, open features that made me think of deep fjords and sunshine, although I quickly shifted to a more interior image when her lips parted and she started making little yelps and moans.

She took up the rating with her hips and began to

move faster, and I began to move faster, too. Then we were both moving at the same speed until she started moving faster still, then I caught up and started moving faster, then she caught up and started moving faster, and pretty soon I couldn't have told you one single thing about Karen Petersen from the Beacon Society for the Blind, because she was moving so fast she launched me into orbit, and I headed for the moon.

As he turned into the avenue, the rain, like a dog recognizing its master, leaped up at Bonnard, licking at his face. He hurried toward the cafeteria, pushed through the doors, and looked around, brushing water from his sleeve.

The end booth was empty. The man was late.

He moved toward it, swung his long frame into the rear seat, and carefully placed the cloth bag he carried on the other side of him near the wall.

He ordered coffee from a bored waitress but didn't touch it when it came, just sat there silently in his black homburg and dark topcoat, his eyes bright sparks in his pale, gaunt face.

Two women came in through the door, then a man, and immediately Bonnard knew it was the one he was waiting for. He was huge, shaped like a barrel, and with sparse hair on a massive head which had a mouth that seemed to be all teeth.

He came toward the doctor, moving slowly, as if all that weight were an effort to carry around. The teeth flashed.

"I think we got a date, right?"

"Sit down," Bonnard said. It wasn't an invitation; it was an order.

"They told me I should look for a guy real tall and thin," the big man said, pleased with his correct guess. "You were easy to spot."

He didn't seem to notice Bonnard's cold stare, or his lack of response, but went on as if he were delighted to meet somebody he'd heard a lot about.

"My name's Pinzon, Johnny Pinzon. It's Spanish for finch, you know what that is, a little bird?" He grinned and slapped a hand to the shoulder of his dripping trench coat. "Funny name for a guy built like me, huh?" He looked down at the cup of coffee steaming in front of Bonnard. "You drinking that?"

"No."

"You mind? I could use it. Little damp out there tonight." The big man reached for the cup, dumped sugar in, gave it a fast stir, and drank it in two gulps. "So," he said, running a hairy wrist across his mouth, "you got a guy you want leaned on, right?"

There was no response from the surgeon, but it didn't seem to matter to the other man. He craned forward and jerked a thumb at his barrel chest. "Let me tell you, mister, you got the best working for you tonight. When Johnny Pinzon leans on a guy, he stays bent for a month."

Bonnard, a sharp edge of distaste in his voice, said, "I don't want this man beaten. I want him unconscious."

Pinzon laughed. "Way I work, it's the same thing."

"I want it done quickly. A single blow if possible."

"You want him out cold with one shot. No problem," Pinzon said, his teeth shining. "What's he like? A big guy? I like 'em big. More fun that way."

"I've never seen him," Bonnard answered in his cold, precise manner.

"You ain't seen him?" Pinzon looked surprised. "Then how do—"

Bonnard cut through him. "He won't be hard to spot. He wears dark glasses and carries a white cane."

"A what?"

"He's blind," Bonnard said.

Slapped sideways by a swirl of wind, rain hosed the window for a moment, then was torn away again. On the other side of the glass the smile on the hired man's face seemed to have been extinguished by the gust.

"Blind? Nobody told me that."

"Now you know."

Pinzon's teeth worked at his lower lip, his head shaking from side to side. "It don't seem right, boppin' a blind guy."

"You're being paid," Bonnard told him, the words hard and flat.

The other man was quick to show he understood. "Look, I know that. I'm only doing my job. But a blind guy . . . it's gonna be a walkover."

"We're wasting time." Bonnard grasped the little cloth case and began to move out of the booth. "You have a car?"

They left the cafeteria and went quickly through the wet streets to a parking lot.

"Where to?" Pinzon asked.

"Twenty-fifth Street. Corner of Second Avenue."

Driving across town, Pinzon, not saying anything now, turned on the radio, clicked impatiently through the dial, turned it off again, and settled for the sound of squishing tires and the steady hum of the windshield wipers.

The wind had dropped, and the rain faded to a fine sprinkle as they turned off Second into the cross street.

"Three Twenty-five," Bonnard murmured. "The apartment house right there."

Pinzon drifted the car past it, slipped into the curb, and stopped. He twisted his huge body, took a look at the building. A thin yellow light came out from the lobby, spilled feebly onto the sidewalk, then tapered off into the darkness of the street. He twisted back and faced the tall man beside him.

"How do you want to play it?"

"We'll go up to his apartment. Once we're inside I want him unconscious. You'll do it quickly and quietly. Then you'll come back here to the car and wait for me."

Pinzon shrugged; he no longer liked this job. He'd never done anything like it before. He glanced at his companion; he'd never worked with anybody like this before either. The guy was spooky. For the first time he noticed the little bag on the seat, a soft cloth case with twin handles.

"What's in the bag?"

Bonnard watched the rain pattern on the windshield. "Nothing that need concern you. I suggest we start." He was reaching for the door handle when Pinzon, turned in his seat again, stopped him.

"Wait! Look, that guy. Coming out on the side-walk. . . ."

Bonnard swiveled and saw for himself: The man was coming through the door of the apartment house, a white cane in his right hand. His dark glasses were already beginning to spot with rain.

"Jesus, we missed him," Pinzon said. But Bonnard took no notice.

He spoke quickly. "Do you have a flashlight?"

"Sure. In the glove compartment."

With an unblinking gaze Bonnard watched the man move down the middle of the opposite side-walk, his cane scanning in front of him. He let him pass them and get a little ahead, then ordered Pinzon to follow.

The car, its dark metal shining in the rain, eased out from the curb and settled in, ten feet behind the man on the sidewalk, stalking him like a jungle beast.

Bonnard peered through the drizzle at the street ahead: parked cars; wet pavement; the dark facades of buildings. There were no people; the only sign of life was the red neon of a bar at the end of the block.

The car crept another twenty feet, nosing through the thin curtain of rain, the low purr of the engine blending in with the slow footsteps on the sidewalk.

Bonnard squinched his eyes, checked both sides of the street, but couldn't see what he wanted. "Stop here," he ordered. He grasped his bag, slid out of the car, ducked his head back in, and spoke quickly to the man behind the wheel. "Drive to the end of the block and park, then walk back toward him. I need a side passage or a basement doorway. If you see one, signal me. Bring the flashlight."

He closed the door and, as the car sped off, crossed to the sidewalk. He was about twenty feet behind his quarry, about where he wanted to be, and he slowed his pace to maintain the gap.

From somewhere down the block came the chunk of a door slamming. Pinzon? He couldn't see. Then, with a suddenness that surprised him, a car spun around the corner, roared by, bursting through puddles, turned off, and was gone. But its headlights had lit up the huge figure of Pinzon less than thirty yards away. Together they moved through the rain toward the man in the middle.

Bonnard searched the buildings ahead, saw nothing that would do, then stopped dead when he heard the noise. The man's cane had spanged against a bicycle chained to a railing, and the sound gonged through the night like the first sudden cry of an alarm.

But that wasn't the only noise that stopped him; the other was a high, toothy whistle.

Pinzon had found a place.

Bonnard watched the man in front feel his way around the bike and continue his slow progress toward the corner.

The doctor shifted the little case to his other hand and followed, lengthening his stride, drawing closer. He still couldn't see Pinzon, the rain diffused the streetlights—one of them was out altogether—but he knew he couldn't be far. He checked behind him. Nobody. Nobody in front either; nobody out walking on a night like this. People stayed indoors or got cabs.

The couples banging out the door of an apartment house were a surprise. Two couples, talking in loud voices, down the block ahead of him. He could just make them out getting into a car.

He relaxed. They weren't going to be a problem; they were leaving.

He heard the whir of a car's starter, but the engine didn't catch. It whirred a second time with the same negative result. There was a ten-second pause, the driver resting the battery; then he tried again, but there was no answering roar. The car wouldn't start.

Bonnard made a small angry sound; that car had to be almost next to where Pinzon was waiting, and if it stayed there, they'd lose their chance at the blind man. Once he made the avenue there'd be too many people around, and it was less than fifty feet away now.

In his anxiety he'd increased his stride and was almost on top of the other man, who still moved at the same slow pace, oblivious of what was happening around him.

Bonnard saw Pinzon then, standing at the entrance of what looked like an alley between two buildings—it would have been ideal. He slapped his side in frustration, and the blind man might have heard the noise if it hadn't been covered by the starter whirring again, a harsh, impatient sound.

Nothing.

Bonnard couldn't believe it. A perfect chance ruined by a rained-out car.

The red neon of the bar on the corner got closer. It was no good; they were going to lose him.

But the thought was canceled immediately. The car, so dead a moment ago, suddenly burst into life. The engine caught and revved; the car's headlights sprang on; it swung out, made the green light on the avenue, and vanished uptown.

Pinzon lumbered out of the doorway directly in front of the blind man. "Give you a hand, buddy?" He took a fast look up and down the block.

The man stopped. "Thanks, but I'm fine."

"No trouble. Here, lemme take your arm." Pinzon reached for him. "Wet night like this, you could run into things."

"It's kind of you."

"Happy to help."

They had only to move a little to be opposite the narrow side alley which ran between two tenements.

Bonnard, a few feet away, checked the street quickly, then said, low, "All right."

Pinzon leaned his weight against the blind man, moving him sideways into the dark mouth of the passage.

"Hey! What—?"

Something heavy in Pinzon's hand swished through the air and thunked against bone.

The man staggered back, his glasses shocked off his head, his cane tumbling from his grasp. He sprawled against a garbage can, rolled, and thwacked down on the cement.

Bonnard hissed at Pinzon. "Fool! You'll wake everybody."

The big man looked surly. "You wanted him out cold, right?"

"Get him in farther. No noise."

Pinzon reached down, grabbed the man under the arms, and hauled him farther into the alley.

"Over there. Lay him down."

Pinzon lowered the man's shoulders. His head bumped back on the alley floor and flopped sideways, his left cheek lying in a puddle of water.

Bonnard crouched beside him, brought his cloth case around, began to unzip it. He spoke urgently. "The flashlight. Shine it here."

The big man dug into his trench coat, clicked a button, and a beam lit the rain sifting down in a fine mist. It played on the bag the doctor hinged open.

"What the hell's all that?" Pinzon asked.

Knives, scissors, forceps flashed and gleamed in the light. Retractors, hemostats, a plastic box of amazingly thin curved needles, everything had its own special place, fitting snugly into cloth loops on each side of the bag.

Bonnard brought out two small folded towels. "On his face," he snapped. "The light. Follow my hands."

He took hold of the man's chin, turned the head, placed a towel on each cheek.

"Listen," Pinzon said. "What's going on?"

"Move the light. I told you, I want you to follow my hands."

Bonnard's words were crisp, demanding. The beam danced on stainless steel again as the doctor slipped a fat little can from its loop, then followed it to the man's face.

"What's that for?"

Bonnard ignored the question as he pressed down on the can and squirted a frothy liquid around the man's eyes, rubbing it into the skin with his fingers. He returned the can and selected another, a smaller one with a nozzle as thin as a nail and bent at the top into a right angle.

Deftly, with a long thumb and forefinger, he parted the man's left eyelid, half rolled it back, held the nozzle to it, and squirted a thick brown liquid into the eye. He did the same with the right eye, then replaced the can.

The man's eyes stayed open, the elasticity gone from the skin where Bonnard had massaged it. The brown liquid lay on the eyes in a thick film, turning them into copper coins. The doctor reached for something else, something that looked like the handle of a fork. He slipped it out of its little plastic scabbard and turned it in his hands, examining it. As it came front on, its razor edge, incredibly fine, perfectly honed, disappeared.

"You gonna mark him?" Pinzon asked.

Bonnard slid a tiny flat silver spatula out of its loops; it was almost as thin as the scalpel. He laid in gently on the man's left eye, depressed the eyeball slightly, then worked the tip just under the upper eyelid. He moved the scalpel in his right hand so it rested flat on top of the spatula, then, very slowly, and very carefully, slid the blade up under the eyelid.

"Jesus, what the fuck you doing?"

"Hold the flashlight *still*," Bonnard snapped.

He eased out the spatula, placed it down, and got on with his work.

With a steady, even pressure the scalpel moved down toward the corner of the eye, and Bonnard's long, bony fingers tensed as they met resistance.

A trickle of blood, heavy like dark syrup, bubbled up and started down the man's cheek toward the towel.

"Jesus. I'm gonna puke."

"Hold the light *steady*."

Like a man paring an apple, Bonnard, with immense care, brought the blade in a circular motion around the corner of the eye, slicing through the supporting muscles. The eye began to fill with blood, which spilled over and seeped into the towel and kept flowing as the blade traveled along and under the bottom eyelid, working toward the inner corner.

"Oh, Christ. . . ." Pinzon sucked in breath. "Nobody never. . . . Oh, Jesus. . . ."

Again Bonnard, with the merest amount of extra pressure, lanced through tiny muscles, turned the corner of the eye, kept the blade moving up and around till he'd come full circle. He withdrew the scalpel, wiped it quickly on the towel, and left it there.

"Bag," he said sharply. "On the bag."

Pinzon directed the beam. He was making little snuffling noises and breathing heavily through his mouth.

Bonnard growled at him. "Get a grip on yourself."

The flashlight followed his hand, lit up the small glass jar he'd chosen. With two fast turns he unscrewed the lid and placed the open mouth of the jar on the bottom of the eyelid.

He picked up the spatula, angled it into the outer corner of the eye, and, with the gentlest lateral pressure, started to work the spatula up and down.

The eyeball pressed against the lids, growing larger.

As it swelled and pushed against them, the lids began to open wider.

With his left hand Bonnard took hold of the little glass jar, pressed its rim against the bottom eyelid, and levered with the spatula.

Like a soft boiled egg squeezed from its shell, the eyeball emerged.

There was a tiny sucking noise, then a sound like a liquid sigh, and the eyeball, trailing little white strings, slid down into the jar on a jelly of red and brown ooze.

Pinzon gulped and swallowed. "Oh, Jesus," he breathed. "Oh, Christ." He went on saying it over and over as Bonnard repeated the operation on the other eye. He held the flashlight steady but kept his face turned away, taking breath in short bursts. He didn't look again till he heard the lid being screwed back onto the jar.

Bonnard placed it in the bag, wrapped the two instruments in a cloth, put them in, too, then closed and zipped up the case. He stood and began to walk out of the alley, but Pinzon didn't seem to be able to move. He stood there, rooted, the beam still shining on the thing lying on the wet cement. The face looked as if two heavy bullets had smashed into it each side of the nose. The rain had washed some of the brown coagulant down into the ears, where it had collected in little dark pools. The two towels sat on the cheeks like bloated leeches and, above them, beneath the eyelids, some blood, dispersed by the muscle relaxant, had formed a delicate lacework mask.

Bonnard turned, hissed at the big man, "Turn that thing off."

Pinzon killed the light, stumbled up the alley, the trembling beginning to creep through his body.

Ahead of him, striding purposefully back toward the car, the doctor was turning up the collar of his topcoat.

It had begun to rain hard again.

15

"MAX! MAX!"

I came back to the world slow and groggy and without the first idea of what, where, or who, only that I couldn't get my breath and that sweat was flowing down me.

Then I knew what had happened.

It must have been the small hours of the morning. We'd made love for quite a while, then fallen asleep—with the dinner, the booze, and the sex we were ready for it—but I hadn't been ready for the way it was interrupted.

"You had a nightmare," the girl said. "You cried out."

I didn't reply. I gave a pretty good imitation of a blind man feeling his way across a room, went into the bathroom, splashed water on my face, and looked for the answer in the washbasin. After a while I went back into the room.

"Max. You okay?"

"Sure. Just a dream."

"You sounded terrified."

"It's a kind of terrifying dream."

"You've had it before?" she asked.

"We're old friends."

She gave it a moment then said, "You called out a name. It sounded like Ollie."

"He was my brother."

Her voice quieted. "Was?"

"He's dead."

I sat down on the sofa with my back to her and ran a towel over my neck, wondering if I was going to have to start buying little white packages to get away from the dream.

When she asked me how it had happened, I started to tell her without even thinking about it. Maybe I had some idea that if I heard it out loud again, hung it up, and examined it once more, I might be able to reach some new conclusions.

"I was nine. Ollie was two years older, so I was the kid brother, but we still shared things, played together a lot. We were always playing What Woulds—what would you have if you could have anything in the world? I knew what I wanted, a Schwinn. That was a bike they used to build then. Heavy as lead, but they looked like the Superchief. Ollie knew what he wanted, too, a Daisy air rifle. A Red Ryder Special. There was no TV then, and a kid's heroes were in comic books, or on radio serials, or in the Saturday afternoon movie serials. Anyway, a kid could earn one of these air rifles if he delivered a zillion copies of a newspaper that was owned by the people who put out Red Ryder comics. Ollie worked his tail off, it took him forever, but he made it, and I remember when the letter came telling him the rifle was in the mail.

"I don't think either of us slept for two weeks.

And I remember Ollie unwrapping it the day it came. Shiny steel barrel and a real wood stock with Red Ryder's signature burned into it. I couldn't get over it, a real gun that fired real bullets, even if they were just BBs. We were out of the house and round to the Blackberries in a minute flat."

The girl said softly, "The Blackberries?"

"It was a big vacant lot next to the local movie house, the Kings. There's a clothing factory on it now, and the movie house is gone, but back then it was a wild half acre of high scrub and blackberry bushes. It was the Chisholm trail, the Panhandle, and the Badlands for Ollie and me. He was always Red Ryder, and I was always Buck Jones; only this time he was really Red Ryder because he had a rifle that could hit things, and it had his name on it. I was busting to try it, but he didn't let me till he'd shredded about a dozen tin cans and a bushel of leaves, and by then it was getting dark."

I stopped for a moment, thinking about it. God, it was clear. I won't say it was as if it had happened yesterday, because it wasn't like that at all; it didn't seem to fit into any time frame. It was more as if it had always happened, if that makes any sense.

Karen told me to go on.

"I'm still not exactly sure about the next part, but I know we started playing again, fooling around. Ollie was behind a tree, and I think I tried to shoot his hat off, like they were always doing in the movies; only he jumped out suddenly, and I got him in the face. In the eye. Pretty good shooting, huh?"

She didn't say anything, just put a hand on my arm and left it there.

"He lost the sight in that eye. Needless to say, that was the end of the Daisy air rifle, and Ollie was far more upset about that than he was about his injury. It didn't seem to make an ounce of difference to him; in fact, he got to be a kind of celebrity among the kids, a kid who'd actually had his eye shot out. It went a bluey yellow color, and he was proud of it.

"Things went okay for a while, but then his other eye started to go on him. My folks took him to a specialist, and he did what should have been done in the first place, removed the sightless eye. But he couldn't save the other one. Sympathetic ophthalmitis, they call it. A little while after that Ollie was totally blind."

I toweled the moisture off my head. I'd started perspiring again.

"Well, that did make a difference. A hell of a one. With one good eye he could do anything the other kids could do, but when that one went. . . . My folks helped him all they could, of course, carted him around, did everything for him except the one thing they couldn't do for him. But Ollie still seemed cheerful and seemed as though it wasn't bothering him that much. But less than a year later, on a real hot July day, a bunch of us went out to the lake, and Ollie came with us. We chose sides for a ball game, and whenever we did that, somebody would always suggest that Ollie should umpire, and Ollie would always laugh.

"We played the game; then I went looking for Ollie because I couldn't find him. I thought he might be sitting on the lake bank where it was cool, but all I could find were his clothes. We finally found him just before it got dark. He'd floated under a boat dock. Everybody said he must have got too hot sitting there on the bank, decided to cool off, and got into trouble in the water, and that was the explanation my folks believed, thank God. I believed it, too, till I was old enough to think it through. Ollie hated the water. He was one of those kids you'd have to throw in to get wet.

"And when I realized it, I started having the dream. Only once a year, maybe, but always the same. Always trying to run across the lake that was as solid as ice, struggling to get across it as if a cyclone was blowing against me. Then reaching the other bank, finding his clothes and his cane, and calling out for him.

"Pretty soon I was getting it twice, three times a year. Then every month. And lately it's been like twice a week, and the thing's starting to change. Those clothes on the bank, for the last couple of months they haven't been Ollie's, they've been mine."

I don't think Karen said anything right away. If she did, I didn't hear her; I was thinking about the change in the dream, the meaning of which was hardly buried in any obscure symbolism. I wished it had been.

I became aware of the silence lying heavy in the room, then Karen's voice.

"It was an accident, Max. It wasn't your fault."

"That's right," I said. "It was just an accident."

I woke up to the sound of Karen's radio and an early-morning breakfast type telling me that it was seven-thirty, and I should be up and doing. Easy enough for him to say; he was already risen, showered, dressed, and coffeed. I caught up with him on the first three things, then the fourth when Karen handed me a cup of Nescafé.

The atmosphere was nicely domestic. She kissed my cheek, buttered my toast, and said she had to fly because she was a working girl. She promised to see me that evening and advance the cause of science another rung up the ladder.

Fine with me.

She hadn't been gone more than fifteen minutes when the doorbell rang.

I asked who it was and got a one-word answer.

"Police."

Right then I got another example of what a blind person has to contend with. In New York you never open your door just because somebody on the other side says he's the police; all too often he turns out to be anything but. What you do is check through the peephole or slip the door chain in and open the door a few inches. Neither of those two things being possible, I just had to trust to luck, which, after my burglary, I didn't feel much like doing.

"What do you want?" I called, testing the response.

"We want in, whad'ya think?"

It had to be the police; muggers aren't that rude. I let them in.

"Max Sinclair?"

"Yes?"

"You know a guy named James Keitel?"

At first it didn't register.

"A blind guy like you." There were two cops, and I think they were patrolmen out of a cruiser. They had the same grace and charm.

"Keitel. . . ." I remembered, the guy I shared those classes with at the Beacon. "Yes, I do know him. Why?"

"He ran into a little trouble last night."

"Is he hurt?"

"You might say that, yeah."

"Where is he?"

"On his way to Emergency. He had identification on him, no address though. You know where we might contact a relative?"

I gave them the Beacon's address and asked how they knew I'd known him.

"We found this package beside him. Got your name and address on it."

"You'd better open it," I said.

I heard paper being ripped; then one of the beefy-voiced cops said, "I think it's one of them blind books," and put it into my hands. He was right; it was a braille primer. I remembered Mrs. Trumbull saying she was going to let me have one. Keitel lived only a couple of blocks away—he'd told me that the first day in class—Trumbull had obviously got him to bring the book around as a practical exercise for him. Whether he'd got the wrong apartment or whether I just hadn't heard him at the door, being wrapped up with Karen, didn't make much difference now.

"What happened to him? How bad is he?"

I heard one of the cops suck at his teeth. "I don't

know what this town's coming to. Ten years on the force, and I ain't seen anything like it."

"Animals," the other cop said. "That's what we got on the streets today, animals."

"You know what they did to that guy?" the first one continued. "Some maniac cut his eyes right out of his head."

"What did you say?"

"I didn't believe it either. Holy Christ, what a mess the guy was. Holes where his eyes shoulda been. They only just found him, lying in an alley down the block. It's a wonder he ain't dead."

I had so little voice I had to have two tries at it. "Somebody . . . somebody cut out his *eyes?*"

"Can you beat it? Doin' that to a blind man? I tell you, this town. I don't know what it's coming to."

The cops left a few minutes later, but I honestly couldn't tell you anything they'd said after that. I was shocked numb.

It was horribly clear somebody had mistaken Keitel for me. And it was horribly clear why.

They were after the eyedrops.

That junkie I'd surprised in my apartment hadn't been a junkie; he'd been somebody searching for the drops. When he found I didn't have them, that they were impossible to get hold of, he'd gone after the next best thing: the things the drops were in. There'd still be a trace of them in my eyes, enough for a good chemist to get a breakdown of the formula.

I realized something else, too: As soon as this person found out his mistake, he'd be back to correct it.

I had to get out of that apartment, and fast.

I found my jacket, found my cane, and had the

door open before it occurred to me that the guy could have been standing there, waiting for me to come out.

I froze. I tried to swallow and couldn't. I waited a beat, then plunged out into the corridor.

Nothing.

I slammed the door behind me, tapped my way to the elevator, and made it down to the lobby. I suppose I should have gone straight into the Carsons', but I wanted to get out of that building, out of that neighborhood. A hundred miles wouldn't have been far enough. I had to call Gallo and get tucked away somewhere safe.

I was so scared and confused and horrified I wasn't thinking straight, and when I got to the sidewalk, instead of heading for the bar, I went off in the opposite direction.

But that wasn't the worst of it. That was stupid enough, but I'd done something far more stupid: I'd been so desperate to get out of the apartment I'd forgotten all about the pill. Maybe it wouldn't have worked, so maybe it wouldn't have done me an ounce of good, but if it *had* worked . . . but wait, it wouldn't have had any effect for two hours anyway, so I would have still been doing what I was doing then: half walking, half running in a blank white world.

I should have gone back and got it, I knew, but there was just no way I was going back to that apartment; the guy might already be waiting up there for me. Or in the lobby. Or right behind me.

I would have sold my soul for just five minutes of sight. I wouldn't have been any more vulnerable if

I'd been in a wheelchair or had two broken arms. The only thing I could think of was to get to a phone before that guy got to me. There were footsteps coming toward me. "Can you help me?" I said. "I'm—"

"Beat it," a man growled.

I stopped somebody else. "Please, I need a phone."

Some kids laughed. "Try the phone company."

I couldn't believe it. What was I, some staggering wino? Some drunken bum? Couldn't they see I was blind?

I got going down that sidewalk, scanning with my cane and cursing my mistake. If I'd turned left instead of right, I would have been halfway to the bar, traveling over territory I knew. As it was, I only knew I was on Second Avenue, but I hadn't a clue to the immediate geography. I might as well have been in Tokyo or Paris.

All my knowledge, all my training went out the window; I was doing everything wrong, doing things so badly I almost fell over the curb.

A hand grabbed my elbow, and I nearly died.

"Help you cross?"

I think I did die a little because I knew that voice. I was sure of it. Whose? And why didn't he say that he knew me, greet me? I couldn't answer, couldn't speak. My voice seemed glued to my throat.

He steered me across the street, my cane tipped the opposite curb, and I stepped up onto it, but the hand didn't go away.

"Okay now?"

Christ damn it, who *was* it? I suddenly couldn't stop trembling, and I could hear it in my words.

"A phone. I need a phone."

"A phone?" He said it reasonably, as if it were the most natural thing in the world. "There's one just down here." And he started to lead me off.

Where to? A parked car? An alley like the one he'd led that poor guy Keitel into? I wanted to yell for help, but I didn't seem to have anything in my throat except a large lump, so I was led like a lamb down the sidewalk, the hand on my elbow gripping me firmly.

"Right here," he said.

"What?"

"The call box."

I heard hinges squeal. I felt with my cane, touched the open space between the doors. What could he do to me in there? It had glass windows, didn't it? Or were they covered with ads? Maybe that call box would make a nice little operating room.

"Here, let me help you."

That firm grip propelled me forward, and I was inside the box before I could do a thing. He didn't try to get in with me, but maybe he had a reason, maybe somebody was walking by, watching us. And I couldn't shut him out because the door wouldn't close properly. I pushed and shoved at it, but it would go only halfway.

I groped for the phone, grabbed the handpiece, dug for coins, and fumbled them in, but I might as well have been hooked up to outer space for all the response I got—somebody had ripped the guts out of the thing.

"No luck? Let me try."

I heard the door hinge back.

I shoved at him, bulled past him, and ran. That's what I did, white wall and all; I ran out of that busted phone box and plunged off the sidewalk because the guy was going to cut my eyes out.

The one thing you never do if you get confused on the street is panic. I must have told blind people that a hundred times, and here I was dashing into an avenue full of rush-hour traffic. It sounded as if half the cars in New York hit their brakes at the same time. I can't be sure, I wasn't taking too much notice right then, but I think they'd all just started maybe half a block away on a green light, so they must have been coming down at me in a solid line.

I still probably would have made it if it hadn't been for some hotshot on a motorbike. I heard his engine cut and his tires screech; then something that felt like an office safe slammed into me, and I was on my way to the ground.

There was nothing but a confusion of voices and honking horns and somebody asking me over and over was I okay. Hands came under my arms, and I was lifted up, no doubt by the hotshot worried about his no-claim bonus.

"You okay, champ? You okay?" He was practically willing me to say yes.

"I'm fine," I said. "Fine." Which was ridiculous because I was blind as a bat, there was a maniac after me, and I'd just been run down in the middle of Second Avenue. But I didn't want to lie there and hear that voice I knew say, "I'm a doctor, I'll take care of him. Help me get him into a cab."

I wanted to get into a cab alone.

"Get me a cab. Just get me a cab."

The horns were going wild.

"You sure you're okay?"

"Yeah. Just get me a cab."

The hotshot got over his shock in a hurry and went straight into relief. "Ya dumb bastard, get a dog, for crissakes."

But one of those honking horns must have belonged to an empty Checker because a minute later I was bundled into a large back seat and whisked away.

"You all right, mister? You want Bellevue?"

"Grand Central."

"You sure? You really went down."

"Grand Central."

"You're the boss," the cabby said.

I didn't feel much like the boss; I felt like the lowest paid rickshaw man in Asia. The shock of getting hit was starting to seep through me, and I didn't dare feel my side, afraid it would be just one big hole. But it wasn't my side I was worried about; it was still my eyes. I wasn't out of it yet, because the cab suddenly stopped.

It couldn't have made more than thirty feet before it had turned off the avenue and pulled up, and a man on foot could cover that distance in no time.

"Let's go, let's go," I called.

"Traffic's backed up," the cabby told me.

"Where are we?"

"Corner Twenty-fifth and Second."

I couldn't believe it, didn't want to believe it. I'd spent the last, what, ten minutes trying frantically to put distance between me and my apartment house, and here I was sitting right outside it.

I slid down in the seat, hunching myself into a corner. The guy would have had to have seen me knocked down and put into a cab, had to have seen it turn off a block later and stop. And we were still stopped.

I fully expected the door to be wrenched open any second, and when it didn't happen—when the cab jerked forward and kept going, instead—the relief almost brought on a heart attack.

We swung onto what had to be Third Avenue, hit a string of green lights, took a left, and barreled up what I guessed was Forty-second.

The taxi slowed, swerved in, and stopped, and the cabby told me I had the station door right ahead. I got out to pay the guy, and it was then I discovered I was really hurt. A flash of pure pain stabbed into me. I put my hand to my side, and oh, God, it felt like a coat hanger inside my shirt. That ace on the motorcycle had cracked one of my ribs.

When I started moving across the sidewalk, I found out another charming piece of news: my cane was still lying in the gutter back on Second Avenue.

There wasn't much I could do about either problem, so I just held one hand over my rib, thrust the other out in front of me, and walked into the crowds streaming out of the station.

I couldn't imagine a worse place for a blind man; the sidewalk was solid with people, and I must have bounced off every other one of them. If I had any doubts about my rib's being cracked, I lost them in a hurry when some dashing commuter belted into me, and I thought I was going to drop.

But I had to get away from the guy I was certain was still behind me. It wouldn't have been hard for him to grab a cab and follow me. I still had to get to a phone, and Grand Central had dozens of them, which is why I went on trying to force my way through the crowd.

It was like running a gauntlet of teasing, pushing bullies who kept swatting me with briefcases and newspapers and handbags. Every shot jarred my rib, slowing me down, and it took me an age to make it through the doors.

I stepped out of the stream of bodies and took a fast breather. I was a bit calmer now because I knew Grand Central like the back of my hand and had no trouble visualizing the waiting room with its high ceiling and long wooden benches. I knew the layout, too: toilets at both ends, a newsstand near the entrance, and, most important, a bank of phones against the far wall.

I managed to reach them without tripping over any feet, located an empty booth, and started searching for money. I didn't have any. I'd given my last bill to the cabdriver. I forced down the panic that started up inside me again, forcing myself to think. There was only one person who was going to get me out of this, and that was Gallo. I had to call him, but I couldn't do it without money. And there's only one way to get money in a hurry if you're poor and honest and blind.

I groped my way back to the mainstream, put my back against the wall, and held out my hand.

"Cup of coffee," I said. "Cup of coffee?"

I didn't think anyone would even be able to hear me in the echoing bedlam of the rush hour, but somebody did and responded to my plea. But not in the way I wanted. I was after a quarter, but what I got was a fresh apple core. New York, you're beautiful.

I guess the charmer who did it figured he knew a con when he saw one. I didn't even have a cane, just the shades, and anyone can put on shades. Also, I must have looked like a bum because my shirt was torn over my rib and the shoulder of my jacket had come away where I'd hit the road.

But as scared and as beat and frustrated as I was, I couldn't help thinking about the change in my situation: Less than a week back I'd been a middle-management guy with a good solid job at a prestigious Wall Street brokerage firm, and now I was standing in Grand Central bumming for the price of a phone call to stop a man cutting my eyes out. How could my life have changed so fast? And how could I have let it change so much?

"Coffee? Cup of coffee, please?"

"Here!" a woman said. She sounded exasperated as if I'd run after her for two blocks tugging at her sleeve. But I didn't care; she'd given me some coins.

I felt my way past people back to the pay phones. Now I had money for the call, and I had the piece of paper with Gallo's number on it, so all I needed was somebody to read it for me. For once my timing was great.

"Can I help you with the call?"

For every three or four thousand New Yorkers

there's one with a heart of gold. This one sounded like an elderly woman. I didn't mind if she was a hundred and eight, just as long as she could read.

"That's awfully kind of you. I really appreciate it." I thrust the piece of paper at her and the coins. She took a minute to dial, then put the phone into my hand.

"It's ringing," she said.

A woman's voice answered, but it wasn't the voice of Gallo's operator. It was another voice I knew.

It was Karen Petersen.

"Karen . . . !"

"Max! Is that you, Max?"

"Yes, but what's—"

"Where are you? Are you all right?" She sounded as if she wanted to climb down the wire to me. Fine, but what the hell was going on?

"Karen. I don't understand. . . ."

"I'm at your apartment, Max."

"My apartment?" Even as I said it, I knew what had happened. There were two phone numbers on the piece of paper I'd handed the woman. One was Gallo's; one was the apartment's. He'd included it when he'd written down the address for me. The old lady had called the wrong one.

"Max, something awful's happened. I came back for you as soon as I found out. Where are you?"

"Grand Central. The waiting room. You mean about Keitel?"

"The blind man, yes. They must have thought it was you."

That floored me. Why should she think that?

"Karen—"

"I'm working for Gallo, Max."

"You're with *Gallo?*" I went down for a second time.

"Stay where you are, darling. Stay right where you are. I'll have somebody pick you up. Fifteen minutes."

Then she hung up.

You could have hung me up, too, I was that limp. Karen working for Gallo . . . what a stopper. And what a fabulous one—I was safe, as long as I could survive for another fifteen minutes. That wasn't long, fifteen minutes, and that guy couldn't hurt me if I stayed where I was in that crowded waiting room, could he? Not if I sat on one of the benches in plain view of everybody.

I felt my way around people, found an empty spot on a bench, and sat myself down. My whole left side was starting to pound, and it hurt like hell to breathe. My rib needed strapping up, but I couldn't give that much thought because of what happened then: A man sat down next to me.

Don't ask me how I knew it was a man, I just knew. I told myself there was nothing wrong with that; that's what you did in waiting rooms, sat down next to people and waited. Except my mouth didn't get the message and got a bad case of the dries, and I suddenly didn't want to sit still anymore. I wondered if I wasn't making a mistake staying out in the open. Maybe I'd be safer hiding in the john.

I got up and started to move, changed my mind, and sat down again. I wasn't thinking straight; a toilet cubicle, a locked private place with room to wield a knife—I was better out in the open.

Then somebody sat down next to me again.

I don't know how I thought I could identify a man just by the feel of him sliding into the seat next to me, but I was positive it was the same guy I'd just left.

The point was, was it *the* guy? The one whose voice I knew but couldn't place.

I had to know. I couldn't keep stumbling around that waiting room, and I couldn't just go on sitting there, waiting for him to press a knife into my side and force me to leave with him. I sat on my hands to stop them from trembling and turned my head to the right.

"Pardon me. Could you tell me the time?"

The high voice of a teenage girl said it was five of nine.

I don't know what she must have thought when I let out a huge breath and said, "Oh, thank you. Thank you so much." What's that line about the only thing you have to fear is fear itself? I was being my own worst enemy.

"Mr. Ellis?"

A man's voice, sharp.

"No," I said in a reflex action. Then I thought again. If he'd called me Ellis, he had to be from Gallo. I changed my answer. "Miss Petersen send you?"

"Yes."

"Thank God," I said, and if he hadn't helped me up, I don't think I would have made it under my own steam.

I took his arm. There wasn't much meat on it, he must have been pretty slim, but he could have been an African pygmy or a circus giant for all I cared, just as long as he had a pair of eyes.

"I'm parked just outside," he said. He had a clipped, precise way of speaking which gave me confidence. He certainly guided me through the doors smoothly, and going out was a lot less painful than coming in had been.

His car must have been double-parked, quite a trick for that time and place. I heard him open the door; then he helped me in. It was a big car, lots of room, and nicely insulated, and when it moved off, there was very little noise from the street. I asked him where we were going.

"Westchester, sir."

That sounded far enough away to be safe; anywhere up there would do me fine. All the same, I asked him why Westchester.

"I don't know, sir. All I have is an address in Mount Vernon."

I figured Karen must have given it to him, although he didn't sound like any of the government men I'd been around.

"You're with Gallo?"

"Paramount Limousine Service," he said from the front seat.

"This is a limo?"

"Yes, sir."

That surprised me till I thought about it for a second. If Karen had come tearing out of the apartment house to come and get me, she might have been followed by the guy with the knife. He could have seen us together the night before if he'd been watching. So she'd got a limo service to pick me up instead—

smart. I settled back in the comfort of the soft uphol-
stery and took the pressure off my side, thinking
about the guy with the knife. I couldn't be sure the
man who'd chased me *was* the guy with the knife.
Come to think of it, I couldn't even be sure he'd
chased me. I'd only suspected him because I'd been
certain I knew his voice, and as I sat there turning it
over, I knew who he had sounded like.

My boss at the office.

My God, that's why I'd thought I knew him. It
hadn't been my boss, and it hadn't been anybody after my eyes either. It had only been someone trying
to be helpful. That's who I'd run away from, and it
had got me a busted rib for my trouble and taken
two years off my life.

What a prize dummy I'd been. I'd done it all for
nothing. Although it didn't change the fact that
there was still somebody who'd tried to maim me
and would no doubt try again if he could. But unless
he was riding in the trunk of the limo, I could forget
about him for a while. In fact, now that I was safe I
could forget about everything for a while, something
my badly overworked brain needed to do.

I leaned back and gave myself up to the soft mur-
mur of the car, but I couldn't turn my head off any
more than I could stop my side from beating like a
bass drum, so I thought some more about Karen and
Gallo and Keitel and the whole insane exercise.

One thing I knew, it was all over for me as far as I
was concerned. I assumed Gallo would be waiting
for me at Mount Vernon, and if he didn't want to
give me a pill, I'd choke one out of him. I was
through being a blind man; I was going back to the

sighted world and staying there. As long as that pill worked, of course.

I worried about that till I got tired of it and asked the driver where we were. I was surprised when he told me.

"We're just turning off the parkway, sir."

"We're at Mount Vernon? That was quick."

"Not much traffic going north this time of day, sir."

We did some stopping and going after that in what I assumed was suburban traffic, then picked up speed for maybe a mile or two, then slowed and took a sharp turn. Again I asked the driver where we were.

"The Oakdale Country Club, sir."

It made sense; a country club, some place out of the way that you could throw a wall of men around. I felt the road rise into a sloping hill then peak, and again the car slowed for a turn.

The driver anticipated my question. "We're going through gates, sir. Big ones. Wrought iron."

"Gates?"

"There are houses around the golf course, sir, This could have been the original one; the grounds are quite extensive."

"Can you see the house?"

"Yes, sir. An old house, white wood frame. Very large."

I knew the type of house he was talking about; there were thousands of them sprinkled through Westchester: two main stories and a full attic; a wide veranda running all the way round; big sash windows which, in the summer, would each have its own striped awning. Most of them were built as summer homes in the twenties, big, sprawling places that went on forever. This one certainly must have, I could hear the tires crunching gravel on what had to be a circular drive, and it was a good two minutes before we stopped.

The driver volunteered the next piece of information, which was a surprising one.

"There's a sign, sir. It says Mount Vernon Blood Donors' Association."

A blood clinic? Was Gallo trying to be witty?

The driver helped me out, guided me up some steps and across a porch, and rang the doorbell.

"Will you be all right now, sir? I was told there'd be somebody here to receive you."

"Fine. Thanks for your help," I said. I heard him go down the stairs and drive off. Then I found he was right about there being somebody waiting for me.

The door opened, and I heard a voice I definitely knew.

"Max, baby. You made it."

Jake McCone.

16

McCONE'S BEING THERE was a bigger surprise than Karen's being in my apartment, and I had a hard time with it for a moment.

"Jake? It's you?"

"Nah, it's Barbra Streisand."

I felt his heavy paw on my elbow. "Come on in, pal."

He guided me through the door, closed it behind me. I had a hundred and forty questions to ask me, but he beat me to it. "Hey, kid, you look all shook up. What happened here?" He tapped my busted rib. A tap from McCone was like a slap from anyone else, and the pain made me cry out.

"Hey, I'm sorry. What happened to you?"

"Some ace on a Harley took a piece out of me. What the hell are you doing here?"

"Long story. C'mon in here, and we'll get you a Band-Aid."

He led me through the house and down what I took to be a long carpeted hall. I bombarded him with questions as we went.

"Jake, for God's sake. I mean, who are you and what are you doing here?"

"I'm Jake McCone, your friendly neighborhood booze artist. And I'm here because you're here. And you're here because Karen sent a limo for you."

"You're with Gallo, too?"

"Sure. Isn't everybody?" We stopped, and I heard him open a door. We went through, and my shoes squeaked on linoleum.

"Jake, have a heart. I don't understand a thing."

He chuckled. "Okay, it's like this." But before he began, he sat me down on what felt like a padded table, helped me off with my jacket, and eased open my shirt. The place couldn't have been anything else but a clinic, there was a lingering smell of methylated spirits and a feeling of pristine cleanliness as if the air itself had been washed and dried and put into a sterilized cabinet.

"Karen and me," Jake said, "we work for Gallo. He wanted somebody around to keep an eye on you. You're a pretty valuable guy, you know. So Karen was with you some of the time, and I was on your hammer whenever you went for a walk."

"Wow!"

"Surprises you, huh? Didn't you never think you was gettin' a lot of freedom? Valuable guy like you?"

"I suppose. But I just never thought I'd have a bodyguard."

McCone's voice hardened. "That other poor bastard shoulda had one, too. You know about him?"

"The cops told me. Is he going to be okay?"

"Got a fractured skull, and he's in shock, but they reckon he'll pull through."

I heard the tearing sound of plaster and the snip of scissors.

McCone said, "You came to the right place. The joint's a blood donor center when it's open. They got all these tables and bandages and stuff." He stretched plaster over my side. "Karen should really do this. She used to be a nurse."

"Where is she?"

"She'll be along."

"And Gallo?"

"In town tryin' to get a lead on Jack the Ripper."

"What's going on, Jake?"

"Beats the hell outa me. All I know is we got a leak like the day the damn burst, and we need a plumber fast." He tapped my shoulder. "All through. Lie back on the table and get a little rest."

But I didn't get the chance. Gravel squished on the drive, and I heard a car pulling up.

"That's probably Karen now," McCone said. "I'll go see."

I heard doors open and close far away, two voices, then footsteps running down the hall and into the room.

"Max!" she cried, and then her arms were around me. It hurt my rib like hell, but I wasn't complaining—I was patched up, I was safe, and I had a gorgeous girl who cared about me caring about me.

She hugged me some more, put her face against mine. "Darling, I was so worried. I didn't know what had happened to you."

"Neither did I," I said.

"When I heard what happened to that poor man, I realized it was supposed to be you, so I rushed back to your apartment, but you'd gone. I called Gallo, and he told me to stay there in case you came back."

She moved her face away and must have spotted the plaster.

"My God. What happened?"

I told her about the accident, leaving out the part about running from the phantom knifer; I wasn't feeling too proud of the episode. We asked each other all kinds of questions, most of them overlapping; then we got in some more smooching. I hadn't heard McCone come back into the room—very tactful of the guy. I think he knew that Karen and I were more than just good friends.

She took my face in her hands, her voice serious. "Max, there's something I want you to know. I was supposed to stay close to you, but sleeping with you, that wasn't orders. I did that because you're a lovely man and I wanted to."

I held her to me in spite of the pain in my side. "Then I'm glad I'm a lovely man."

She kissed me and took my tongue in her mouth, and it was like licking into a soft, ripe papaya. I felt like forgetting my ruined side and taking all her clothes off, right there and then.

She moved her head, cradled it on my shoulder. "That poor man, Max. It could have been you. I wish this was all finished, I hate it. And I hate working for Gallo."

"Welcome to the club."

"God, he's insufferable. He treats everybody like a child. Do you know he wouldn't even tell us why we're looking after you? We know about the eyedrops, of course, but he wouldn't tell us what they do."

I had to laugh. That was Gallo, all right.

Karen laughed, too. She nuzzled my neck. "How about putting a girl out of her misery. What are those damn things for?"

"The drops?"

"Yes."

I gave a little shrug. "You know Gallo. He wouldn't even tell me."

"Max, you dope. Stop kidding."

"I'm not kidding, Karen. I honestly don't know what they're for."

I felt her draw away, and I knew she was looking at me.

Then she got off my lap, and McCone spoke. He said, low and hard, "Bullshit you don't. And you're fuckin' gonna tell us."

When Karen had told me she was working for Gallo, I'd accepted it. It had floored me, but I'd believed it. And I'd accepted McCone's meeting me at the door and his explanation of what, why, and how. And I'd certainly accepted the reunion between Karen and me. The warmth had surprised me a little, it's true, but I was very flattered to have this girl worried sick about me, so I accepted it because I wanted to. But when she'd asked me the sixty-four-thousand-dollar question about the eyedrops, I knew I'd been kidded about everything. And do you know why? Because she didn't say Simon says.

Remember that game? Simon says stand up. Simon says sit down. Simon says put your hand up. Put your hand down. And if you did, you were out, because Simon didn't say to put your hand down. That's what struck me about Karen and her question:

She'd slipped it in there so nicely and neatly I wasn't supposed to notice.

But I did.

Was I amazed that Karen and McCone had turned out to be playing for the other club? I don't think so. Not really. The two of them being against me made as much sense as the two of them being for me. The point was, I was in deep trouble. As Mc-Cone made pretty clear.

"Listen, kiddo, this place ain't open today, so we got all kinds of time."

I knew that had to be true; I hadn't heard a sound from the rest of the house since I'd first walked in the door.

"But," McCone went on, "we got better things to do than hang around here, so make it easy on all of us. Tell us now. You'll save us all a lot of time, and you'll save yourself a lot of pain."

As levelly as I could I said, "I'd tell you if I knew, Jake, but I don't."

McCone's breath came very close to my face; I don't think he brushed after every meal. "Hey, fella, you ain't readin' me. I'm talkin' about *pain*," he said, and I felt his thick, stubby fingers grab the plaster on my side and savagely rip it away. It almost took my rib with it, and I cried out, really yelled, clutched at myself, and folded over on the table.

Old Jake, the friendly barfly, gave me a minute to recover, then said, "So how about it, buddy boy? What are the drops for?"

"I don't know."

"Look, I'm not kidding here." His voice was getting angry. "I got a fortune ridin' on this thing, and no blind skinhead bastard's gonna lose me a fortune. Now you tell me what them fuckin' drops are for or I'll tear your fuckin' rib right outa your body."

"That's enough!" Karen's voice, hard and sharp.

"Stay outa this."

"Don't hurt him anymore."

"Look, I'm gonna do it my way, okay? Nobody's beggin' you to stick around."

"That's not the way to do it."

"It's always the way to do it. I found that out in Nam. The slopes, they wouldn't even tell you their name at the start. Five minutes was all it ever took to change their minds. Like Max here is gonna change his mind. Now get outa here."

I heard her stumble, and I think he must have shoved her. When she didn't come back at him, and I heard her walking away and the door close, I thought I was going to pee my pants. It was going to happen; this gorilla was going to put me through the wringer.

That's when I found out just how brave I was. I yelled, "No!" and jumped up and ran.

God knows where I thought I was running to, but I didn't get very far. McCone grabbed me, hefted me up, and slammed me down onto that clinic table like a sack of corks.

I though my rib was going to go through my flank. It was such an insanely colossal burst of pain it fogged my senses, and I was only vaguely aware of McCone tying my wrists down to the table.

I think he used bandages. Then there was a hazy few minutes during which I got the impression he'd left the room and come back in again, which turned out to be correct. He'd gone to get something.

"Okay, Max, baby." He was back to being his lovable old self. I think he was looking forward to the fun. "You're gonna take a little lie detector test. I ask you a question, and if you tell the truth, fine, everything's dandy. But if you lie to me or clam up, then you get this broom handle I got here in my hands. Understand how it work, Max?"

My head was still full of buzz, but there was no question of my not understanding; it was abundantly clear. I was going to suffer, really suffer, and I was so scared I wanted to break down and weep.

"You didn't get to Nam, did you Max? Nah, you didn't. We used to do this all the time. Get a slope in there, wounded maybe, shot in the arm or the leg. You'd ask him a question, and when he didn't say nothin', you'd remind him he had a wound with your rifle butt. Now I ain't got me a rifle; all I got is this broom handle. And if you lie to me, I'll tickle your rib for you, got it, Max?"

I said nothing. I didn't have to, I understood fine.

"So here we go. Easy one to start with. What's your name?"

"Max."

"Right. The needle on the machine points to truth. You see? Tell the truth and no pain. Next question. What's your last name?"

"Ellis."

"Smart boy, Max. If you'd said Sinclair, the little needle would've pointed to lie, and you would've got a little reminder. But the limo driver, the guy picked you up, he called you Ellis, right? So you knew we knew."

McCone was dead right about that, but I didn't bother to tell him.

"Okay. Before Gallo hooked you in on this, you could see perfect, right?"

"Right."

"Needle points to truth. You doin' fine, Max. Now, in the hosiptal there, they put the drops in your eyes, truth?"

"Truth."

"And the drops made you blind, right?"

"Right."

"Now. Big question."

To underscore that, he thumped the broom handle on the floor. He was doing a pretty good job stretching the questions out, letting them build, keeping me wound up, waiting to find out what that broom handle would feel like prizing up my rib. I think I would rather have found out than go on wondering. I was sweating so hard my socks were sticking to my ankles.

"Answer this one right, Max, and you're home free. What do the drops do?"

"I don't know," I said, but the last word came out as part of a scream.

I guess the most pain I'd ever felt was a few years back when somebody accidentally slammed a car door on my fingers. If you've ever had something like that happen to you, then you know how much it hurts—the shock wave of pain charging through you, the weakness in your knees, the feeling you're going to gag, it's pretty exquisite stuff. But I can tell you that compared to a broom handle stabbing into a busted rib, smashed fingers are about as painful as chapped lips. It was like a pure white tongue of fire bursting inside me, and every nerve ending in my body hit the alarm button.

"Little needle says that one's a lie, Max. And you were doin' beautiful, too."

McCone's voice chilled me through the pain. There was a slow patience in it which let me know he had all the time in the world and that there were plenty more licks where the last one had come from.

He went back and started the questions all over again, asking them in that same slow, coaxing manner. Oh, he was a real sweetheart, McCone was: the kindly executioner, the sympathetic inquisitor who's really rooting for you to come through so he can stop doing this thing that's hurting him more than it's hurting you. I'd never been interrogated before, so I was no expert, but I think Jake McCone could have had offers from the pros.

"Gallo wanted your help, truth?"

"Truth." It was only a mumble.

"On something really big, right?"

"Right."

"Some kind of drops for your eyes, truth?"

"Truth."

"Okay, Max, this time we're goin' all the way, all right? Just tell the truth like you been doin' and we'll shut the machine down and we'll all have a drink, okay? Now, what did Gallo tell you about the drops?"

"He said they were top secret."

McCone wasn't expecting that answer, but it didn't

delay him very long, and that's all I was playing for: delay.

"Sure they're top secret. Right. Machine says truth. But Max, what do they do?"

I took a big swallow. "They made me blind."

"Yeah, I know that. I know they made you blind. But why did they make you blind? What are the drops for?"

I shook my head this time because I knew I'd need all my breath for another scream, and I was right, because when he jabbed that broom handle halfway through my side, it was either yell or go crazy bonkers with the pain.

Belt your thumbnail and you can at least suck it or blow on it or flap your hand, comfort it in some way, but with my wrists lashed to that table the only release I had was a verbal one, and as releases go, they're not up to much. I could have saved myself all the agony by simply telling him, of course, just as he'd said. I didn't think he would have killed me if I had—it was true I knew who they both were and could have turned them in, except I was pretty sure the two of them would have been long gone before I would have got the chance. But I was holding out for a reason.

It had nothing to do with Gallo, God, and Country—it certainly wasn't in my contract to stand up to some goon trying to tear out my side—it was simply because McCone and the girl had faked me out of my shoes, conned me stupid. And they'd done it so easily. They'd run up a huge score, and I hadn't even known the game was scheduled, let alone started.

But the game wasn't over, that was the thing; it wasn't over yet. But it would be if I gave them the answer. Final result, McCone/Petersen 109, Ellis/ Sinclair 0.

And I didn't want the loss. And I didn't want to settle for a draw.

I wanted to go for a win.

Yeah, I know that sounds crazy. Blind, half dead, lashed to a table, and with a gorilla to get past. But I knew what their weapons were, and they didn't know about mine. They didn't know I had one, and they wouldn't unless McCone got it out of me. That's why I had to keep it from him.

I was fully aware that even if I got the chance, it would be hours before I could use it, and I wasn't sure I could last another five minutes.

"How about it, Max? What are the drops for?"

Or even another two minutes.

"Gallo didn't say."

McCone lost his cool, blew the lid right off it.

"Fuckin' bastard! What're they FOR?" He brought the broom handle lashing through the air and slammed it into my rib as if I were a log he was trying to chop in half.

There was too much pain too quickly, and it fused something somewhere. My brain winked out, and I went falling down a long, beautiful, painless drop . . . down, down, down like Alice on her way to Wonderland.

I thought it was a cat licking my face, but it turned out to be a cool, moist cloth moving over my forehead. Somebody held my head, put a glass of something to my mouth, and I drank it—brandy I think it was. It made me cough and brought me back to the world, a fact I was sorry about because I wasn't too crazy about the world right then. It was one huge pain in my side where a shark and two tigers had bitten me.

I could feel something working there, and I thought it was friend McCone patting a divot back into place and getting ready to tee off again, but the treatment was a lot gentler.

I heard the sound of scissors and plaster; I was getting another tape job.

"How are you feeling, Max?" Karen's voice.

"Just grand."

I felt the cloth on my chest and the nub of a towel following it around. She sponged and dried the sweat off my skin, soothed my shoulders, patted my underarms. McCone had said she'd been a nurse, and I could believe it. The tape job was a good one, too. I was still breathing daggers, but they weren't nearly as sharp.

"I'm sorry about all this, Max."

"Me too."

"It's so unnecessary."

"That's what I keep trying to get through to Mc-Cone."

"It's pointless to try to make out you don't know, Max. Those drops made you blind. Nobody would let that happen to him without knowing why."

She was talking in a quiet, reasonable manner and sponging my chest in slow circles. It felt good. I decided to reward her by lying, but only a little. I figured it would sound more like the truth if it were *almost* the truth.

"Believe me, Karen, I tried to find out why. I told Gallo it was my eyesight that was being screwed around with, not his, so I had a right to know. But he just kept saying it was top secret and he couldn't tell me. He just kept talking about the ten grand they were going to pay me. He knew I was broke; he knew I'd have to do it for the money."

"I don't buy it, Max. I know you worked at the Sight Center, and nobody who's worked with the blind would ever sell his sight for money. Not for ten thousand. Not for a million."

"But I didn't sell it for good, just for a couple of weeks. There's a pill that can restore my vision anytime. Look, all I know is they wanted someone they could run some tests on, someone who could handle being blind for a couple of weeks. So they chose me."

"But why do they want you blind, Max? Why do you have to be blind?"

"I'm still waiting to find that out. I keep asking Gallo, and he keeps reminding me of the deal we made. Ten grand and no questions asked."

"Max, I don't believe you."

"Karen, if I thought it wouldn't hurt me, I'd shrug and say sorry."

She went on with the sponging, moving the cloth and the towel over my neck and shoulders. She continued talking in that same civilized, no-reason-why-we-can't-be-friends tone.

"Let me tell you what happened, Max. A man came to see me. Well built, fair hair, spoke with an accent. Apart from that, I don't know anything about him, except that he knew about you and Gallo and the eyedrops, and he wanted me to find out what they're for, why they gave them to you. He also hired McCone for the same reason. I don't know McCone very well, but what I do know I don't like. He's a professional hood, I think."

"He told me he was a college professor."

"Max, I'm serious."

Oh, sure. I was enjoying this in a curious kind of way; it was nice to be conned for a change and know it. She was supposed to be tender and soothing after the ravages of the beast, and I was supposed to go for it out of sheer gratitude and relief. Fine, on with the show. It was better than being bayoneted with a broom handle.

And it was also using up daylight.

"This man said we should try to get our hands on the drops, although he didn't think there'd be much chance of that. But he'd still pay money to find out what the eyedrops did. It's a fortune, Max. It'd buy a lifetime on the Riviera."

"That's why you're doing it, because you like French cooking?"

"Everybody needs money, Max." She paused for a moment, then continued in a different kind of voice, a touch of humility in it. "I'll tell you something," she said.

Here it comes, I thought, confession time.

"A man once offered me a thousand dollars to fly down to Puerto Rico with him for the weekend. He was a nice enough guy, and I certainly could have used the money, but I said no because I'd never thought of myself as being on the block. But this isn't a thousand dollars, Max; it's the kind of money that can change your life, make you part of a world ordinary people only read about. I would have been crazy to turn it down, Max. You understand that, don't you?"

"Tell me something. That was you in my apartment that night, wasn't it? Looking for the drops."

"Yes. I took the radio to make it seem like a simple break-in."

"It didn't feel very simple to me."

The cloth stopped on my chest. "I'm sorry I had to kick you. But I couldn't risk you catching me."

Quite a girl, our Miss Petersen—one night she has her knee in my crotch, the next night her face.

"So where do we go from here?" I asked.

"What's wrong with the Riviera?"

"You mean the two of us?"

"Why not? Would it be so bad?"

I didn't answer, and the cloth started moving again in slow circles, moving from my chest down to my tummy. Moving in *very* slow circles.

Her voice was lower, a little husky. "It was good together, Max, wasn't it? And it can be good again. That money could buy us anything we wanted. And we'd be together . . . you and I."

So slow, that cloth.

"I'd like that, Max. I really would."

Barely touching me, she ran a finger from my navel down to my belt.

"You'd like it, too . . . I'd make sure of that."

And began to undo it.

"We'd have money, we'd have each other. . . ."

She began to undo my zipper.

"And all the time in the world."

And those were her last words on the subject for a while. Oh, Mother Nature, what are we going to do with you? Sex was absolutely the last thing I was ready for right then, but when Miss Petersen lowered her head to her favorite part of me, her favorite part of me started to respond.

She must be terribly insecure, Mother Nature must, the way she's made us capable of propagating the species at all times, and she also must be pretty dumb. How she expected me to propagate anything lashed to a blood donor's table and sporting a fractured rib, I don't know. But at the same time, I have to give her credit, she certainly knew her man, because I must admit that I possess what surely must be one of the most combustible fuses in America. I'm not saying I'm a satyr, only that I've always had the physical ability to respond to a female whenever and wherever the occasion presented itself. In short, while most men have a sexual drive of one degree or another, mine is more of a sexual smash. But I wasn't giving any of this an enormous amount of thought right then because my attention was taken up by the supermarvelous things Karen Petersen was doing. Her tongue was fluttering, darting, and swooping like an electric butterfly, and for the first time that morning I let out a moan that wasn't on account of pain.

When she heard it, she knew she had me, and she did a very smart thing. She left off what she was doing.

Oh, no! The last thing I'd wanted was for her to

start on me, but now that she had, the last thing I wanted was for her to stop.

"I'd do this to you whenever you wanted, Max," she murmured. "I know how to make it last."

And she showed me how, and my gosh, I wanted it to last forever. She was taking things far slower than last night, nibbling at me one second, devouring me whole the next, gumming me and worrying me like a dog with a bone, then sucking in a slow, circular motion. I'd never experienced anything like it, and my moans were pretty regular now.

Then she stopped again, and I gave myself away again.

"Don't stop. . . ."

Her voice purred. "Tell me what the drops are for, Max. Then I can get the money we'll need. To be together. And do this all day long."

And that squishy-soft papaya mouth closed over me again.

She was so *good*. If I'd been in danger of dying from pain earlier on, I was close to expiring from the exact opposite now, and one was almost as bad as the other.

"Do you like this, Max?"

"Oh, yes. . . ."

"And this?"

"God, yes. . . ."

"What are the drops for, darling?"

"The drops. . . ?"

"Tell me, darling."

"Don't stop."

Tongue, teeth, lips.

"Tell me, Max. Just whisper it."

"Don't stop. . . . Please. . . ."

"Then tell me what they're for."

And I knew then, the realization was there, half drowning in the ocean of pleasure flooding my brain, I knew I was going to tell her.

I couldn't help myself. Not as long as she kept me suspended in such unbelievable toe-curling ecstasy. And that's what she was doing, keeping me suspended, bringing me up to the brink, then easing off, then bringing me back again. She had such fantastic control over me that I wasn't going to release until she wanted me to, and that wouldn't be till I'd answered her question.

So I was going to tell her because she was mouthing and chewing and tickling me into a semidrugged state, and I wasn't going to know what I was saying.

I had to stop myself from doing that. I had to climax. But she wouldn't let me, holding me back, balancing me on the edge.

"What are the drops for, darling? You can tell me."

"The drops," I moaned. "They make me . . . they let me. . . ."

And guess who came riding to my rescue?

No, not Gallo, not Weyland.

Bev Jordan.

Remember my dream girl at the Sight Center? The one with the body that just won't stop? She came to my rescue. That wasn't Karen Petersen down there; that was Bev Jordan. Bev with those fantastic, wonderful knockers, and that incredible ass, and those long, smooth, creamy legs that were wrapping around me and getting tighter and Bev and those breasts and thighs and, oh, Jesus, BEV!

Petersen knew she'd lost me, and she knew there wasn't a damn thing she could do about it, because once the express is on the tracks, it's coming down the line, boy, and you can forget about signals, switches, gates, anything.

She barely had time to jump out of the way and throw the towel over me, and then the earth moved, and also a few of the planets.

The welcome I got, when I finally made it back from outer space, wasn't the kind it's nice to come home to. The girl was furious, raging.

"You rotten little—" She went off into an insane tirade, calling me all kinds of names, including one which, considering her recent performance, applied far more to her than to me. She was so mad. Screamed at me, yelled at me, then stepped around and started to slap me wildly in the face, bam, bam, bam, back and forward, still yelling obscenities at me. Now I know there are guys who pay good money to be tied down and slapped by sexy little blondes, but I doubt the young ladies hit as hard as Miss Petersen did.

I was kind of anesthetized anyway, after her and Bev Jordan, which was a good thing because she'd done her nut and just went on lamming into me, busting my mouth all over the place. McCone finally came rushing in and stopped her. I guess he thought the laying on of hands was his department and Karen wasn't union.

I heard him bustle her out the door, and I think he must have threatened to belt her one because when they came back in, she didn't say a word. But I could hear her breathing hard, and she must have really been breathing hard for me to hear her because not all that much was getting through to me, what with my spent body and my head ringing like a temple bell.

I said weakly, "Hey, Jake."

"Yeah?"

"Would you help an old soldier?"

"Sure. What?"

I licked the blood on my lips. "Pull up my pants, will you? I feel naked without them."

He did it, too. Heart of gold, that one.

My dark glasses had been knocked sideways, and the daylight was killing me and making me wince, but it didn't give anything away—I had plenty of things to wince about.

"And my shades, huh?"

"Sure."

He put them on straight, then said, "So, you ready to play Truth or Consequences again?" He whacked the table I was lying on with the broom handle. Even that hurt.

"Why not?" I said. It was only a ploy. I didn't think I could take another session of McCone and his lie detector, so I tried a kind of reverse Br'er Rabbit, hoping I wouldn't get the thing I was asking for.

"You're pretty good with that broom handle, Jake. I bet when you played stickball, you could hit three sewers."

He grunted at that. "You're a tough little cookie,

Max. I'm surprised. But you're a dumb little cookie, too."

"And just how do you figure that, Jake, ol' buddy?"

"Because you're a goodie, and it don't pay to be a goodie in this world."

"What makes you so sure I'm a goodie?" Keep him talking, keep the clock going. Come on, sun, get down that goddamn sky.

"Because you're fulla crap ideas, that's why. My Country 'Tis of Thee, and all that shit."

"You're the dummy, Jake. You're beating a dead horse here, but you don't know it. I don't know what the drops are for. Gallo wouldn't tell me. But you won't believe it, so why don't you start in again with the stick, and when the pain gets too bad, I'll make up an answer."

"Nah," he said. "I'm wastin' time whackin' on you. But if I was to whack on somebody else, I think you'd maybe tell then."

That was a surprise. Somebody else?

"If you're talking about Miss Petersen, you can throw in a Chinese burn for me."

"Not her," McCone said. "Although it ain't a bad idea."

"Shut up!" Karen told him.

She was clearly simmering over her recent failure, and she didn't take too kindly to his criticism. I had an idea he was glad she'd failed; he wanted to be the one to crack me, not only because it would be more fun for him that way, but also to establish himself as boss of their little act.

"We got a friend of yours here, Max," McCone said to me.

"No!" Karen, very sharp and emphatic.

"Why not? It can't hurt."

"He doesn't need to know about them." She said it in a hiss.

Those two certainly weren't getting any crazier about each other, which was fine with me. The more they argued, the less time they'd have to pick on the kid. But what the hell was McCone talking about?

"Look," he said to the girl. "How about we do it my way for a change? You bombed out already."

She swore at him, but he only grunted, and I heard his heavy footsteps going up the room to what must have been another door. When I heard it close, I said, "I don't think he likes you, Karen."

"Shut up!"

Her dialogue really hadn't changed.

"I wouldn't trust him," I said, trying to stir things up. "He's the type that likes to end up with all the marbles."

"I told you to shut *up!*" Her shoes clicked angrily across the linoleum, and I braced myself for a back-hand, but she held off. I think she heard the same thing I did: McCone coming back. There was another voice, too, and it sounded as if they were arguing.

". . . your hands off her!"

"Don't do that, buddy." McCone's voice. "That's the way people lose teeth."

Then something I couldn't catch, the first voice raised, a slapping sound, then McCone saying, "Son of a *bitch!*" There was the sound of a blow and a thud like a chair going over.

A woman cried, "Stop it! Stop it!" Then the door at the end of the room opened and closed, and I heard a key being turned. Footsteps came toward me, and I could hear McCone breathing heavily and a woman sniffling and choking on words.

"Little bastard bloodied my nose," McCone said.

Karen shot back at him. "Serves you right. I told you to leave them out of it."

"Don't hurt him," the other woman wailed. "Don't hit him anymore," and I recognized the voice. Muriel Carson wasn't talking about me; she was talking about her husband locked in the other room.

"Just worry about yourself," McCone said to her. Then, to me: "We got your neighbors here, Max. Old home week, huh? Now I'm gonna tell you something. I'm through beatin' on you, like I said, but if you don't come up with a real answer, I'm gonna start in on Grandma here."

I could hear Muriel Carson whimpering softly, but I was pretty sure it was for her husband, not for herself.

McCone said, "You want I should start now?"

I told him no.

"You see?" This must have been to Karen; there was triumph in his voice. He said to me, "I told you you were a goodie, Max."

I was in a bind. I didn't doubt for a moment that if I stayed silent, McCone would beat the daylights out of fifty-five-year-old Muriel Carson and have fun doing it. So it looked as if it were all over. I'd have to tell them. They would have got it out of me sooner or later in any case; my powers of resistance had been only hair-thin before, and Miss P.'s double workout hadn't strengthened them any. So on paper it made sense for me to quit while I could still speak. Besides, I didn't have any other way to go— my idea of trying to hold out till sundown, like a besieged fort, seemed ludicrous now; it couldn't even have been noon. But ludicrous or not, it was still the only shot I had, and I hated like hell to give up on it, so I decided to try freezing the ball till the end of the quarter and see what happened then.

"Give me five minutes alone with her, Jake. How about it?"

"No!" Karen spat out the word, and I was glad to hear it.

It gave McCone a chance to override her, and I could tell he enjoyed doing that.

"C'mon," he said. "It's time for my booze break anyway."

"I don't trust him," Karen said.

I had to laugh at that. *"You* don't trust *me?"*

She argued with McCone, but it didn't do her any good. She'd lost the leadership because of her failure with me, and McCone was in the driver's seat now. She clearly hated playing second fiddle, but she must have known that if she came on too strong, she'd be risking that whack in the mouth he'd half-jokingly offered to give her, so she had to cool it. But I figured it would only be for a while; if I'd been McCone, I wouldn't have counted on being the boss on a permanent basis, not around a pretty little coral snake like Karen Petersen.

They left the room, still arguing, and I could hear

them at it as they went into another part of the house. Then I was able to check on Muriel.

"I'm all right," she answered, "but poor Ralph. . . ."

"What happened? How did they get you here?"

I heard her move, flop into a chair. "I don't understand. It's like a nightmare."

"Tell me what happened."

"That awful man came to our apartment last night. He said you'd had an accident, that you'd been taken to a hospital in Westchester, and that you'd given him our names. We came, of course, but when we got here. . . ." She caught her breath on a sob. "He beat Ralph. Oh, how he beat him. That awful man. He kept asking about you, wanted to know what you'd told us about your eyes. We didn't know what he was talking about, but he wouldn't believe us. Then when he did believe us, he was so angry he just kept hitting poor Ralph."

Her voice broke, and I think she was sobbing into her hands. I caught the word "nightmare" again, then just sharp, little intakes of breath.

"What's it all about, Max? I don't understand."

I didn't relish an explanation. How was I supposed to say that I was sorry and that they were in this thing simply because they'd been nice to a guy?

"Muriel, I'm doing some work on a government project. McCone and the girl, they know about it, but they don't know all about it. The girl tricked me; so did he. I told her about how I was spending my days, about you and Ralph having me in, and I guess they thought I might have told you about the project. I guess they thought that grabbing you two was worth a try, that it would be easier than grabbing me because they probably thought I was being watched."

"Government work?" She didn't sound as if she'd taken it all in.

"All those two know is that I was given some eyedrops, but they don't know why."

"He kept talking about eyedrops. I thought he was mad, because you're blind."

"They're trying to find out what they do, Muriel. That's what this whole thing's all about."

"Don't tell them, Max." Her voice was fierce. "Don't tell them anything."

"It's getting hard not to, Muriel. They've both been trying to persuade me."

I heard her chair scrape back, and perhaps she really looked at me for the first time. She found the facecloth Karen had been using and dabbed at my ruined mouth and the bubble of blood at my nostrils. I heard her suck in breath and knew she'd spotted my rib.

"That man did that to you?"

"He didn't help it any."

"They're vile people, Max. Don't let them win. Let him hit me. I'll mend. Don't tell them a thing."

Fifteen years older than me and thirty times braver.

"Muriel," I said, "if I wasn't tied down, I'd hug you."

The statement seemed to trigger something in her, as if she'd only just realized I was a prisoner. I heard her move away quickly; then she was back again.

She'd found the scissors Karen had used to tape me up.

I said stupidly, "What are you doing?"

"You've got to get away, Max. You've got to try."

The scissors snipped at the bandage around my left wrist, freed it.

"The windows," she said urgently, "they're only locked from the inside. You could get out, go for help."

Poor old Muriel, she had guts but no brains. The limo driver had told me how big the grounds were; the nearest help had to be at least a couple of hundred yards away.

"I wouldn't get twenty feet, Muriel. I don't even have a cane."

"Oh, God. . . ." She said it in despair. She must have been half out of her head worrying about her husband. I think she'd forgotten I was blind.

She wailed softly, "Then these are no use."

"What aren't?"

"His car keys."

"His what?" I'd heard her perfectly the first time.

"He left them in his jacket. In the other room. I took them."

"Muriel. . . ." I made three distinct syllables out of it. She cut the bandage on my right hand, and I sat up, swung my legs down, and went on talking through the wave of giddiness that washed through me.

"Help me to the window."

"It's no good, Max. You can't see."

"You can."

"I can't drive."

"I'll drive. You can be my eyes."

"No. I'm not leaving Ralph here."

"Muriel, listen to me." I heard my voice shaking with excitement; I had a chance to do it, actually to get away. Two minutes ago the idea of being able to run from McCone would have been in the realm of fantasy, but now it had suddenly become a glorious, stunning possibility—as long as I could get Muriel Carson to help me. I spoke fast.

"They'll be back any second. We don't have time to argue. They don't want Ralph, they want me. If we can get off the grounds, they'll know the first thing we'll do is call the police, so they'll take off quick. They won't bother with Ralph."

"I can't leave him, Max."

I eased myself off the table and onto my feet and had to grab for the table again. The pain in my side made me gasp, and I had to bite down and understand fast that it was going to feel like this as long as I was upright, so I'd better get used to it.

Muriel Carson took my elbow to steady me, and I clutched her wrist. "You won't be leaving him; you'll be getting help for him. And you can't do that by staying here."

I started to move to where I figured the windows had to be, half being supported by her, half tugging her along.

"Show me the window, quick."

"I shouldn't leave him. It's wrong," she moaned.

I didn't have time to try to talk her into it anymore; I just bullied her. I squeezed down on her wrist hard.

"Come *on*."

She must have been half persuaded and a little frightened of me, too, a blind man clutching like a leech. She moved with me, guided me around some tables, led me across the room to the window.

"I can't budge it," she said.

"Put my hands there."

I knew these old-style windows; they locked by a circular catch that had to be rotated. It was stuck pretty hard, but by getting both hands onto it, I was able to push it around. Then the main problem became the window itself. I got a good grip on it and heaved upward, and for a moment I thought McCone had started on me with the broom handle again. I had to stop till the pain subsided; then Muriel and I tried it together. It took a lot of heaving and pushing, but together we got it open, but then the real hang-up presented itself: getting Muriel Carson to go through that window.

"Go on, Muriel. Go *on*."

"No. I can't leave Ralph."

I was practically wrestling with her. "Muriel. It's the only way to get help for Ralph."

The words "help" and "Ralph" must have decided her, because she stopped struggling, and I heard her grunting her way over the sill.

I followed, feeling with my foot for the ground. It was only just below, but the effort was still good for another knife attack in the side, and I had to stop again to let the pain recede.

I felt earth under my shoes, then grass, and grabbed at Muriel Carson. "Where are we?"

"Side of the house. We need the front."

We started off in a sort of trot. I had one hand on

her arm, the other bent across me holding my rib, and I was having a lot of trouble moving. Even so, I tried to put my training to work and made an attempt to get my bearings by locating the sun from its feel on my face. But I couldn't feel any warmth at all, just a chilly wind that were right through my shirt. My ears weren't much help, all I could hear was the sound of our shoes stumbling over grass, but at least my nose told me something: I was getting a strong whiff of fertilizer, so I figured the earth I'd stepped out onto must be a garden border that probably ran around the whole house. And seeing the smell wasn't fading any, I guessed we were running parallel to the border. Other than that, I had no idea of the layout, but we had to be passing other windows, and we must have been able to be seen through them. I expected any second to hear a roar from McCone, but I planned to keep going till he stopped me, although the going wasn't that great. Every step was murder, and my breathing was giving me fits. It seemed to be all out of sync, no rhythm to it, as if I'd forgotten how.

"Where are we?" I was panting badly. "Where are we now?"

But Muriel Carson, trotting beside me, was either too out of breath or too scared to answer. And that was when something slammed into my knee.

I went down hard and pancaked on my bad side. I'm sure being struck by lightning couldn't have hurt worse. I felt Muriel's hand on my elbow; I grasped her hand and used it to struggle upright. We started trotting again, but I was limping now because my left leg felt as if it were going to come off.

Muriel panted out an apology. "Sorry . . . didn't see it . . . wheelbarrow."

Screw the wheelbarrow, where was the car?

"Muriel . . . where's the car?"

"Just ahead . . . I see it." Then she said, "Two cars."

One had to be McCone's; the other Karen's.

A few more yards, and we stopped, both of us grabbing for breath. I heard her opening a car door.

"Get in," I said, pushed her ahead of me, and felt my way in after her. "The keys. Put 'em in. Hurry."

She reached across me, fumbling around. "I don't . . . it won't go in."

"Wrong key. Try another, quick."

Panic tinged her voice. "It won't fit. It won't go."

I groped for her hand, snatched the keys, tried to insert them myself. There were only two, and neither of them fitted.

"Muriel! Whose car is this?"

"What?"

Jesus God.

"Get out. Quick. It's the wrong car."

I tumbled out of there, heard her moving, followed the sound, and banged into the fender of a car parked behind. I felt for the handle, opened the door, got in, slammed the door as she slammed hers.

We weren't going to make it. McCone couldn't have missed all that noise. He was probably coming now, running through the house, out onto the porch, jumping down the steps.

"The ignition. Where's the ignition?"

She took my hand, guided it. I slipped a key in, felt for the selector, couldn't find it.

"Muriel. Where's the selector? Put my hand on it."

"I don't know," she gabbled. "I don't know anything about cars."

I felt with my feet—two pedals; it was a manual. I rapped my hand against the stick shift on the floor.

"Take the wheel. You're going to have to steer."

"I can't. I don't know how." Her voice had risen, fear popping into it.

Mine wasn't too normal either. "You're going to have to do it, Muriel. Just keep it on the road. That's all you have to do."

I turned the key, and the engine caught. I slammed it into first gear, spun the wheel to the left, and took the car away, but I didn't burn any rubber. I couldn't. I had to get around the car in front, a car I knew was there but couldn't see.

I made a big loop to get past it, straightened the wheel, and then I was lost.

"Where, Muriel, where? Steer the car."

"I'm trying!"

I felt her hands come tentatively onto the wheel. I was still in first gear and crawling, but what could I do? I didn't know where I was headed.

"We okay, Muriel? We okay?"

She cried out, her hands stiff on the wheel, "Too far left."

The car slumped to one side, and I heard branches breaking as the wheels lost traction. We had to be in a flower bed; the drive must have had a border, too.

I fought the car back onto the gravel. "Crissake, Muriel, steer it!"

"I can't," she called back, near to sobbing. "I don't know how."

"Just guide it, that's all," but as I said it, we slumped off into the border again. I wanted to yell at Muriel, scream at her, but I didn't because I knew it would panic her, and I was close enough to that for both of us. She'd picked a hell of a time to take her first driving lesson.

I got the car back onto the drive. "I'll steer, you guide me. Left? Right? What?"

"Left. It bends left."

"Now?" I couldn't keep my voice down, and hers rose with mine.

"Yes!"

I turned the wheel.

"Max!"

Branches belted against the fender; then we slugged into something that stopped us cold.

It was insane; we weren't escaping, we were floundering. We couldn't have come fifty yards from the house. McCone would be on top of us any moment.

I restarted the engine, dug for reverse, couldn't find it, tried again, couldn't find it again. I let out the clutch, stomped it back in again, and lifted, pulled and smashed that gearshift into reverse, then trod the gas pedal.

The car bucked and sawed and dragged itself free, snapping branches. I got it back into first and up on the drive once more. I shifted to second and turned the wheel gently this time.

"Okay? We Okay?"

"Yes. We're okay."

"Tell me when to straighten. Now?"

"Not yet . . . now."

"Is he coming? McCone?"

"I don't see him. No."

"We okay? We heading straight?"

"More to the right."

I corrected.

"No. Too *much*."

The way she shrilled the words I thought we were on top of something, so I swerved.

There was a crunching sound, and a shock, then the crunch again.

"Trees, Max. There are trees!"

I swung away, off to my left.

"The flower bed! Watch the flower bed!"

That was the whole point, I couldn't watch anything except the white sheet in front of my eyes.

"Careful . . . watch it!"

"I can't see," I yelled. "I can't damn well *see*."

Then we plowed into something so hard I nearly went through the windshield.

I was close to tears, close to going to pieces. I would have happily agreed to spend the next ten years in a salt mine in exchange for two minutes, one minute, of clear, unobstructed sight. I've never even wanted anything so badly, and because I knew I couldn't have it, I almost went ape.

But Muriel Carson saved me; her words pulled me out of it.

"It's not far, Max. I can see the gates. We're almost there."

I got the car going again, backed out up onto the drive. I could feel for it, listen for the crunch of gravel under the wheels, but once there, I was lost, and Muriel Carson, a frightened, flustered non-driver, seemed to be incapable of guiding me.

"How far?"

"Not far. Keep straight."

I heard her turn in her seat and draw in breath. Her voice climbed. "Oh God, he's coming!"

I hit the gas pedal. "Keep us on the road."

"Go right. No! Too much! Left! Now straight. *Straight!*"

I fought the wheel; the car was swaying from side to side.

I yelled at her. "Where is he? How far behind?"

Her voice shrilled. "He's gaining! Coming fast!" Then it shrilled higher, jagged edges in it. "Max! The gates are closing!"

"Hold on!"

I tromped the gas pedal, clutched the wheel, felt sweat stinging my lousy useless eyes, hunched into myself for the crash.

Muriel cried out, but the crash didn't come.

"We made it! We made it, Max!"

"What about McCone?"

I heard her turn in her seat again. "No. . . ." It was a keening wail. "He's going to make it, too."

"Where are we? Tell me!"

"Careful, Max!"

"WHAT? WHERE?"

"The *fence!*"

The car jumped and spanged into metal, slewed around, and stopped.

I couldn't start it again—the overheated engine just did not want to start.

"McCone. Where's McCone?"

"Coming fast!"

Her voice matched mine. We were screaming at each other.

I fought with the engine, yelled at her, "How far behind us is he? How far?"

"Oh, about twenty-four inches," McCone said from the rear seat.

17

WHAT AN ACTRESS MURIEL CARSON had turned out to be. Star quality. She'd simply kept me crisscrossing the drive out of one flower bed and into the other. I must have had a pulse rate of 109 trying to move that car, thinking I was only an ace away from a suburban street and houses, and a phone, and help, but I couldn't have been more than a hundred feet from the front door of the clinic the entire time.

I was pretty certain it had been McCone's idea because I don't think he was kidding about having been in Vietnam. I knew that one of the interrogation techniques used by both sides was to let a prisoner think he'd escaped, to let him think he was home and dry, then to yank the string on him. Well, I don't know if it worked in Vietnam, but it sure as hell worked in Mount Vernon. When McCone had spoken from the rear seat, and I'd understood the score, I'm afraid I gave him exactly the reaction he'd been after: I started to cry, just put my head down on the wheel and bawled like a kid, because the rage, and the disappointment, and the helplessness, and, above all, the cruelty of what they'd done just destroyed me.

It wasn't just the crushing disappointment of having victory snatched away at the last moment; it was the knowledge that I'd never had a chance anyway, that while I'd been busting a gut and sweating blood in an agony of effort, McCone had just been sitting back, laughing at my comical antics. That's what really drained me, and I was totally demoralized. So he had me exactly the way he wanted me: a nice round blob of silly putty ready to be worked on again.

He didn't even bother taking me into the house to do it, just hauled me out of the car, tossed me down onto the grass, and started in asking me the same old question while he carefully, almost lazily, kicked my busted rib.

But I didn't tell him.

I held out.

Because the pain became a part of me. I was getting used to it. I never knew a person could do that, but you can. It's not the pain that gets worse, that stays the same; it's the idea of it that gets worse, the knowledge that it might not stop and that if it doesn't, you'll go crazy.

But I wasn't thinking about going crazy. I was thinking about something else: the way they'd made me look a fool for a third time.

They'd made a dummy of me, an idiot, not once but three times, and they'd done it with one hand behind their backs.

Max the dunce. Candy from a baby. Almost a shame to take it. I couldn't forgive them that; they'd been too mean.

So I didn't tell McCone even though, technically, I

was fresh out of resistance. I just lay there hating them all, and every time he kicked me I yelled and cried out, because they could have all the moans and screams I had in me, because they weren't going to get the thing they wanted because they really wanted it, and I didn't think they'd done a thing to deserve it.

McCone didn't understand. I should have been babbling by now, and he was getting mad. He fetched me a couple of kicks that blacked me out, but that just gave me a rest, and he knew it, so when he finally realized there was no percentage in kicking me to death, he quit.

And that was when my troubles really began, because Karen took over.

McCone lifted me, carried me maybe twenty yards to the house, up the porch steps, and tossed me down. I thought he'd put me on another table, but it was a trolley, and I felt myself being wheeled through the house and, I was fairly sure, back into the room I'd been in before.

McCone tied my left wrist down—again with a bandage, I thought, although it felt a little different—then stretched my other arm out at a right angle to my body and tied that wrist to what felt like the hard wood armrest of a chair. I was less than fully conscious, but I was taking it all in, and everything registered.

Something metallic was moved near my head. I heard cupboards opening and closing and a series of snaps and clicks; then Karen Petersen spoke. Her voice was crisp, efficient, very professional.

"Ever given blood, Max? If you haven't, you're about to."

It seemed reasonable enough; after all, this was a blood donor center, so they were going to use the facilities. And that meant they were settling down for the long haul. They hadn't been able to storm the castle with the battering ram, so they were going to camp outside the walls and starve it into submission.

I suppose the medieval reference occurred to my foggy brain because of the auto-da-fé I was being treated to. There can't be too many people who aren't sorry they weren't around when the Inquisition was playing. I recalled reading about one poor Calvinist who was lashed to the wheel and left without "a single unbroken bone or unruptured vein."

That thought presented itself when Miss Petersen felt for a fat one in my arm, and I recognized the steely bite of a metal-tipped tube.

But that still gave me only one broken bone and one ruptured vein, so I was way behind the Calvinist.

Part of the horror of the Inquisition must have been the total bewilderment of so many of its victims—this was being done to them by the Holy Mother Church? Font of all mercy and forgiveness?

It was easier for me. I knew this was happening because of Holy Mother Money, so I didn't have to suffer the bewilderment, only the pain.

Nurse Petersen went on in that same crisp tone. "This is what's going to happen, Max. For every second you hold out on us now, you're going to lose blood. We're through fooling around. You can either tell us or bleed to death. It's up to you."

She didn't say anything more, and McCone didn't comment. I heard them leave the room, and somebody else come in.

It was the only member of the gang who hadn't said hello to me yet.

"We're down to the wire, Max. You know that, don't you?" Ralph Carson asked.

I was through knowing anything. I just kept quiet.

"If you don't tell us, you'll die."

I must admit that got to me a bit. If it had been in Karen's icy manner or McCone's Yonkers Raceway accent, that would have been one thing. But delivered as it was in Ralph Carson's meek little bookkeeper voice, the effect was chilling.

"We've told you a lot of lies, Max, but we're not lying now. This is the truth."

I knew it was, too. They'd run out of weapons.

"So how about it? Tell me what the drops are for, and I'll have this stopped immediately. When we're safely away, I'll let Gallo know where you are."

I didn't answer; my phone was off the hook.

I heard him start to walk away, but he stopped and had one last try at it.

"Nobody will think any the less of you if you tell us, not with your life on the line. Whatever the drops are for, it can't be so important it's worth dying for, can it, Max?"

I assumed Carson gave a sad little shrug before he left the room. I heard the door close behind him, and I was on my own for a change.

I could have answered yes when Karen Petersen had asked me if I'd ever given blood. I'd got roped in once when some idiot had pledged the entire office, so I knew what was going on. I could picture the tube in my arm running up to the plastic sack, and the metal stand that would be holding the sack. And I could hear the soft whump-whump of the electric machine, the little teeter-totters they use to help pump the blood. I tried to recall how much blood a person has in his body. Was it a gallon?

How much of that could you lose and still be able to stand up? I remembered you gave one pint when you donated, and that could leave you feeling dizzy. Maybe two pints was the limit for being able to function.

Let's see, say twenty minutes to pump a pint, I had about forty minutes to do something or forget it and just go on doing what I was doing, which was dying on a blood donor's table in Westchester.

Forty minutes. The night had to be a lot farther off than that, not that it mattered much anymore. I was going to run out of blood before I ran out of time.

But looking on the bright side, at least I was getting a rest, something I hadn't had much chance to do lately. It was nice and quiet in the room, the little pump humming to me, my ruined body supported by a soft, comfortable trolley; I could have gone to sleep if it hadn't been for the blowtorch in my side.

It was also the first chance I'd had to think about the avalanche which had swept down on me. McCone, Karen, the Carsons—not a bad team. McCone to pour drinks into me at the bar, maybe get me drunk enough to let him in on a cute liddle ol' secret; the Carsons next door to lull me with home cooking and the warmth of the hearth, a mom and dad to confide in; and Karen, the classic pair of lily-white thighs, in whose thrilling grip I might tell all. Only they didn't get a chance to stick with their game plan because the guy with the knife had spoiled it.

He was competition; that's why they'd had to grab me.

So that was somebody else who knew about the eyedrops and was after them. So much for Gallo and his leak-proof security. Two groups then, not just the one. Although one was plenty for me at the moment.

I lay there thinking over it, listening to the song of the vampire pump. The time slipped by; then I heard the door open and the click of Karen's heels.

She turned everything off. I heard the plastic bag being unsnapped and a fresh one being hooked up. She switched the pump back on and checked the tube in my arm, wiggling the metal tip a bit just to let me know she cared. She left without saying a word.

She hadn't had to, her actions spoke for her, and they were pretty eloquent: one pint down, seven to go. Or maybe only three or four. I wondered how much blood you could lose and still go on living and what it would feel like when it happened. It'd have to be painless; I'd probably drift off into unconsciousness until it became a permanent state. I also wondered what was going on outside with the others. It would have been fairly pointless their staying in the room watching a blind man bleed to death; it's not the kind of sport you'd be able to sell franchises for. I figured they'd wait till I'd lost a second pint, then come and ask me how about it. If I was right, I had about twenty minutes in which to be dynamic and do something.

But I didn't feel like doing anything except go to sleep, and I might have dozed, busted rib and all, if I hadn't started to feel chilly. With my central heating system being drained I was beginning to shiver.

But not to do anything would have been un-American. I had to strive against pain, run for daylight, get tough and get going, and all the rest of that Vince Lombardi crap.

I started by trying to assess the situation and approach it logically.

On the negative side, I was blind, injured, tied down, and slowly losing all my blood.

On the plus side, I wasn't really blind.

But I needed the night not to be really blind, and that was hours away.

Therefore, I had to hurry the night along, which was impossible, or make my own night, which wasn't quite as impossible.

But to do anything at all, I had to stop being tied down so I could stop losing all my blood.

I've always been a clear thinker. Not too bright, but clear. I concentrated on my left wrist. McCone had tied it to a wheel of the trolley; I could feel the rubber of the tire on the back of my hand. That was interesting. And I had an idea it wasn't a cloth bandage he'd used, but an elastic one. Which was even more interesting.

It was tight now, but if I could move the trolley,

get the wheel to turn a bit, the bandage might stretch.

I tried it. I pushed on the chair with my right arm, and the trolley moved a half inch, the left rear wheel moving my left hand the same tiny distance. Still bracing against the chair, I tested the bandage.

When I felt it stretch a little, it was like winning the Cadillac in the hospital raffle, because what could stretch a little could stretch a lot.

It was my first piece of luck in what seemed like twelve years. McCone using an elastic bandage, a tiny thing like that was going to mean the difference between staying where I was and getting free. When I realized it, I was like Popeye after he downs the can of spinach—a ship's whistle blew, steam came out of my ears, and my biceps inflated like balloons.

I gathered myself for a big effort, braced my right arm on the chair, and really pushed this time.

It wasn't nice because tensing my arm tensed the veins in it, and I could feel the fine steel tip of the tube sliding deeper into me. But then pain and I had been seeing a lot of each other lately, so it was like meeting an old friend. The wheel moved, and my wrist with it, a good six inches. I kept the pressure on my right arm and tried pulling my left hand through the bandage.

It was coming. The bandage crept up from my wrist to my thumb. I couldn't sustain the pressure, so I had to let go, but the bandage stayed where I'd moved it.

I tried again, braced, squeezed my hand a bit farther out, let go. I was back to a familiar routine, breathing and sweating as if I'd been cutting down trees. And trying to ignore the stiletto twisting in my arm.

I took a breather. I was going to do it this time because I wasn't sure there'd be a next time.

I braced, pushed, and pulled, curving my hand in on itself, making it as small as I could. That bandage must have loved my hand because it didn't want to let go. It clung like a grasping relative, and for a good twenty seconds there was a shaking, trembling tug-of-war.

Don't let anybody tell you that you can feel only the greater of two pains. I felt two very clearly: my rib gouging into my side and that vicious little steel tip working its way farther into my vein.

I thought I was going to have to quit, and I would have if the bandage hadn't started creeping up over my knuckles. It held on for a last reluctant second, then collapsed on itself, and my hand jerked out as if it had been fired from a gun.

I gave my rib a few moments to get over its protest demonstration, then nearly made a big mistake. I turned on my right side and was feeling for the tube, intending to pull its bloodsucking head out of my arm, when I realized that would have left me with a dark-red fountain spraying everywhere, and no way to turn it off, so I had to let the lousy thing go on sucking away my life while I worked on the other bandage.

McCone was no sailor; the knots were tied like a kid's shoestrings, but it was still damn difficult with only one hand and one set of teeth and no sight to see what I was doing. It ended up costing me five minutes and a couple of fluid ounces of blood.

I whipped the bandage off and, with the greatest of pleasure, slid the tube out of my arm, shoved my thumb over the hole, and bent my arm back on itself. Then I swung my legs down and sat up.

What a mistake.

Ordinarily when you get up quickly and you feel a little dizzy for a moment, it's because the blood takes a second to rise to the brain. But since I was a couple of pints short, it took my system a lot longer to make the trip, and I nearly passed out.

I waited till I'd stopped swaying, got everything under control, then slid off the trolley onto my feet.

Another mistake.

I would have folded if I hadn't grabbed the trolley with both hands. That, of course, released the fountain in my arm, and things were getting messy.

I dug in my pocket for a Kleenex, balled it up, slapped it over the puncture, and bent my elbow back on it. I needed a pressure pack, and while I was sure I could have found some tape and bandages, I couldn't spare the time to look. I had to get out of there.

I planned to make for the door at the other end of the room, the one McCone had come through to start the Muriel Carson Show. God knows where it led, but it had to be a better bet than the main door.

I started for it, one step, two steps, three steps, like that. I was awfully wobbly, but I was staying upright, and that's all I cared about. It was just too bad that I couldn't seem to breathe.

I felt my way along a row of padded tables, found the far wall, found the door, unlocked it, and went through. Nobody laughed, swore, cried out, or grabbed me, so I kept right on going.

I bumped into a chair, caught it before it fell, moved forward, and felt the cold metal of a desk or filing cabinet. Behind it I felt a window, then a long space to the end wall. The room might have been an office, but whatever it was, it was too big for what I wanted to do. I needed a much smaller area.

I made a circuit of the wall, reached a door, stepped through it, and groped into emptiness. I felt a slight movement of air on my face and carpet underfoot, so I assumed I was in an extension of the corridor McCone had led me down when I'd arrived.

I don't know why, but I got a horrible feeling he was in there waiting for me, watching me come toward him. I knew that's the way he'd do it, stay silent and let me blunder into it. "Well, if it ain't Lady Macbeth." That's what he'd say, something like that. On purpose I took a deep breath, and the pain from my side hosed the image away.

I was moving at a turtle pace when my foot bumped on wood. I waved my good arm in front of me, stretching it out. It slapped against something: a newel-post. Stairs. That's where I'd find a smaller room, upstairs. A bedroom, maybe. If I could make the climb.

I took hold of the stair rail with my left hand, the only one I could use, put my left foot on the first step, and hauled.

I made it. One whole step.

I brought my right foot up onto it, rested a moment to let the dizziness pass, then tried the next one.

It was like carrying a trunk up the Washington Monument. It was certainly as slow, and a lot more tiring.

I must have been a scary sight, dragging my body up those stairs. I must have looked like the heavy in a horror movie, slowly climbing toward a sweet young thing with big boobs and a twisted ankle screaming her lungs out on the landing.

The thought triggered another one about an old movie I'd seen. Richard Arlen was a fighter, and his pal, Andy Devine, gets himself knifed, I forget how, so Arlen immediately donates some blood for him. Arlen's due at the Garden in an hour's time, but he won't call off the fight because the kid's got guts, so he leaves Andy at the hospital, goes to the arena, and gets into the ring minus a couple of pints of grade A. He gets plastered all over the place for eleven straight rounds, does nothing but take them on the jaw because he's weak as a kitten, naturally. But then Devine pulls through, so what do they do? They rig up his bedside phone so that it comes over the PA system at the Garden. And when Arlen hears Andy's crackly old voice saying that he's okay, and to go, man, go, he uncorks one punch, the first he's thrown all night, and knocks his opponent cold.

I thought it was a pretty fantastic trick when I saw it at the age of twelve. And right then I knew just how fantastic. It was *very* fantastic.

It was taking me too long to mount those stairs. I was moving slower and slower, and I knew they'd have to find me gone soon. I still couldn't hear a thing from the rest of the house, but the silence wouldn't last for long when they went in to check on me. They'd rush through the house searching, and when they did, they'd only have to look up to see me, and I was tired of their seeing the same old me. I was dying to show them the other me, the nighttime guy. The thought of that was like a hand pushing me from behind, and although I was close to conking out, the stairs stopped before I did.

I felt my way along a wall until my hand brushed against a doorknob. I turned it and went through, easing the door shut behind me.

The room had a dusty, enclosed smell, which was a good beginning. I groped across it, found a window, then another about ten feet away, then the wall ten feet from that.

Good. Better than good, because the windows had louvered shades on them; I'd felt the cords.

I moved to them, found them, eased them away from their spring holders, lowered the blinds, pulled the slats closed. Then I took off my dark glasses.

It wasn't the dead of night, but it was plenty dark enough for me to operate. I could see fine, and oh, what an incredibly beautiful thing that was. To say I drank in the room with my eyes wouldn't be far wrong; I was parched for sight, the way you can be parched for drink, and seeing again was like draining a long, chilled glass of beer after crawling across a desert. I gazed around that little room as if Leonardo had painted frescoes everywhere. Even a corny floral wallpaper looks superb when you've seen nothing but a blank for hours. Listen, next time you spot a blind person with a cupful of pencils, buy them, buy the whole fucking lot, because there *is* nothing worse than not being able to see.

I took a little tour. It might have been a bedroom once, but it was empty of furniture now save for a single chair. There was a washstand in one corner, a closet next to it, a bricked-up fireplace, and that was it. There was no sign of the two things I needed: a bandage for my arm and a weapon of some kind.

I went over and checked the closet. It was a big one, and deep, and had been turned into a storeroom for office supplies. The shelves were full of paper clips, pencils, typing paper, envelopes; unless I could scare McCone off with a poison-pen letter, I didn't see anything that would make a weapon. But I did see an answer to my other problem. I unbent my elbow and took a look at my arm. It was still bleeding, and it wouldn't be stopping without a pressure bandage, so I made one out of office supplies. I found a big soft rubber eraser, pressed it onto the wad of Kleenex I'd put on my arm, and bound it down tight with a reel of half-inch Scotch tape.

Then I took a look at my side and was immediately sorry I had. It looked every bit as bad as it felt, black and blue and swollen to the size of a cantaloupe. The plaster Karen had put on was missing, no doubt torn off by McCone when he'd been kicking me around the lawn, so I went at it with the Scotch tape, winding it tight around and around my body.

It took a terrible twenty seconds that was worse than being poked by the broom handle because I had to press the rib back into place and keep holding it down. But it was far easier to breathe when

I'd finished, and I wanted to be breathing nice and normal for Karen and McCone.

Now the only problem I had was to find a weapon.

I checked the shelves again, but there was nothing, so I got out of the closet and took a look at the chair. No go. It was a saggy old cane chair McCone could have bitten in two. That didn't leave much else.

I went over and checked the washbasin, and that was more promising. The shelf above it was a piece of marble, a solid piece about three and a half feet long and six inches wide. It would make a hell of a baseball bat if I could lift it. It wasn't attached to anything, just resting on heavy metal wall brackets. I got one hand on each end of it, heaved it up, staggered with it, lowered it to the floor, and nearly joined it there. I really wasn't in shape for weight lifting, and I had to put my back against the wall until the dizzies went away. But I'd proved that I could heft it. Now if I could just swing it, I had myself a weapon. That left me with one last job to do.

I hadn't planned on doing any more climbing till the next centenary, but I still had a little to do. I got the rickety old chair, moved it to the center of the room, and very slowly clambered up onto it. It creaked and groaned and sagged on its frame, but it held, and by stretching up carefully, I was able to get a hand on the light bulb that was dangling in a shade and unscrew it.

I was glad the chair was there for another reason: I needed it when I got down. I sank onto it and did my famous impersonation of an exhausted man. But I was a thinking one, too. Now that I had some kind of a trap I had to entice the rats to come into it.

That part didn't bother me; the trick was going to be making sure they didn't all come at once. McCone was going to be the big problem, of course. And in my present condition, Miss Petersen would be a problem, too, although, let's face it, she could probably have taken me the best day I ever saw with her range of cute little moves.

I was less worried about the Carsons; they weren't the physical type. In fact, they were altogether different from the others, ordinary folks, I guessed, who'd been seduced into this by the lure of rich retirement years in Florida. I somehow doubted that Karen needed much persuasion; this couldn't have been the first time she'd strayed off the straight and narrow, she was too slick. I knew now she was mean as hell, but when I first met her, I would never have believed it. I think that little girl had had a lot of practice using her body to get what she wanted.

McCone wasn't anywhere near as complex; he had to be hired muscle, pure and simple. But together they were a pretty formidable combination, so if I was going to stay in the game, I had to make sure one arrived before the other.

But as I sat there in that cane chair, it became increasingly evident that nobody was arriving at all, and a hideous thought popped up: It couldn't be another trick of theirs, could it? One more jerk of the string? If it was, and they laughingly came and dragged me back to that table, I would have been happy to put the tube back in my arm myself.

But I was saved from doing that.

From downstairs came the noise of doors slamming and people running around, so I knew they'd discovered the rock had been rolled away.

I struggled up, moved the chair aside, hefted one end of the marble slab, dragged it over, and leaned it against the wall near the door.

I opened the door an inch so I could hear better, propped myself against the wall, and waited.

Doors opened and closed, and McCone's voice yelled something, sounding angry. Then I heard it coming from outside the house. I guessed he was thinking I'd got out the window I'd used before, which was a real break.

A minute went by; then I heard a door open right underneath me and somebody starting up the stairs. It sounded like Karen's swift, efficient steps.

I put my mouth to the crack in the doorframe, and when the footsteps drew level, I said quickly and urgently, "Karen!"

The footsteps stopped dead.

"Karen. Don't call out. I'll make a deal with you."

"Max. . . ?"

"In here. Don't let him hear you."

The door was slowly pushed open. I heard the click of the light switch, but there was only one light in the room, and the bulb was in my pocket.

"Max. . . ?"

The open door let some light into the room, but not much, and Karen followed it in.

I swung the door shut behind her, and the room went black again. She caught her breath and stood there trying to see through the dark, straining for perception. She took a hesitant step, her movements unsure. Poor kid, she couldn't see a thing.

I kept my voice low and full of money. "Karen, I'll make a deal with you. You get me out of here, and I'll tell you about the drops. McCone doesn't have to know we're gone. You can cut him out of it."

Surrounded by darkness, she had no need to disguise her reaction. Her eyes lit up, and her smile was about two hundred thousand dollars wide.

"We could still be together, Karen. Go to Europe and live our lives in the sun, just like you said. We could forget what happened here, put it all behind us."

"Max. Darling. That's what I wanted all along." She moved a tentative foot toward me, toward the sound of my voice. "I wouldn't have let you die, you must have known that. I was coming in to free you when I found you'd gone."

Another step.

"I never wanted to hurt you, darling. It was McCone. He forced me to."

I let her find me, move her body tight against mine. Her mouth pressed against my neck, moved up my face. Warm breath, warm voice from deep in her throat.

"We'll get out of here, take my car. We'll be gone before he knows it, darling."

"Let's go, Karen. Fast." I started to move back, but she clung.

"Tell me first, darling. Tell me about the eyedrops."

"We've got to go, Karen. He'll catch me. Start hitting me again."

"We'll go, Max. Right now. But tell me about the drops."

"They're for the Army."

"The Army! Yes. . . ?" Her words came quickly.

I moved her away, turned her. "We've got to go. There's a door through here."

"The Army, Max. What do the drops do for the Army?"

"They're for soldiers. Infantrymen."

"Soldiers. Yes. . . ?"

"This way. There are backstairs."

"Tell me, Max. Tell me!"

"They work on a soldier's eyes. Stop him from crying."

"Gas warfare! Is that it?"

"Through here, quickly."

"His eyes won't tear if he's gassed, is that it? Is that why they stop him from crying?"

"No. They stop him from crying," I said, moving her ahead of me, "if his sergeant gives him KP." Then I stepped back, closed the closet door, and locked it.

There was a half second of stunned silence; then the closet exploded. I'd never heard a woman say the things Karen Petersen said then. Boy, she was rude. And loud. Kicking and beating on the door, and yelling . . . it solved any problem I might have had attracting McCone into the room. I heard his heavy footsteps taking the stairs two at a time and got ready behind the door.

He burst in as I knew he would, throwing light into the room, and made straight for the pounding coming from the closet.

I pushed the door closed, plunging the room into darkness again.

He stopped, whirled around fast.

"Hi, Jake," I said casually.

He stood very still, wary, his head cocked slightly, trying to get a bearing on me.

"Max, baby. Kinda dark in here, ain't it?"

"I thought it might even things up a bit."

"Uh-huh," he said. "A blind guy's gotta have a big advantage in the dark, right?"

It was the first time I'd got a look at Jake McCone, but there were no surprises: big and heavy with thick, sloping shoulders, a beer gut on him, arms like thick cables, and a face that had had a lot of things thrown at it.

The noise from the closet got louder. Karen must have heard his voice.

"What's Karen doin' in there?" It was just a stalling question; he wanted to keep me talking.

"She went to hang up her coat."

McCone yelled at her to shut up, and she did. Then very slowly he took a step toward where he thought I was.

"I can hear you moving, Jake. I wouldn't do that. I found me a golf club up here. Feels like a five iron. You try to reach me and I'll brain you."

"A five iron, huh?" He was very quietly slipping off his left shoe. "Wouldn't want to run into one of them."

I closed my fingers around the marble slab.

"How many times did you kick me, Jake?"

"Coupla dozen, maybe."

"How many times did you hit me?"

"I dunno. Who keeps score?"

He eased his right shoe off, put it down silently.

His hand went to his back pocket, moving in slow motion. It came out again holding something.

He said, "Why you askin'?" but only to cover the click of the switchblade springing out.

"No special reason."

I sucked in a breath, held it, and lifted the mantelpiece onto my shoulder, trying not to grunt with the effort and trying not to fall down under the weight.

McCone was sliding toward me in his socks, crouching slightly, one hand holding the knife, the other held in front of him like a feeler.

I kept the slab balanced on my shoulder with my right hand and, with my left, felt in my pocket for the light bulb.

"You still there, Jake? I can't hear you."

He was about ten feet away. I watched him tense, getting ready to rush me. He hunched up and ran his tongue around his lips, his eyes squinting, and that's when I lobbed the light bulb.

It hit the wall to his right and popped like a gunshot in the silent little room.

McCone whipped around, surprised as hell, then immediately spun back toward me, but by that time I had the marble slab off my shoulder and was swinging it at his head.

I mentioned earlier that I thought the thing would make a great little baseball bat, but if I'd been swinging at a baseball, instead of Jake McCone, I wouldn't have hit a four-hundred-foot homer. It would have been one of those sad little rollers back to the mound.

Mickey Mantelpiece.

The thing was too unwieldy, and it twisted out of my hands and more or less glanced off his ear on its way to the floor. But it was so heavy that he still took a pretty good shot, and he fell down and rolled over, not out, but not in either.

I was pretty close to falling down, too; I was swaying like a sailor in a storm. But I kept my feet because I knew I had to do something about McCone before he recovered. I had to lock him in that closet, and I already had a live one in there, which meant I'd have to take care of Karen all over again. She'd heard the thump and crash of the marble falling and had naturally assumed it was all over for me.

"McCone," she yelled, kicking the door. "Let me out."

I hobbled over to the closet, turned the key, opened the door, and Karen took a step forward. Her cheeks were a bright red color that didn't go with her hair.

"Turn the fucking—" My palm in her face cut her off. As her hands flew up, I drove a set of stiff fingers into her solar plexus, and the air whooshed out of her. She sank back into the closet and collapsed onto the floor, trying for breath that wouldn't be available for a few minutes. It was the first time I'd ever raised my hand to a woman—I loved it. I owed Miss Petersen just as much as I owed McCone, and I found both payoffs very satisfying.

McCone was on his knees now, shaking his head like a bear with a fishbone caught in its mouth. I crossed to him, took his elbow, and he staggered to his feet, fell down, and got up again. His semiconscious condition was a lucky thing for me because I would never have been able to drag his two hundred pounds across that room.

We stumbled in tandem for a few steps; then I gave him a gentle shove and added him to the office supplies. I locked the door on the pair of them and sagged against it, trying to keep my spaghetti legs from looping underneath me. There was still the Carsons, but I doubted they'd give me a hard time, and as I was thinking that, I heard Ralph Carson calling up the stairs.

"McCone?"

He sounded frightened.

I eased my way over to the door, opened it, and called down.

"Come on up, Ralph. Bring Muriel. We're having a party."

Whatever we were having, the Carsons didn't want any. They must have heard all the thumping and bumping, and how they imagined I'd got the better of McCone I couldn't say, but they weren't about to come up and find out.

A minute later I heard a car start up and drive off. So long, Carsons. They were probably heading for Altoona to hide out with a sister-in-law or some dumb thing like that. They weren't very bright, although that Muriel Carson should have gone on the stage.

I went over to the window to check the light. The sun was going down, but there was still too much day for me to see, so I lowered myself into the old cane chair and just sat there.

McCone was coming around, and Karen was screaming at him, tearing strips off him. I could hear him groaning and muttering. When he'd recovered enough, he started kicking at the door, but it didn't worry me; the house had been built back when real carpenters used real materials. The closet door must have weighed forty pounds, the lock was big and heavy, and the hinges were probably solid brass. He wasn't going anywhere, and when he found it out, he switched to a verbal attack, and I'm sure Karen Petersen learned some newies.

An hour later I was downstairs moving like a sleepwalker through the house. It wasn't quite night yet, but it was dark enough for me to see, and I found an office and some notepaper with the clinic's address on it and called Gallo. He wasn't there, so I left a message for him to come out and get me as soon as he could, then went in search of the kitchen and raided the icebox.

What I needed was a gallon of chicken soup, a couple of steaks, and some medicinal bourbon, but I had to settle for milk and Oreo cookies. There were lots of those two things, kept, I assumed, to restore the donors after they'd given blood. Well, the clinic had a couple of pints of mine, so I qualified.

I did a lot of resting and a lot of thinking after that, mainly about how I'd come to be where I was.

It was clear that whoever had hired McCone and company had inside information, knowing about Gallo and me and the eyedrops as they did. But it was limited; they didn't know what the drops were for. On the other hand, the other group—and I had to assume the guy after my eyes was working for somebody else—did seem to know what the drops were for. That's why they were interested only in my eyes, not the rest of me. And that thought bothered me, because it seemed to point to the fact that this second group was getting its info from a higher source.

Maybe from somebody high enough to intercept the message I'd just left for Gallo.

The possibility of that happening really made my day.

I tried to discount the idea, tried to talk myself out of it, because I wanted to feel I was safe now, that it was all over. But it wouldn't let me alone. It nagged at me, keeping time with the bass drum in my side, and I spent twenty minutes worrying about it.

I finally decided the best thing to do, the safest thing, would be to get out of the house. I couldn't take either of the cars in front because headlights blinded me at night, so I hauled myself back to the office and called a local cab company. They said they'd be over for me as soon as they could, and ten minutes later I heard a car coming around the drive.

I put my shades back on and weaved out onto the porch, holding onto things. I hated to put those glasses on again because they cut down on my vision, but I felt I had to go on playing the blind man, at least till I got to my apartment, crossed my fingers, and took that pill.

I made it down the steps onto the drive and watched the car swing toward me. God, I was happy to be leaving that place. I hated all clinics, all twenties wood frame houses, and all Mount Vernon.

The car stopped a few yards away, and I saw that the driver already had a passenger. He got out and started toward me, a very tall, very thin man wearing a black homburg and carrying a funny little cloth bag. Then things got confused because the driver got out, and he didn't look like a cabdriver; he looked more like a wrestler. And he didn't ask me if I'd called for a cab. Instead, he pulled something out of the pocket of his topcoat, and by the time I saw it was a piece of pipe it was too late, because he was already hitting me with it.

I should have expected it, of course. I should have known I wasn't just going to step into a cab and be driven away from all that mess—not that day. Unh-unh. No way. The fates were doing a number on me, and they don't fool around. When it's your day to be picked on, they just go right on picking on you, and you can cry, "Enough, already," till you're blue in the face, but it doesn't do any good. They just pile it on all the more, and they don't stop till they're good and ready. So when that big guy started hitting me with the pipe I was hurt, defeated, exhausted, all those things.

But I certainly wasn't surprised.

18

I NEVER WAS A FAST LEARNER.

That thought occurred to me on my way to the ground.

How could I continue to be so dumb? If I'd thought there'd been a possibility of that phone call to Gallo being intercepted, why the hell had I gone strolling out onto the drive when I'd heard a car coming?

I didn't have to wonder who the new visitors were, the lead pipe and that little cloth bag kind of gave me a clue, but the knowledge still didn't spring me to my feet. The guy had got me in the neck, just where it joins the shoulder, and my body felt like a bundle of washing.

He treated it like one, too. He grabbed one of my limp arms, pulled me up, and hefted me onto his shoulder—it was no trouble for him—and started to follow the tall man up the steps to the porch. I assumed they thought the house would be a perfect place for an eye operation—it was a clinic, after all, and it was clearly empty, every window being dark. There wasn't a sound coming from it either, McCone having given up kicking the door a long time back. So I was on my way to surgery when the guy carrying me stumbled on the top step.

I bounced up and down on his shoulder and came down on my rib, and it must have come within a hair of going through my lung. The pain was so spectacular it shocked me right out of my stupor, shocked my eyes wide open. My shades had come off when he'd hit me, so I could see pretty well, and as he lugged me through the front door, I reached out, grabbed both sides of the doorframe, and heaved myself forward.

Clutching me as he was, he had nowhere to go but backward, couldn't keep his balance, and went down under my weight. I scrambled up, lunged for the steps, hit the drive, and ran.

When I say ran, I don't mean like Man o' War, I mean ran like a zombie in a sack race. My shoulder seemed to have risen under my right ear, and I couldn't hold my head straight. And with my rib hurting worse than ever, plus my wobbly pasta legs, and the rest of me getting by on six pints of blood, I was a stumbling, shuffling disaster. I went along the front of the house, around a flower bed, making for the corner. I'd been right about its bordering the house, and right about the house itself; in the fast glimpse I caught of it, it was very much the same as the one I'd imagined: big; sprawling; with windows everywhere. The grounds were also as advertised, a circular drive, then nothing but lawn for a hundred yards. But being able to see all this for myself didn't make much of an improvement in my situation—I was still a half-ruined computer programmer being chased by a thug in good condition, and I couldn't hide from him because it wasn't all that dark.

For the second time that day I found myself desperately needing a weapon, and I knew I wasn't going to find a heavy mantelpiece in the garden. A rake or a shovel maybe—I would have paid a hundred dollars for something like that. When I stumbled around the corner, I thought I'd found something. It had a handle all right, two of them, but on the other end was a wheelbarrow, no doubt the one Muriel Carson had so sweetly led me into.

I stopped and grabbed it. It was no big decision, I could hear the guy coming fast, so I would only have had a few more yards of freedom anyway.

As he burst around the corner, I shoved the wheelbarrow at his legs, but I didn't have the strength to push it hard, and he saw it coming and tried to leap it. He didn't make it, though; he caught a foot and tumbled over onto the grass, but by that time I was off again.

Off? I got about twenty more feet before I slowed and stopped, just the way a windup toy stops when the spring's all unwound. I wasn't going to get an inch farther down that garden because I'd run out of motive power.

But at least my body had chosen a good spot for its breakdown: right outside an open window. And I was pretty sure it was the same one Muriel Carson and I had "escaped" through.

So I did a funny thing.

I got back into the house.

That lousy house of horrors, the place that those two guys were *trying* to get me into, I went back into.

And in a curious way.

I managed to get my head through the window and one leg over the sill, but my other leg didn't want to swing up, just did not want to move, so I was left straddling the windowsill like a shot burglar.

As I said, the night wasn't that dark, and when the guy in the garden spotted me, he charged. But he was clumsy and, I'm sure, mad about the wheelbarrow, so when he lunged at me, he succeeded in doing what I hadn't been able to: He pushed me over the sill and got me into the room.

He had a problem getting his huge body through the window and an even bigger one when he got inside. It was dark in that room, and he couldn't see a thing. But I could, crystal clear, and I would have known that room anywhere. There was the stretcher with the elastic bandage on the wheel, and almost a pint of my blood hanging in a plastic bag above it. There were a dozen padded tables, glass cabinets full of tape and bandages and all the trappings, rubber tubes and metal stands. But as I had been once before that day, I was interested only in getting out of the room, and the guy by the window was interested only in stopping me. He could hear me dragging myself across it, but he couldn't do much about it because he kept bumping into the tables and getting angrier.

"Inside!" he yelled. "He's inside!"

I left him trying to find a light switch, went through the door at the end, and recognized the corridor and the stairs leading off it.

Don't ask me how I got up those stairs—frontward,

backward, maybe I did it standing on my head—but I can tell you why I got up them: because I had to if I wanted to get any help. Outside in the garden it had been easy to collapse because I was going nowhere. But now I had a goal ahead of me, and with a goal you can always promise yourself a rest after you reach it.

The goal, by the way, was the closet.

I was going to let McCone out.

That idea might strike you as a touch strange, but what were my options? I couldn't hide in the house, not when they started turning the lights on, and I couldn't do the mantelpiece trick again because I couldn't have budged it now. So I had to use something else to stop those two guys below from getting me onto a table.

You're right, that would still leave me McCone and the girl to contend with, but I'd spent all day with them, and they hadn't killed me yet. Maybe they wouldn't.

I staggered into the room, bent down for the key on the floor, took an age to straighten up, weaved over to the closet, and got a nasty shock.

I suddenly couldn't see very well. The light on the landing outside had been switched on from downstairs, and it was spilling in through the open door, robbing me of half my vision.

I tried and I tried, but I couldn't seem to get that key into the closet door, couldn't seem to coordinate my hand movements. I don't know what McCone thought was happening, maybe he thought I was teasing him, but he started to yell and thump on the door, and they must have heard that down below below because a door banged open and heavy footsteps started up the stairs.

I was still trying to fit the key into the hole, but it was like trying to thread a needle in a thunderstorm. And those footsteps were maybe halfway up the stairs before I got it in. McCone must have had the handle turned, because as soon as the lock snapped back the door flew open and sent me flying. I wrapped up against the wall and, as my knees started buckling, slid down it as slowly as a blob of honey.

McCone charged out of the closet, looking wildly around. Karen close behind, her face tight with fury. He stopped and snatched up something from the floor, and I knew it had to be the knife he'd dropped when I'd clobbered him.

He turned, saw me sitting propped up against the wall; then things got hazy.

It wasn't just my eyes; it was my whole body. It was closing down, switching off, going bye-byes.

You'd think a man could stay awake for his own execution, but I didn't seem to be able to. I was beginning to doze off like a husband dragged to an opera.

My hearing was the last thing to go, and I think Karen cried out, or somebody cried out; then it wrapped up too, and I was falling down that long dark hole on my way to Wonderland again. It wasn't fair. My brain could have quit anytime in the last fifteen minutes, and here it was doing it right at the most exciting part.

But that's show business.

19

I KNEW I WASN'T DEAD BECAUSE I CAME TO, but that didn't mean I wasn't dying.

I looked and I felt, but there wasn't any knife sticking out of me, so I assumed the pain was just my rib acting up in the cold weather.

That was a surprise. Was old Jake going to turn out to be just a bully, after all, and not a killer? And where was he anyway? Where was Karen? And the tall man, and the heavy? The house was dead silent. It sounded as if no one were in it. I wondered how long I'd been out of things; quite a while to judge from my body, which felt as if it had been starched and ironed.

It took me about five minutes to get up. Using the wall as a crutch, I found a light switch on the landing, killed the light, then saw I'd been wrong about there being nobody in the house.

The big man, the one who'd chased me, was lying in a pool of his own blood at the top of the stairs. It was pretty thoughtless of McCone to leave him where somebody could fall over him.

I grasped the railing, edged down the staircase, then crept around turning lights off.

The tall man was in the carpeted corridor, still wearing his homburg, a dark two-inch slit near the second button of his topcoat. Old Jake sure did neat work.

There was no sign of him or Karen, and when I checked outside, I found their cars were gone. That was okay with me, but it still didn't explain why McCone hadn't come back upstairs and made it three in a row.

But then I remembered the cab I'd called. McCone and the girl had probably made the same mistake I'd made: seen or heard the cab coming up the drive, figured it was help for me, jumped into their cars, and taken off. It sounded likely.

There was a strange glow in the sky I didn't understand till I realized it was the morning waiting in the wings. Wow, that meant I'd been out for almost twelve hours, which would explain the feeling of rigor mortis in my body.

I lowered what was left of it onto the porch and had a little think.

What I should do, I knew, was call Gallo and resign, give up my apartment, and take a lease on two rooms in an intensive care ward. But I was thinking about that security leak. There was a chance I could find out who it was if I wanted to try. I recalled Gallo telling me there weren't more than a dozen people who knew any details about the project, and of the others I'd met only Weyland and kindly old Dr. John. Plus the two doctors who'd run the tests on me at the Beacon. So it was odds on I'd never met the guy who was tapping Gallo's phone. Which gave me a fairly bright and suicidal idea.

I jacked myself to my feet and hobbled back into the house bent over like a ninety-six-year-old man. I found I could move best with one hand holding my rib and the other against a wall or a table, struggling from one support to another. There was a speedway driver when I was a kid who I always liked because of his name and the ad painted on his car: Satan Brewer. Running on Kendall oil. I knew what they could have painted on me right then: Max Ellis. Running on pure adrenaline.

I called the cab company again, and a sleepy-voiced operator confirmed what I'd suspected: The cab had arrived just as two cars had taken off. The driver had knocked on the door, and when nobody had answered, he'd figured that whoever had called had got a ride in one of those cars. The operator was a bit mad at me, but I gave him an excuse, ordered up another cab, and promised to pay a penalty for stiffing the first one. Then I made a few adjustments around the house which were part of my plan for later.

Poking around, I found a walking stick, and as I'd already found my shades out on the front porch, I was back to being a blind man when the cab came ten minutes later. I needed the glasses because the sun was coming up and my vision was going to bed. I wanted to go to bed, too. I dozed off in the cab on the way back to Manhattan, and the driver had to shake me awake when we got to the apartment house, which was a switch because I'd shaken him when he'd first seen me. He told me I looked as if I'd been in a train wreck, which is exactly how I felt, but of course, I didn't tell him the truth, and he was diplomatic enough not to ask.

He helped me to the elevator, but I rode up alone and wobbled and hobbled down the corridor to my door. I let myself in, felt my way to the kitchen, and didn't fall over a single dead body. Nobody started beating on me, either, or tried to pluck out my eyes.

There's no place like home.

I found some sliced bread and something that smelled like ham and made myself the biggest sandwich outside of the comics.

I couldn't find the booze I'd bought for Karen's dinner party, but I did find a pint of orange juice, which I followed with three cups of coffee.

Then I braced myself for the moment of truth.

I went into the bathroom, closed the door so I could see, took off my shades, and eased off my jacket and shirt. I almost laughed at what I saw in the mirror: a clown with cushions tucked under his skin. The twelve hours I'd spent flaked out upstairs in that house had given my body time to bruise and swell. I had two fat lips, both caked with dried blood, and my shoulder had ballooned up like my side. And with the Scotch tape around my arm and Scotch tape around my rib cage, I looked as if a Model A Ford enthusiast were battling to keep me together.

I washed my mouth, sponged down my body, and toweled off. Then I opened the bathroom cupboard and took out the pack of Exedrins I'd put there. All the pills were marked with the letter *E*.

Except one.

I tapped it out onto my hand and swallowed it

with some water. It was going to restore my sight, huh? I wondered idly if one of the aspirins wouldn't have had more chance. I'd know in a couple of hours.

I put my clothes back on, got out of the bathroom, found the sofa, and snoozed now and then, pinching my arm every time I was in danger of dropping off into deep sleep.

When I heard the rush-hour traffic outside on the avenue, I thought it was time to get things started.

I still had Gallo's number in my pocket, and I'd memorized it before I'd left Mount Vernon. When I called it, he was there for a change.

"Max! You okay? What happened? Where are you?" His questions tumbled over each other.

"Macy's. They're having a sale."

I don't think he believed me. "For God's sake, Max, tell me where you are."

"I tried to tell you where I was. I left a message for you."

"When?"

"Last night. Around six or seven."

"I never got it."

"Somebody sure did."

He asked me what I meant.

"I got into a spot of bother, and part of it was because I left a message for you. You need a washer on your phone, Gallo. You got a leak in it."

There was a beat. "How's that?"

"You got a bad apple over there. And I know who it is."

"Who? How do you know?"

"One of the gentlemen I was recently associated with told me."

"Max. Give me a number I can call you back."

"I'll call you. Give me a number you know is safe."

He rattled one out, and I got him to repeat it.

"Call me there. Fifteen minutes," he said.

I figured I'd need longer than that, so I told him it was no good. "Half an hour's the best I can do."

"Okay. Half an hour. Don't call me here again." He rang off.

I moved back to the sofa and settled down to wait. I didn't think it would be a long one, and it wasn't.

I was thinking deep thoughts about Gallo's bugged phone when, about twenty minutes later, I heard a key scrape in my front door, and it opened.

"Can I come in?"

The door closed.

"Sure," I said. "I didn't know you had a key."

"Uh-huh."

"How did you know I'd be here?"

"Put a trace on the call you just made."

"I should have thought of that." I already had.

"You look awful," Weyland said.

"That's funny, I feel great."

"What happened up there?"

"Up where?"

"Mount Vernon."

So there it was.

"I went around and around with some nasty types."

"Was it you who killed them?"

"You've seen them?"

"No, we got a report."

"How so?"

"When you called Gallo last night, the call was traced as far as Mount Vernon, but it couldn't be pinpointed. So we asked the local police to report anything out of the ordinary."

"How did they find out?"

"Your cabdriver reported in. He said he'd picked up a blind man six A.M. at a clinic who looked like he'd been in a lot of trouble. The police investigated and found two dead men."

"Then the cops would like to talk to me. Maybe they're on their way."

"No. That's all been taken care of."

"I'll bet it has," I said.

In the silence that followed I thought Weyland would be able to hear the beat of butterfly wings in my stomach. I've already said this was a suicidal idea, but I'd gone too far to back out. I came on strong, instead.

"That was naughty of you tapping Gallo's phone, Weyland."

"Naughty but necessary," he said in that flat voice of his. Then he got down to the nitty-gritty. "You told Gallo one of those men told you who'd hired him."

"You heard it."

"I don't believe you," Weyland said. "I think you were just saying that to see what swam into your net. Am I right?"

"Right." I was amazed at the tone of this conversation, it was so low-key, as if we were discussing gas mileage or something.

"And you think it worked, do you?"

"Well, here you are."

"So I am," he said.

There was a slow, dragging, dreadful pause. I was certain he was reaching for a gun, and if he had been, there wasn't much I could have done against something like that.

But there was no need for him to use a weapon, as he then pointed out.

"My being here hardly constitutes proof."

He was right. All it proved was that he was tapping Gallo's phone. And he'd probably already removed the tap, so even that couldn't be proved. The guy was safe, and he knew it.

And if he was safe, I was safe.

"You're going to be meeting Gallo shortly, aren't you?" he said.

"That's right."

"When you tell him it's me, I doubt he'll believe you."

He said it walking away, walking toward the door.

"Hold it," I said. "Those two dead men. Who were they?"

"I wouldn't know."

"Didn't the police find any identification on them?"

"No. None at all."

"But one of them would have been a doctor, wouldn't he?"

"I really couldn't say," Weyland answered. Then the door opened and closed, and he was gone.

For the third time in twenty-four hours I thought I was going to be killed and hadn't been. But I felt no burst of wild relief; it was just one more anticli-max to add to the day's collection.

I got up off the sofa, feeling a lot more wobbly than when I'd sat down, and called the number Gallo had given me, surprised I hadn't forgotten it.

He picked it up on the first ring.

"Max?"

"Hi. I've got news for you."

"How soon can you meet me? Midtown. East Side."

I told him half an hour. He gave me an address and hung up. I shuffled back to the sofa and just sat there, my mind totally wrapped up thinking about Weyland and what he'd said. And what he hadn't said.

20

I GOT A CAB TO THE ADDRESS Gallo had given me, turned out to be an apartment house. I went up to the fourteenth floor, where he'd said he'd be waiting. As I stepped out of the elevator, he grabbed my elbow.

"Max! My God, what happened?"

"You're the second guy to ask me that."

An apartment door opened, loud laughter behind it, people coming down the corridor.

"Come on," Gallo murmured. He led me away through a door to the backstairs, helped me up them, and guided me through another door, which brought us out onto the roof.

Traffic sounds came up from the avenue below, and I could feel a weak sun on my face. The air was chilly.

"Christ, Max, I hardly recognize you. What happened?"

"I look a little different, don't I?"

"My God, yes."

"Trouble is, Gallo, I don't look different enough."

It was a moment before he understood what I was

talking about: I was still wearing shades and carrying the walking stick I'd found at the clinic.

His voice had a low tightness in it. "You saying you took the pill?"

"Yep. And I'll tell you something. I don't think you should go national with it."

I don't think he knew what to say. But I had plenty to say.

"Isn't that a kick? How about that for a flying finish? The project's over, but the guinea pig's going to be blind half the time for the rest of his life."

"Max, I—"

"Oh, no, please. Spare me the sympathy. I'm going to be a rich man, remember? That's what you promised."

"That's right," he said quietly. "You'll never have to worry about money again."

"Gallo, there are a lot of things I won't have to worry about again. Like wasting five bucks on a lousy movie. Or having to line up to rent a car. Or getting a warm beer at the ball game. All I'll have to worry about is hoping the sun goes down on time. I'm going to be a rich mole, Gallo; only I'll have to wait till night to count my money because I won't be able to see to count it in the daytime."

"Max, listen—"

"I'm listening. What are you going to tell me? Remind me of Helen Keller maybe? Tell me it won't be so hard because I make a damn good blind man? I got screwed, buddy, up, down and sideways. But don't feel sorry for me, for crissakes, don't feel that, because I'm going to be a big celebrity. Max Ellis, the nighttime guy."

"Look, Max—"

"It's so fucking unfair, Gallo. So fucking un*fair!*"

I brought the walking stick lashing down onto the roof so hard I almost snapped it.

Neither of us said anything for a long time; then Gallo spoke, very quietly.

"They'll be working on that pill constantly, Max. They could get it right within a couple of weeks."

I was quieter, too. A lot quieter. "Sure. A couple of weeks. Or a couple of months. A couple of lifetimes." I blew out a long breath. "Anyway, you didn't come to hear about my problems. You came to hear about yours."

Gallo waited for me to go on.

"You know about Mount Vernon, do you?"

"The two dead men. Yes," Gallo answered.

"When I told you on the phone that one of them had told me who'd hired him, it wasn't true. That was a little trap I set, and guess who walked into it."

"Who?"

"Weyland."

"*Weyland?* You're kidding."

"He's your leak. I know it, and he knows I know it. And he knows I can't prove it."

"It can't be Weyland, Max. No way. He's been with the department fifteen years."

"Fifteen years, fifty years, you told me yourself this thing was worth a fortune. Anyway, knowing who it is doesn't help you. Like I say, there's no proof. The only guys who worked for him are dead."

"Listen, what happened out there? Who beat you up?"

"Another bunch. Those two dead guys just tried to steal my eyes. Do you know who they were?"

"They had no identification. They're still checking."

"Like that, huh? But I guess one of them had to be a doctor."

"It looks that way," Gallo replied.

"Does it?"

"What?"

"Look that way. The guy was a doctor?"

Gallo took my arm. "I've got a cold. Let's move out of the wind a little."

He walked me several steps; then we stopped, and he answered my question. "So they figure."

"The Mount Vernon cops told you that?"

"That's right."

"What made them think he was a doctor?"

The wind swirled up, brisk and chilly, bringing with it a chorus of horns from the street fourteen stories below.

"Goddamn wind," Gallo said. "Let's move to the other side."

He guided me across the roof; then we stopped, and I felt the cold stone of the parapet under my hand.

"The guy seems to fascinate you, Max."

"I'm always fascinated by people who try to maim me. What made them think he was a doctor?"

"They found his instruments," Gallo said. "His bag."

"Then those cops must have been feeling hungry."

"I don't get you."

"Before I left that house this morning, I hid his bag in the vegetable crisper in the refrigerator."

"You hid it," Gallo repeated slowly.

"And their identification."

"Why do a thing like that?"

"Because I thought there was a chance somebody might tell me what you just did. Only the person who hired that man would know he was a doctor."

Gallo grunted. "You're a suspicious guy, Max. And a changeable one. You just got through telling me Weyland was the boy."

"I honestly thought he was. I asked myself who was in the best position to intercept your calls. The answer was your boss. He came to visit me just now, and when he'd gone, I got to thinking some more, and I realized that you were in an even better position to intercept your calls."

"Max," Gallo said. He put his hand on my arm. "You've been through a lot. And you've just had a god-awful disappointment. It's making your thinking fuzzy. Come on, let's walk a little and clear the cobwebs."

"I like the cobwebs."

"Then at least come out of the wind. I'm going to start sneezing."

I let him walk me a little farther along the roof, his hand on my left elbow. I had the stick in my right hand, tapping it against the parapet. I listened to him explain.

"You're basing this whole thing on the fact that I said the cops found a doctor's bag. It was all pure assumption on my part. I assumed the man was a doctor, so I assumed he'd have instruments. And I assumed the police would have found them. That's all."

Gallo stopped, and I turned toward his voice. "That's not the same as saying they did find them, like you told me." I was letting my walking stick swing gently in my hand. On its backward swing it hit the parapet; only it didn't clunk on cement, it made a metallic pinging sound, the way it would have hitting a rail. The kind you might use to cover repair work.

"I meant I thought they would find them," Gallo answered.

"Why?" I asked. "What made you think he'd be a doctor anyway?"

"Because," Gallo said from directly in front of me, "I saw the report on that poor guy who lost his eyes, the one they must have thought was you. The report said his eyes had been cut out with a scalpel, so it was natural to assume it'd been done by a doctor."

"Yeah, well, I'll tell you, Gallo. You might know a lot about weapons and warfare and things, but you don't know beans about eyes. And I do. There are only six little muscles you'd have to cut to remove an eye, and it'd be impossible to tell whether it had been done by a scalpel or a sharp knife. Because that's all a scalpel is, a sharp knife. So you've said too much, fella."

There was a long moment of heavy silence; then Gallo said, "So it seems." Then he added," However, I'm not the only one who's said too much."

His voice was coming from a little farther off— he'd taken a step away from me.

"I have a confession to make, Max. I lied to you. I

haven't been moving you along because of the wind. I've been moving you so you'd be standing right where you're standing now."

"That's funny," I said. "Because I've got a confession to make, too."

But Gallo wasn't listening anymore. He was already lunging at me.

His outstretched hands were less than a foot away when I kicked my body to the right. His left hand grabbed at my arm, but his momentum was already carrying him past me, and all I had to do was knock his hand away, and he was crashing through the metal barrier of the broken parapet.

He was so surprised at my move that he didn't start screaming until a moment before he hit the roof of the adjoining building about six floors below.

I knew he couldn't hear, but I completed my confession because they say it's good for the soul.

"I was lying, too," I said. "The pill works."

Epilogue

So THAT'S HOW IT WAS, that's how it went, and that's how I came to be alive and kicking on my back in a hotel pool in Florida.

I got down here forty-eight hours after I was checked into a small and discreet hospital in Rockland County where I allowed skilled paleontologists to rebuild my body.

Weyland picked up the tab and also arrived on the second day with a briefcase full of one-hundred-dollar bills. Although that wasn't the first time I'd seen him since he'd left my apartment the morning I'd got back from Mount Vernon. I'd seen him about sixty seconds after Gallo had tried to push me off that roof. He'd come strolling out as casually as a man getting a little air after a heavy dinner, walked to the broken parapet, and looked down at Gallo's body as if it were somebody's hat that had blown there. I'd gaped at him, and said, "You just get here?"

"I was right behind you."

"You saw it all?"

He nodded, still looking thoughtfully down at the roof.

"Well, thanks for the helping hand. Hell, that could've been me down there. I didn't even have a weapon."

"You had an excellent weapon," he said, and he reached out and took off my shades.

That shook me—George Weyland, dull and plodding, Korvette's suit and size twelve Florsheims, had known I could see.

"How did you know?"

"It stood to reason the first thing you'd do when you got back to your apartment was take that pill. It was supposed to work, so I assumed it had. I knew for sure when you thought I'd come to kill you. I moved my hand to my jacket as if I were reaching for a gun, and you almost jumped out of your skin."

"But what made you think I'd try to fool Gallo? I'd just accused you."

"You weren't sure of me," Weyland said. "I didn't give you the right answer about that man being a doctor. I didn't know if he was a doctor, but I could tell you certainly thought he was."

As I said, dull, plodding George Weyland.

"Then you knew it was Gallo who was pulling strings?"

"Well, I didn't send those men to Mount Vernon. It had to be him."

"But you must have suspected him. You tapped his phone."

Weyland shook his head. "I tapped every phone in my department. Those drops are worth millions, and I figured somebody might be tempted to try ripping them off." He nodded down at the crumpled body below. "I was right."

I gave him the whole story about McCone and Karen Petersen and the Carsons, but as I write this, only the Carsons have been picked up. Boarding a bus for Atlantic City, would you believe? They didn't know the man who'd hired them, but the description they gave tied in with the one Karen had given me: fair-haired, athletic-looking, an accent. It was enough for Weyland to have him identified; it wasn't hard because he was on top of the list of people who'd be interested in a hush-hush project. He told me his name later: Plesek. He made it out of the country and back to his embassy in Ottawa, but the State Department is putting pressure on, and the guy's going to be thrown out of Canada. It's going to take a bit longer to catch up with McCone and Petersen, but I don't think it will matter. Sooner or later the McCone's of the world end up dead in an alley. And girls like Karen don't last a minute longer than their looks, so I don't think she has much of a future either.

As far as my own future goes, I'm going to tan my lumps and bruises for another week down here; then it's back to the grind.

So that about wraps the whole thing up, although I do have one little postscript to add. A happy one, too.

Remember Cy Green, boy psychologist? It was his party I'd been to the night before I rode the subway to the tax office and first met Gallo. I ran into him in a restaurant a few days back. It wasn't so surprising; half the people in Miami Beach are from New York.

"Max," he said. "I didn't know you were down here. How are you anyway?"

He'd noticed my limping walk, so I told him I'd had a small auto accident, nothing serious, and had come down here for a little R and R.

He commiserated with me about that, then asked how things were otherwise. "You sleeping okay?"

"Sure. Why?"

"Only that the last time we spoke, you had a problem with a dream."

"A dream. . . ."

"About your brother."

"Oh, I know which one, but it just struck me . . . I'd almost forgotten about it." I started to smile, my first one in I don't know how long. "As a matter of fact, I don't think it's going to be back."

"That's fantastic news," Cy Greene said. "How did you get rid of it?"

"I took your advice."

"My advice," Cy said, nodding. He'd forgotten what it had been.

"You told me I didn't have a debt to my brother, but if I couldn't help thinking I did, then I'd have to find a way to cancel it."

"And that's what happened? You found a way to cancel it?"

I thought for a moment, a long one. "I guess I did. Either that or it found me."

"That's terrific, Max," he said. "Tell me what you did. I have a couple of patients with a similar problem. Maybe I can recommend the same thing to them."

But I didn't tell him.

Cy's a nice guy, and I didn't want him to lose his practice.

MAX ELLIS
Miami Beach, May 1977

Special Preview Excerpt

A NERVE-SHATTERING RACE
AGAINST ULTIMATE TERROR IN THE
MOST HIGHLY CHARGED BLOCKBUSTER
SINCE *EYE OF THE NEEDLE* AND
THE DAY OF THE JACKAL

THE 81st SITE

by Tony Kenrick

AN ORIGINAL HARDCOVER NOVEL FROM
NAL BOOKS (N) MAY 1980 RELEASE
H379/$10.00 ($10.95 in Canada)

NEW AMERICAN LIBRARY

TIMES MIRROR
NEW YORK AND SCARBOROUGH, ONTARIO

"All things will pass away.
Nothing remaining but death and
the glory of deeds."

—ADOLPH HITLER
quoting from the
Scandinavian *Eddas*

PART ONE

THE SEARCH

IN LONDON . . .
the mysterious explosion had killed seven people, sending American insurance agent **Jim Pellham** and a beautiful secretary into a nerve-shattering race to save London from ultimate, final terror.

IN AUSTRIA . . .
aging, desperate Nazi pilot **Willie Lauter**—unable to accept Hitler's defeat 33 years after the war—had finally discovered at THE 81st SITE the long-missing cache of V-1 rockets with which to launch a one-man nuclear attack.

IN THE SKY . . .
the final battle would be fought within sight of London, between a propeller-driven Focke-Wulfe fighter, a V-1 rocket with a nuclear warhead, and a modern phantom jet—in the most climactic air battle ever waged . . .

CHAPTER ONE

Lauter—April 1945

The bombers, Junker 88s, were parked in neat, orderly rows on an airstrip not far from the Austrian border. There was no tarmac, no concrete, just a flat grassy field, part of which had been covered with tarpaulins to keep out the weather. The field was dry enough now, had been for some time, but the planes hadn't moved from their positions for two weeks.

Under the wing of one of the bombers a cow grazed on the new grass, which had pushed up from underneath its blanket of snow, long since melted. A cow on a Luftwaffe airfield! Somebody would get in trouble. Probably.

A chilly spring breeze skitted over the field, humming through the aircraft's aerials and tugging at a piece of fuselage torn where a Mustang's 20-mm shell had ripped through it weeks ago. The bomber parked next to it had its starboard engine mounted on a mobile winch waiting to be refitted. Of the ninety-two aircraft on the field it was the only one which wasn't operational, although, had there been an alert, there was no way any of those planes could have taken off and flown for more than a few miles.

One hundred yards away, the men who normally would have been bustling around the aircraft, revving up engines, loading bomb bays, feeding in long spaghetti strings of machine-gun bullets were playing at being builders, working on a new messhall for Kampfgeschwader 56. The bomber squadron didn't need a new messhall, but they had the materials, and the men had to be kept busy. Only the aircrews escaped the chores. They were like passengers on a boring, bad-weather cruise, waiting out the clock till mealtimes. They lounged around their wooden

286

barracks rereading the same old magazines, walking outdoors to look up at the same empty gray sky, or watching the slow progress being made on the new messhall.

When the officer in charge of the work called a halt for the mid-morning break, the men lined up for hot cocoa, then stood together in little clumps, warming their hands on the tin cups; backs turned to the silent airfield, "the Museum," as somebody had christened it.

The mood was surly; they resented the work they were doing, men who'd been trained to send bomb loads five hundred miles and back reduced to the role of common laborers.

In one of the groups, a stocky, thick-shouldered man swirled the cocoa in his cup and squinted at it sourly. "Look at this stuff," he invited anybody who cared to listen. "Thin as piss and just about as tasty." He looked up as he heard somebody running toward them and snorted through his broken nose. "Well, well, if it isn't Obergefreiter Lauter. Now my day is perfect." He tossed his cocoa onto the ground as the running man came up, out of breath from his long jog across the field. With his cheeks flushed, two red spots glowing in their hollows, he looked younger than his nineteen years. He had a slim, bony face, a slim, bony body that seemed to be the wrong shape for the baggy blue-gray uniform he wore.

"Hans," he said, excited. "It's true. The rumor. I just heard."

The man he'd spoken to, a big, hulking farm boy about his own age, frowned at his friend. "What rumor?"

"Not that shit about the fuel again," the broken-nosed man said tiredly.

Lauter ignored him and burbled on to his friend. "The colonel's orderly told me himself. It's all true."

Again the other man commented. "The only rumor I want to hear is true is the one about our glorious leader."

The excitement fled from Lauter's face as he rounded on the man. "I warned you yesterday, Wyss. Any further derogatory references to the Fuehrer and I'm reporting you to Oberleutnant Hoffman."

The other man looked as if he'd bitten into something

hard. He made a noise that was supposed to be a laugh, then addressed the group in general. "You hear that? The kid's threatening me with the fucking SS." He turned back quickly. "Lauter, you were born stupid. If it turned out that that madman in Berlin really is dead Hoffman would—"

He didn't get a chance to finish saying that Hoffman would buy the whole squadron a drink because Lauter, fury pounding in his face, was rushing at him.

He got only a few feet. With a fast sideways lunge, his friend, much bigger and stronger, grabbed him, smothering him in his arms. "Willie! Forget it, Willie!"

Lauter struggled wildly. "Let me go!"

"Yeah, let him go," voices called. A fight would have relieved the tedium a bit, although it wouldn't have been much of a battle. But they were disappointed. The farm boy wrestled Lauter away from the crowd, bundled him round behind a hut.

Lauter couldn't do anything but protest.

"Forget it, Willie. Wyss will kick your head in."

"I don't care. He's a *traitor*."

The big youth held him locked in his grip for a few moments then said, "I'm going to let you go now, Willie. All right? You okay now?"

He slowly released his friend but kept a restraining hand on him.

Lauter was panting with anger, but the blind rage was ebbing.

"Did you hear what he called him, Hans? The Fuehrer. The greatest German who ever lived. . . ."

"He'll keep, Willie. Tell me the news. What did you hear?"

Lauter let out a long breath, recovering slowly. He straightened his uniform as his friend released him, and as the anger drained from his face, his earlier excitement surged back.

"It's fantastic, Hans. We're being transferred. All of us. Over the border into Austria."

"Why? What's in Austria?"

"The flying bombs. They've built launching sites there.

Hundreds of them, all in secret. We're being transferred to operate them. The orders just came through."

Hans, doubtful, swept an arm at the airstrip. "But what about the planes?"

"We're abandoning them. All available fuel is to go for the flying bombs. The V-1s." Lauter's eyes were dancing as he raced on. "It's brilliant, Hans. It's the Fuehrer's masterstroke. Our squadron and several others airlifted to Wels on Thursday. A week to be trained in launching procedure, then the next day it starts, five hundred flying bombs an hour, twenty-four hours a day, day in and day out. London will be leveled, obliterated, and the English will have to sue for peace. And they'll force the Americans and the Russians to do the same."

"But Willie." The big man groped for a way to put it kindly. "It sounds wonderful, Willie, but it just doesn't sound possible."

"The Fuehrer makes everything possible," Lauter said tightly. Then, gushing again: "Think of it, Hans. No more waiting around like sitting ducks for the raiders. *We'll* be the raiders. The sky will be black with flying bombs. London will be reduced to rubble, and the war will be won with a single massive stroke."

Hans dropped his eyes to the ground, said uncertainly, "I don't know, Willie. You know what rumors are like."

"But this one's true. The colonel's orderly said—" Lauter stopped as his ears caught the scratchy sound amplified over loudspeakers. It was followed immediately by the blaring of a bugle. The first few notes had hardly sounded before Lauter was talking again, more excited than ever. "General Assembly. I told you, Hans. They're going to announce it now. Come on."

He grabbed his friend and they started off at a trot. All around them men spilled out of huts and converged on the airstrip that doubled as a parade ground. Two corporals were already there, setting up a raised wooden dias on the edge of a perimeter road that was nothing more than a track worn flat by heavy trucks. Boots thumped over grass as a gray sea of men swarmed into the area, jamming themselves into a tight box shape. There was a fast dress, and the lines concertinaed. The parade-ground sergeant shouted orders at them, smartened them up, then turned toward the sound of an approaching motorbike. It wheeled in, stopped exactly in front of the dias; the driver hopped off, ran round, and opened the tiny door of the sidecar, and the commanding officer stepped out and mounted the dias.

He returned the salute of the assembled officers grouped behind him, then turned as the parade-ground sergeant brought the men to attention, heels clicked like gunshots.

The colonel was a tall, straight-backed man, popular with the men because he'd flown one hell of a Heinkel 177 before he'd flown a desk. He nodded to the sergeant who saluted, stood the men at ease, then waited like everybody else. The colonel didn't say anything for a moment but briefly checked the sky, an old flier's habit, then brought his attention back to his command. When he began to speak, his voice was steady, almost conversational, but nobody had any trouble hearing him; the ever-present wind carried his words.

"No doubt all of you have heard a rumor lately to the effect that the Fuehrer is dead. I am happy to report that I have no official confirmation of this." He paused for a moment, wanting to give weight to his next sentence. "And unhappy to report that neither do I have any official denial."

In the middle of the third rank, Lauter shook his head. "He's not dead," he muttered. "The Fuehrer isn't dead."

His friend Hans flicked his eyes at him, then looked back at the man on the dias.

"However, there is another rumor you may or may not have heard about that I have just received definite information."

Lauter nudged his friend, excited. "Here it is," he whispered.

"And," the colonel went on, "it is for this reason I have called this assembly." He stopped and looked over the sea of faces waiting for his news. With no expression in his voice, he gave it to them. "I am extremely sorry to tell you that at eight o'clock this morning the German forces in Europe began to surrender."

There was a moment of iron silence, then a murmured word: "Surrender." It drifted up from the ranks, the faces opening. It was a rumor that had been heard and discounted, and its sudden confirmation was a stunning surprise. The men looked at each other, looked back at their commanding officer.

"The Russians are in Berlin, the American and English spearhead has crossed the Rhine. The enemy is advancing almost unchecked on all fronts. We have no means of stopping them without air support, and no chance of that because our fuel and supplies are exhausted. Furthermore, with no news as to the fate of the Fuehrer we are, for all intents and purposes, leaderless."

When the colonel paused again the parade ground was so quiet that they could hear the sound of the windsock as it filled and snapped in the breeze. The colonel coughed behind his hand, cleared his throat, and continued in the same flat tone.

"Germany fought well and bravely." He nodded at them. "You fought well and bravely. But victory has been denied us." He let that sink in then said slowly, "Gentlemen, the war is over."

He stood very still for a moment looking at them, then turned, stepped off the dias, and headed for the waiting sidecar.

The parade-ground sergeant, as stunned as everybody else, forgot to order a salute and instead, dismissed the men, the edge gone from his voice.

Nobody moved very far. They milled around in small groups, the consequence of the news slowly dawning on them. Most of the men had been in uniform for the last five years, and their life had seemed a permanent one; the thought of a stupendous change, like going back home, going back to a normal life, was too hard to grasp immediately.

Hans was staring at Lauter, trying to get his mind around it. "It's over, Willie. I can't believe it."

Lauter was looking at him but not seeing anything; his

eyes glazed as if he'd been struck. He shook his head, bewilderment stinging his words. "It isn't possible. We can't have lost. How could we have lost?"

"I'll see my parents again," Hans said. "My sister, my brother." The big youth reached a hand out to Lauter's shoulder, smiled, said quietly, "It's over, Willie. The war is over."

Lauter's eyes focused, glared at his friend. He began to shake his head, and kept on moving it in steady denial. "The war can never be over," he said. "Not for me. Never."

CHAPTER THREE

Pelham—London, December 18, 1978

The laboratory that Pelham went to the next morning was situated off Theobalds Road in a curious area made up partly of fine town houses converted into offices, and partly by small factories and beans-on-toast cafés. Pelham had never been to the lab before, but he knew it was supposed to be the best in London, and that it did a lot of investigatory work for insurance firms, as well as certain jobs for the police and the military.

Sitting in the waiting room, he was warmed by the thought of Evans, back at the office, wondering where he was at nine forty-five in the morning. He was looking forward to walking in, cutting off the man's tirade, and handing him Henshaw's head on a platter. There was little doubt in Pelham's mind that the landlord was guilty as hell. He didn't think that he'd had anything to do with the explosion, only that he'd seized a chance to claim for merchandise and fittings that had never been in those houses. If Pelham could prove it, he could probably force Henshaw to drop all claims entirely, save the company a bundle, and emerge a hero. But it all depended on the lab's report, and they'd had the thing for the best part of an hour now.

He picked up a magazine from a table and flipped through it impatiently for a few minutes, tossed it down, and was getting to his feet as a door opened and a short bald man came in. He was wearing a dark blue lab jacket and carried in his hand the frame that Pelham had given him. He said, a little sheepishly, "I'm afraid we haven't made much progress. About the only thing I can tell you is that it's definitely not part of a stove. And it couldn't be the brand you mention anyway because the name is spelt A-G-A. It's pronounced as if there should be an R in it, but there isn't."

Pelham closed his eyes and winced. "Goddammit! You sure?"

"We've been on to some other stove manufacturers and described the object but they say there's nothing remotely like it in anything they make. Or ever has been."

"I was certain it was a vent of some kind," Pelham said. "And with that name on it . . ."

The lab man put the frame on the magazine table and held it upright. "It was a sensible guess. We checked our brands book and found a couple of firms with those three letters in their name, but none of them work in metal."

"Could it be part of some other appliance? An old refrigerator, maybe."

The other man looked unhappy. "Frankly, we're a bit stumped on this one. These metal flanges here suggest some kind of valve system; you can see how they're hinged. Of course, if the piece were intact, instead of being so damaged, its function would be easier to guess. But as it is I'm afraid we have no real idea what it's supposed to do, and therefore can't guess what it could have been part of." The lab man, seeing the effect his words were having on his client, tried to introduce a ray of sunshine. "However, there are one or two facts we've been

293

able to ascertain. Whatever this thing is it was manufactured thirty or forty years ago at least. The metal tells us that. And see this blackened part across the center? That's new, so it's certain it was caused by the blast. The opinion is it was very close to the blast. Also, it was definitely intact at the time of the explosion."

"I see," Pelham said. He didn't sound thrilled.

"One other thing." The lab man turned the frame on its side. "There are some more initials, harder to see than the others. Did you notice them?" He was pointing to the other side of the torn corner.

Pelham squinched his eyes up and read them out. "Erke. That mean anything to you?"

"We think it could be *Werke*, German for works."

Pelham's head came up fast. "Then maybe it's part of an old refrigerator or something that was made in Germany years ago."

The other man began to wrap the frame in the brown paper Pelham had brought it in. It made a sad, dispirited sound. "It's possible, although I wouldn't hold out much hope. I doubt very much that it's part of a home appliance. However," he pushed the parcel across the table, "there is one other thing you could do. There's a man we sometimes use when we need an opinion on something foreign. He's German, incidentally, so he may be able to help you on this."

The man handed over a card that Pelham took, although he didn't want it; if the thing wasn't part of an appliance he wouldn't have a case.

He thanked the lab man, went out onto the sidewalk, and stood there, despondent. He looked at the card in his hand; an address on the Harrow Road. What was the point of going miles out of the way if the thing he was carrying was part of a duct from a German-made boiler, or something, which had been installed when Henshaw had been toddling round in diapers? Pelham swore; he was back to square one, an ace away from being thrown out on his ear.

He found himself walking toward a pub a few yards down the block. He pushed at the door, then pulled at it until he realized it was too early for it to be open. Sixty years back the government had restricted pub hours in order to get the munition workers back to the factories sober, and the same laws were still in force; another little irritant to living in this country. "They'll always be an England," Pelham said out loud, giving the door a final shove.

An empty cab was coming up the road and Pelham flagged it down, stepped up to the driver's window. He was about to say Covent Garden when he changed his mind. "What the hell," he said. "The Harrow Road."

"Aw, shit!" the driver said, a young man already fat. That was another thing that had changed in London, the rude cabbies who drove like bullets. Morosely, Pelham wondered if the reason he was taking such a thrashing was because the London he'd come back to live in, after a visit ten years before, was no longer there. Maybe that was why he was so out of it: London had simply changed the way everything changes, and the town he remembered no longer existed.

He was still brooding about it when the cab eventually made it to the address on the Harrow Road. The place turned out to be a foreign-car service garage, with its entrance around the corner on a side street. It was big and cavernous, full of expensive sports cars, mechanics buried in their open hoods. One of them was revving a Maserati, taking it all the way up and filling the garage with its roar. He wore greasy, double-breasted coveralls and a hat made of newspaper, and he sang along to the car's radio, which was blaring almost as loudly as the engine. It could have been a garage in France or Italy.

Pelham walked by a Porsche Turbo, all black including the chrome, and wondered where some people got the money. The mechanic working on it told him where he could find the boss, and Pelham went up a rickety iron stairway to an office overlooking the repair shop. The door was half open and he could see a desk covered with yellow dockets, the man behind it working an old-fashioned adding machine.

"Mr. Shotze?" Pelham asked.

The man peered at Pelham, mistaking him for a client, and tried to remember what car went with his face.

Pelham introduced himself, told him about the lab sending him over, and apologized for not calling ahead.

"Not at all," the man said. "I'll be happy to help if I can." He spoke perfect English with only a slight accent, but he was unmistakably German: gray hair clipped short, pale eyes, and strong, flat features. Pelham thought he might have been fifty-five or so. He stood the frame on the man's desk and began to unwrap it.

"I've got a toughie for you. I have something here but I don't know what it is or what it's from, and I'd like to. The lab figures it could have been made in Germany."

He stripped the rest of the brown paper away and lifted the frame out.

The German had no reaction for a moment, then slowly rose from his chair.

Pelham pointed his finger. "You can see a piece of a name here, ARG. There's also part of another word here, where the corner's torn. I originally thought ARG stood for Arga."

Shotze was staring at the frame, a strange expression on his face. He looked up and said, "Where did you get this?"

"That's a bit confidential. The point is, can you identify it? Is it anything you've ever seen before?"

"Yes it is," Shotze answered. "I just never thought I'd see one again."

"Is it part of a German refrigerator?" Pelham wasn't trying to influence the man, he just couldn't help asking.

"A refrigerator? No. But it was made in Germany. By the Argus Motorwerke. What you thought was Arga was Argus."

"Argus," Pelham repeated. "Okay, but you still haven't told me what it is."

"It's a valve box," Shotze said. He seemed mesmerized by the object.

"From a heating system?"

The German shook his head. "No, the Argus firm built things like submarine motors, torpedoes, and aircraft engines." He moved his hands over the metal flanges, hinging them back and forth. "What you have here is what's left of the flap valve inlet of an Argus pulse jet."

Pelham squinted at him; it didn't make sense. "That thing's from a jet engine?"

"A pulse jet, remember. Nothing like you're thinking of. These flanges here operate and close to admit air to the combustion chamber." Shotze nodded, confirmed his opinion. "It's from an Argus pulse jet, no question about it." He looked up. "You've found yourself a nice little war souvenir."

"What do you mean?"

The man gave a little shrug. "The Argus jet was only built for one thing, and never used for anything else. It was the propulsion unit for the Fieseler."

"The Fieseler?"

"The V-1. The flying bomb. It did a lot of damage to London. Carried something like a ton of high explosives. It made thousands of people homeless."

The phone rang and Shotze excused himself and picked it up. He didn't notice the look on his visitor's face.

The understanding shocked through Pelham, rocked him like a slap in the mouth. "My God," he said under his breath. "Somebody's trying to start up World War II again."

About the Author

TONY KENRICK was born in Australia and has lived in Canada, The United States, and Europe. He worked for many years in advertising before becoming a writer. He and his Welsh wife and their two children make their home in Weston, Connecticut. He is also the author of 81st SITE available from NAL Books.